THE SELBYS

THE SELBYS

ANNE GREEN

CUTTING EDGE

ISBN-13: 978-1-957868-65-3

Published by
Cutting Edge Books
PO Box 8212
Calabasas, CA 91372
www.cuttingedgebooks.com

CHAPTER ONE

Mrs. Selby hated the American colony in Paris to a man, or rather to an old lady. Why a full blooded American should have disliked her own kind to such an extent was a mystery to her casual acquaintances, but I, who knew her very well, can tell you. This prejudiced but spirited lady said Americans did not "keep" abroad but lost their native flavor, while retaining their exterior characteristics. A European atmosphere slowly corroded them (even when they kept strictly to themselves, robbed them of their native crispness, and left them without a distinct nationality. Or, to quote Mrs. Selby: "neither flesh, fowl nor good red herring." If this argument failed to carry (and it very often did) she hinted darkly that when one lived abroad, preferring Europe to an often and favorably quoted native land, there was usually a disgraceful reason, such as weakness of intellect, humble birth, murder in the family or Negro blood. In fact, the only people she excepted from suspicion were her husband and the Ambassador, the former's business having torn him, unresisting, it must be owned, from Savannah to Paris. Mrs. Selby's last plea was cruel but truest of all. She said that Paris preserved old Americans to a disgusting extent and that they remained hale and hearty there long over their allotted time. She conjured up horrid visions of what would happen to old Mr. Brooks if he returned to New York, or if that queen of bullies, Miss Nègre, went home to New Orleans: one whiff of native air and they would crumble to the dust where they belonged. This Poe-like vision was a very literary one; the old people she had in mind were perfectly harmless and worthy of a doting place in the sun.

Strangely enough, Mrs. Selby was adored by these despised ones, and when she perchance allowed them to call they would sit enthralled by her merry conversation and shrieks of gay laughter. In her day in Savannah the lady who received "entertained." That is, as far as I can gather, offered princely, deadly refreshments quite out of keeping with the slim modern stomach, and did all the talking. It must be admitted that a circle of people stunned into the perceptions and consistency of vegetables by this brilliant flow of conversation was a unique sight in American Paris. Virginia Selby swore that when she first came to Paris and called on sundry potentates that cluster around the Embassy, the most trivial matters had been discussed such as Latin immorality, the awful quality of plumbing in Paris, recipes for cornbeef hash (a vulgar Northern dish) and attacks on Protestant principles attempted by Catholic schools. So much for Americans of elegance. Montparnasse circles, where talk and drinks savored of Greenwich village, she called horrid without giving any old-fashioned reasons except that people, sprawling on divans and drinking brandy, looked hideous.

Her own conversation, it is only too true, was extremely surprising and impossible to quote correctly, for the soliloquy of a versatile mind cannot be rendered. To her enchanted circle an excited silvery voice poured forth daily experiences related in a fancy with a wealth of detail; Negro stories, handed to her direct by Joe Chandler Harris, occasional references to the Civil war delivered with much gritting of teeth and insultingly polite apologies to any present Northerner. She stopped for an occasional pun, quoted Tennyson, had a good hate at the Germans and then laughed until the tears rolled down her cheeks at her own rather foolish but infectious jokes. Alas, that print should sound so cold!

An hour of this amazing rambling conversation, without a single reference to daily trials and events was a tonic for the heaviest minds and although they dimly resented her jokes, the quality of this entertainment (which most people would have called a tea-party) and her evident desire never to see them again, acted as a magnet to most Anglo-Saxons. Mrs. Selby's comfortable apartment was an often quoted but seldom penetrated spot and this small, agile middle-aged woman with a beautiful face dominated men and women who were far better looking, better dressed and far more gifted than she had ever aspired to be.

Her sons lived in America and her two daughters had married in France, one an Englishman, the other a Frenchman. Mrs. Selby found a never ceasing source of joy and pride in the latter, who was as gay as she was herself. He considered himself a citizen of the world because he knew English very well, had traveled in Italy, and understood that bathrooms are the very core of existence. In reality he was the traditional French bourgeois.

Mrs. Selby's sons-in-law adored her. To her they owed their handsome wives whose plastic minds bore the indelible stamp of her molding. Their education was anything but humdrum; they knew what the average French girl achieves, and in this rather dull pudding were stuck here and there plums contributed by Mrs. Selby. To wit: a surprising knowledge of the Civil war, a surpassing but literary hatred of Yankees, a set of proverbs from Georgia, the fruit of Negro and Irish habitants, very, very antiquated slang and strangest of all, many expressions connected with an eighteenth century ancestor of sporting instincts who had dropped dead of apoplexy at a fox-hunting breakfast when only twenty-three. These girls in 1929 knew Gilbert and Sullivan's musical comedies by rote, sung to them slightly wrong and very false by their mother since their infancy. They also had to reconcile Brer Rabbit and Georgia with the fact that Negro ladies and gentlemen are now received in Paris by the *élite*. Their English history and American geography although fairly accurate was much flavored for them by their mother's likes and dislikes, very strong ones, and interspersed by strange anecdotes which she may be suspected of having invented to fit her political tastes. As a luxury a certain amount of the Almanach de Gotha had filtered through Evelyn's and Margaret's minds, chiefly regarding Queen Victoria's progeny and their numerous offshoots.

All this jumble of vague information tended to correct what an orderly French education does to a medium mind. It directs, conducts, but does not encourage flights of fancy; whereas a lot of loose information lends charming confusion to a stolid intelligence.

CHAPTER TWO

This is related to give you an idea of Barbara Winship's future home. She is Mrs. Selby's orphan niece brought up in her native Savannah until the Episcopal High School and Miss Pitzer's Seminary had polished her to a solid if provincial luster. Then it was decided to send her over to Aunt Virginia Selby for whom, as any Georgian will tell you, the French had no secrets. This was true to a large extent for no one loved Latins, or understood them better, than Mrs. Selby.

CHAPTER THREE

Barbara was met at Havre by her placid, kind uncle and agitated aunt. Mrs. Selby felt a gush of warm family feeling when she saw her delicate looking pretty niece standing by two of the largest trunks that ever left America. The feeling was intensified when she realized how shabby the little figure looked and how light the grumbling porters found the trunks. "I shall never be able to do enough for my sister's child, never love her enough, never make up for years of casual if affectionate care from stray relations," thought Mrs. Selby; "the poor child must be starved for want of a *real* home." Just then Barbara remarked, "Auntie, you didn't used to live in You-rup, did you? Cousin John sent you his best and said he sure did remember the good old times when you taught him the two-step." Mrs. Selby's critical sense was rudely jolted. "Goodness," she cried inwardly, "she talks Georgia! Isn't that just my luck? Sometimes those Winships do and sometimes they don't; this one does, anyway. It will take me years to make her drop it and when she goes home she will be considered stuck up." Outwardly she replied: "Yes, my dear, and I hope you have inherited the family's light heels." She added magnanimously, "Let's leave the porter to your uncle, and order lunch at that sweet little restaurant on the wharf. We are not going to Paris on the boat train, there are plenty of others. I want to hear all about Savannah first. I don't want to become acquainted with my niece on a noisy train."

CHAPTER FOUR

Barbara proceeded to spend the most unhappy two weeks of her life. She had left a gay, casual life in Savannah for a strange, and to her insupportable, existence. No more running out to have a banana split at Solomon's and do a movie, no more practical jokes and flirtations with callow youths from college, and no one to talk to. No one, in Barbara's mind, meant nobody of her own age, for Aunt Virginia was kind and affectionate in her absent-minded way. Instead of what seemed to her, in contrast with present misery, a dashing adventurous past, the wretched girl found herself confronted with barriers that were insurmountable. Added to the horror of having her English corrected in a good-natured but firm manner, French was immediately suggested on the strength of "having your mind improved, my dear." When Barbara is an old lady she will still remember the agony of sight-seeing with her aunt or Adèle, the maid.

Of course Napoleon's tomb was fun, not much to see there, and awe-inspiring, but the Louvre! with its miles of slippery floors and thousands of pictures that must be admired. "One great comfort," thought the bewildered Barbara, "is that you can admire anything you like and it's sure to be right." So, accordingly, she clung to village scenes by the tender Greuze and fat pink cupids signed Boucher as a relief from horrible Primitives full of ghastly martyrs and badly drawn saints. All the other museums were full of stuffy dead relics and she hated them as she said she hated everything else in Paris.

Secretly she admitted to herself that the drives down town and walks in the Bois were lovely, but home-sickness prevented her from admiring anything in this foreign world where she must live three years. Three years! Barbara began counting up how many days that meant and wrote each one down on a strip of paper which she hung in a comforting manner near her bed. She struck a day off each evening after she had said her prayers and felt a little nearer her beloved Savannah. Mrs. Selby found this pathetic list one day when she strolled into her niece's room to see if she could improve it for her in some way. Tears came into her eyes when she realized what this seemingly comfortable life meant to Barbara, but with unexpected patience she said nothing and turned the matter over in her mind. "The little fool does not realize what a lovely place this is," she reflected, "and I am too impatient to teach her. What shall I do? My sister's child shall not remain such an ass. But what shall I do?"

CHAPTER FIVE

What Mrs. Selby did sounded cruel to her husband. She took Barbara over to Madame de Malassis' select finishing school for young savages of all races, had a short talk with the lady, said: "Goodbye, Barbara, Adèle will bring over your things this afternoon, come to lunch on Sunday," and departed leaving her niece too dumbfounded even for tears.

Madame de Malassis lived in a pompous wide avenue leading up to the beautiful École Militaire; this street reminded all high-brow Americans of the fact that a Frenchman had planned Washington, for it looked exactly like that city. The house was comfortable and simple, the teachers kindly and the girls extremely nice. At last someone of nineteen to talk to, if only by signs. By Sunday Barbara had cheered up considerably and answered her aunt's questions less sullenly than she had planned. In a month she even asked permission to go to the *Théâtre Français* to see "Le Cid," that super-production of dullness amongst seventeenth century French classics, with two Roumanian girls and a teacher that looked like a rabbit. She grudgingly found interest in things she would have been ashamed to own before her American friends, and imbibed a surprising amount of French. No longer did the meals seem queer when other girls liked them. Barbara's rather strange clothes altered without her realizing it at all and within a few months she looked almost like a Parisian school girl, something very sober, dull yet with a sort of quiet elegance only seen in French circles. Aunt Virginia not only approved but added fancy touches of her own in the most atrocious taste, although she had sworn to Madame de Malassis not to interfere with the transformation of her niece.

CHAPTER SIX

A year in Paris, although it changed Barbara very much outwardly really did very little towards altering her mental point of view. The delicate little face, sallow from years of a southern climate, filled out and acquired a shell-like transparency which idealized the charming, irregular short features and slanting golden eyes. A head of curly hair which she had further frizzled with pins was left to long natural waves and thinned all but a little tail of curls at the nape of the neck. The hairdresser assured her it was the color of summer ermine, *"si à la mode."* Madame de Malassis' prim taste for dark dresses of monastic cut touched up with white collars and cuffs suited her charming, slim figure and she concealed as little of her best point as possible: her lovely slim legs. In fact even Mrs. Selby, whose ideal type of female beauty was the flamboyant Rubens' Venus, was struck by the charming, natural freshness that was Barbara's very essence.

I have purposely said nothing about Barbara's character because she had as little as one can do with, when she came to France. Living with stray relatives and the feeling that she belonged to no one had stunted the affections she could have bestowed on less casual surroundings. The happiest hours of her life, although she did not realize it, had been spent in forgetting that she did not have a home of her own. She forgot it in unsought popularity. The letters her schoolmates wrote her after graduation all celebrated her having more "pep" than anyone else in school.

She was good at theatricals, played the guitar, ragtime and jazz on the piano by ear, was a good mimic, a beautiful dancer and an enthusiastic baseball player. She made fudge divinely, knew how to fry sausages over a box of matches and indulged in the most delightful practical jokes. The crowning joy of Barbara's life was her total ignorance of any book learning. "And proud of it," as the slogan of her "fast" set at school had it, when anything priggish or erudite was said. She also thought she knew everything wicked and low in life and stood at nineteen a most innocent, sweet, shy creature, not clever, but with as nimble a brain and as empty a one as could be found anywhere. To this we might add the obstinacy of a mule from her own state.

When Virginia Selby realized her niece's lack of personality she set out in her determined way to make her one. The year at the finishing school was the foundation of a new life for Barbara and as soon as the wild little thing knew French fairly well, her aunt took her home to launch her into a hybrid but interesting world with the help of her daughters. The latter to be called on only if Barbara proved a difficult case to manage.

CHAPTER SEVEN

Sunday lunch was an important event in the Selby household. Mr. Selby, or rather Uncle George, in his more wicked moments did not attend church but read the papers in the sitting-room until the floor was covered with them, had a mint julep, and played Rossini's operas by ear with a light and feathery touch. Meanwhile his wife sat down and wondered whom she had asked to lunch, and whether her daughters were bringing surprises in the way of guests; they found it a very convenient way of entertaining all manner of people who did not fit in exactly with their very fast and jolly set. Thus it was that Barbara saw very little of her cousins at first, and if Mrs. Selby had had more than an intuitive idea of their rackety conversation and what she termed promiscuousness she would have dropped down dead.

The week after Barbara's return from Madame de Malassis occurred the particular Sunday which proved the beginning of her adventures. It was a soft pale blue day in February when the trees look brown instead of black, and with the stir and bustle in the air of returning spring.

"A few people are coming to lunch, my dear," said Mrs. Selby. "I want you to wear your little red crêpe dress, wash the paint off your face, and talk, damn you," she finished off with vigor. Barbara, quite used to her aunt by now, did not even answer that she put on very little rouge, that she was not going to look like a corpse when the rest of the world wears a gaily bedizened face highly suggestive of great passion or apoplexy, and that furthermore, no one ever managed to put in a word edgeways when Mrs. Selby was present.

She smiled graciously instead, and said: "All right Auntie, I'll talk, I'll talk as like you as I can," and ran out of the room to dress. She paused when she reached her own door and stared in. She had never forgotten her trick as a child which consisted in shutting her eyes and opening them suddenly to see things as if you had never beheld them. Marcel Proust says something very wise to the effect that we arrange a room with loving care and taste, then habit removes all the furniture, for when we are used to things we no longer see them.

What Barbara gazed at was rather pretty. It was an old-fashioned room with the bed in a deep recess or alcove in the middle of a long wall; this recess could be entirely withdrawn from the world by long green chintz curtains. On either side of the alcove were two closets, one a hanging cupboard for clothes, the other a little dressing-room. Two long windows faced the bed and through them could be seen a confused mass of tree tops. The Selbys lived on the fifth floor of an apartment house in the Avenue Henri-Martin, which avenue has four rows of chestnut trees, a bridle path leading to the Bois, and a crazy yellow tram which rambles all over Paris and madly crosses the river Seine twice before arriving at its destination, the Gare de Lyon. So much for the street. The room was papered with chintz flowers, there were fat, comfortable armchairs in front of a small wood fire, a writing table between the windows, where Barbara was wont to pen long letters to her friend and boon companion Cornelia Deluth, a chest of drawers that had seen numerous days of ill usage and a few really frightful pictures on the walls. Barbara had had very little time to rearrange her room according to her own limited taste; she sighed for one just like her new and intimate friend's, Suzanne Talbot: a hideous white lacquered copy of an eighteenth century suite with water colors by Monsieur Talbot and some very ugly lamps, carved gold stands with big floppy pink taffeta shades, the work of Madame Talbot.

Although Barbara did not think much of her aunt's taste, yet she realized a certain intimate and comfortable quality in the rooms she arranged, the knack of making the most inappropriate furniture friendly and inviting, although the thought of keeping to a period seldom crossed her mind. Virginia Selby had discovered the secret usually ignored by the ablest decorators who seldom achieve or even want to get a warm, lived-in atmosphere. A comfortable fireplace group, pretty curtains, powerful lamps low enough not to throw gaunt black shadows on the innocent walls, armchairs by tables, with books and ash-trays; with these the furniture does not really matter and as to styles, if the accessories match, differences in years, even centuries, count for very little. That is providing you prefer a home to a room on an exposition stand or an hotel.

CHAPTER EIGHT

Barbara brushed her eyelashes back with brown kohl, a gift from her dashing friend Suzanne, to give a star-like expression to her eyes, painted her lips a brilliant cherry with an indelible lipstick of the best quality purchased with her uncle's and aunt's Christmas present, and touched up her little cheeks with a pink brick. Then she put on her red dress and waited until a succession of rings told her that the guests had arrived and that her aunt would not be able to send her back to wash her face.

She grinned impishly as she entered the long low drawing-room, kissed Evelyn Delahaye and Margaret Winton, her cousins, embraced their husbands, and was introduced to the other guests by her aggravated aunt. They were three: Madame Langlois, a middle-aged woman with frizzy untidy hair, vague eyes and a huge amber necklace; Monsieur Langlois, celebrated for his travels in the East and the extreme modesty which he showed on all scores in spite of the fact that he had just brought to light a buried town in Persia. He seemed to Barbara all beard and a pair of jolly, shy brown eyes; she took a great fancy to him, paying very little attention to the third guest, Georges Lemoine, a slim youth with a fine Greek head. He was the nephew of the Langlois, who had expressed the desire of meeting the Selbys.

Barbara enjoyed the conversation at lunch when it was not too general. She was not yet accustomed to the delights of roaring at the guests across the table in the true French manner— or hearing ten people all talking at once in what sounds like a heated discussion just short of a fight, and is known as an animated conversation. She sat between Robert Delahaye who occasionally prodded her with his fork and asked her vulgar riddles in Parisian slang, and nice Monsieur Langlois who liked her with her shy, hesitating French and big generous smile as much as she liked him.

They entered into conversation in the most brilliant manner: "Do you have nice dogs in Afghanistan?" breathed Barbara, sinking her voice to a very low pitch in the hopes that rude Robert would not hear her efforts and guffaw. To her joy Monsieur Langlois answered at great length and courtesy.

"Yes, Mademoiselle, but a very strange type; they look like immense greyhounds, with the curly ears of a spaniel, a long monkey tail finished off at the tip by a tuft of feathery hair. They are very wild but affectionate; also, they bite everyone that wears white, because they do not like policemen and that is the way they dress in Afghanistan."

"Rather the wrong people to bite," said Barbara lamely.

"Yes, but we have brought over a couple to France where the *sergents de ville* wear blue; besides they live on the river in our barge, which is our headquarters when in France; a floating home is the only place for two such indefatigable, restless travelers as my wife and myself. Will you come and see our boat, the *Stéphane Mallarmé?* At present it is moored under the Pont des Tournelles as I am working at the Bibliothèque Nationale. If you will come to tea we will glide down to the Quai de Passy quite close to you." Monsieur Langlois added with a rather foolish smile: "Can you imagine anything more convenient than moving up to see your friends with all your belongings?"

Barbara was enchanted. She found herself asking all sorts of foolish questions about boats, how to say thank you in Arabic and a thousand gay, silly remarks that charmed the great savant and refreshed him after much contact with a weary scientific world of desiccated old gentlemen, pert, dried-up young ones and the almost insupportable conversation of beautiful young women who collect oriental antiques. "Those lovely women are the worst bores of all in my dusty world," reflected Monsieur Langlois, as he ate fruit salad with a horrible lapping noise. "Their subscriptions come in very handy for scientific research, but how hard for a man of my age to have to bear their playful allusions to Siva, Kmer smiles and the sacred dancing at Angkor. How much nicer to know nothing at all like this American Barbara. It is like asking a kitten to come and play on the *Stéphane Mallarmé*; she is the only person in Paris who has not asked why my barge bears the ridiculously inappropriate name of a great poet. How glad I am not to have to explain about the alcoholic bargee poet from whom I bought the boat and how he fancied his attacks of D. T.'s made him more and more like Verlaine. What an escape from intellectual conversation! This priceless girl who never heard of either Verlaine or Mallarmé is the very one for Germaine and I to divert ourselves with after stuffy Lord Dinsdale and Sven Galbörg have annoyed us in Arabic all day."

Barbara served coffee dutifully and cunningly managed to slip away unperceived to a concert with Suzanne Talbot, deferring a dreaded conversation about paint with her aunt.

She told Suzanne all about the party and sweet Monsieur Langlois but Suzanne refused to listen after she heard that Georges Lemoine had been present. "I know him, my dear," she shrieked excitedly, "so rude and so handsome! He says the most disagreeable things! He comes to my class of rhythmic dancing and makes sarcastic, biting remarks to everyone; even Jeanne Petitpont, our teacher, is afraid of him and dares not correct his dancing. He has never been known to say a pleasant thing to any of the girls, but we cannot detest him because he has such a charming, cruel smile and lovely yellow eyes, like an eagle, that stare through you as if you had nothing on."

"I didn't notice his looks much," said Barbara half apologetically, "I thought he was rather shy, he hardly said a word."

"I suppose you preferred his beaver uncle," said Suzanne.

"Well," answered Barbara slowly, "he talked so sweetly to me, not at all patronizingly as you might expect from such an old dry-as-dust. And what about skipping out before the Fifth Symphony? We've heard it three times already since October, and we might have tea at Sherry's on the Rond-Point. Only, Suzanne," she added sternly, "you shan't have an icecream soda, or if you do, don't spit it out as you did last time. I was mortified, and what did those American waitresses think when you insisted on ordering a pop-over with it?"

"Well," answered her unfortunate French friend, flushing, "what about the time you laughed openly when my aunt Gobert put rum in her tea? Mamma thought you both rude and ignorant, because everyone knows old ladies won't drink tea unless something is added to disguise the flavor." Etc, etc., until they got to the concert.

CHAPTER NINE

Meanwhile, Suzanne's mother, Madame Talbot, was calling on Mrs. Selby and to the tacit relief of both ladies agreed that Barbara and Suzanne could go out together unchaperoned.

"You see I am giving in to your customs, Madame," said Madame Talbot with an arch, toothy smile. Mrs. Selby bridled: "Indeed they are customs as foreign to me as to you; in my day in America, girls never went out alone except in very small towns. However, I am sure that a little freedom will hurt neither of them." Mrs. Selby refused an invitation to dinner for the coming week on the plea that her husband never went out, a terrible lie, as the poor man was quite sociable; but she rejoiced much when Madame Talbot asked if her niece could visit Suzanne during the Easter holidays at their country place near Bayonne.

Barbara did not yet realize what an honor the Talbots did her by allowing so much intimacy with their daughter, but Mrs. Selby did and was secretly gratified by her niece's success. The Talbots belonged to the *grande bourgeoisie* (anglicè, the upper middle classes) and within this cultured, amiable class they formed the nucleus of a set that prided itself upon not knowing foreigners, and considered France and its favored inhabitants the pivots of the universe. Of course this happens in all countries, but nowhere is delighted ignorance better practised than in France by certain classes sufficiently wealthy not to have been touched by the war. They scorned to profit by the innumerable spiritual and material advantages furnished by contact with other races.

To hear the Talbots and their large family connection talk, their last meeting with their nearest neighbors the English occurred when Joan of Arc hurried them out of France.

The elderly men of these families worked in an elegant manner and went to their clubs in the afternoon, a most fantastic idea when most of the clubs in Paris are flickering out. The younger men, handsome, well-dressed and given to as many sports as Englishmen, rocked by the comfortable assurance of "expectations," languidly considered going into banks or the Stock Exchange, blissfully oblivious of the fact that the best opportunities were taken long ago by more ambitious and pushing compatriots. The women of the family spoke several tongues, were well groomed, well connected and, had they but known it, lived on exactly the same lines as the ignored American rivals of the same class. Owing to Monsieur Talbot's artistic tendencies, which embraced horrible water colors and a free thinking turn of mind, Suzanne had gone to Madame de Malassis instead of to a convent, to become Barbara's intimate friend.

CHAPTER TEN

When Barbara hurried home full of misgivings from a huge and heavy tea at Sherry's, she was immensely surprised at being affably and cheerfully greeted by her aunt, who had in fact for the moment forgotten all about her niece's painted face. It was now flushed and shiny. "You can't count on Auntie's moods or it may be my hoodoo," thought the girl. From her earliest infancy, Barbara, along with several million other girls, cherished the belief that the best way of preventing "bad" things from happening was to conjure them up in the blackest light. Strangely enough this plan often succeeded better than strong-mindedness or Coué.

"Well, Lovey-dove," said her aunt, moving a little on her fat red and blue Chesterfield sofa, "did you think it a nice concert? I have some invitations for you. Monsieur Langlois likes you very much and has asked us to tea on his barge for next Wednesday. You will enjoy that, and Madame Talbot wants you to spend ten days with her at Etche Berria, her place in the Basque country. That is in six weeks, so we'll have Mademoiselle Goudeau in very soon to make you some new clothes. I am feeling very benevolent to-night, so I have decided that you shall direct her yourself, although if I do say it who shouldn't, I had exquisite taste in my time. Never mind, every dog has its day and this is going to be yours; only don't bully the poor old seamstress too much with Chanel models; remember her crowning glory used to be dressing the ladies of the Dutch court."

Barbara was too excited and too pleased to more than mumble, "Oh, Auntie," and run out of the room. Happiness or any emotion left her outwardly unmoved and with a horrible pounding in her throat that she fancied could be seen. Hence a hurried exit to fling herself down on her bed and have her happy fit secretly. Oh, the joy of drawing the chintz curtains around her bed and feeling cut off from the world! Utter darkness and quiet were formed, the only sound to Barbara as she lay on her stomach and pressed her face into the great fat pillows was the surging of the blood in her ears. She was happy and excited, for nothing seemed more splendid than being launched forth into an unknown world. The feeling that several people approved of her and wished to have even more of her company was sufficient to give her boundless self-confidence. Of course, she imagined these strangers' lives as one round of jollification, with nothing of the dullness that went with her own existence, bounded by the ever recurring details that dwarf the gayest spirits.

Dinner with Aunt Virginia and Uncle George came as an anti-climax, as both were absent-minded and quiet. After the meal was over Mrs. Selby disposed of the other two by persuading them to go to a movie, meaning to have a quiet evening by herself.

Her children teased her dreadfully about her "vice," which was a craving now and again for the works of Marie Corelli, Miss Braddon, and, best of all, Mrs. Henry Wood. Quoth she: "My dears, when you come to my age, you will find that what you are pleased to call your brains need a little excitement. Discussions of sex and how to choose your children's parents, descriptions of low life and good society, don't stimulate me. I have seen all the nymphomaniacs, drunkards, drug fiends and general waste of health and manners I wanted. Give me 'Lady Audley's Secret' with a lot of mental agony and genteel sin. Let me revel in Victorian smugness and injured virtue. You think me old-fashioned. I am not, I'm a generation ahead of you; the swing of the pendulum will remove you from indecent modern photographs to vicious, priggish water colors of Edwardian times, and your children, like myself, will revel in books like 'East Lynne' and 'The Sorrows of Satan,' or their equivalents," she added prudently.

Accordingly she took out "Kitty Costello" and read the light prim novel, thinking meanwhile of Barbara and how to smooth the future for her. She knew so well what agonies we can suffer from everything when we are very young, and what an impression is made by our first worldly experiences, because, really, there is a sharply defined line that we must all cross from flapperdom to the magic grown-up world. The start is what matters most and what we call luck is perhaps a good beginning, and the art of showing oneself physically and mentally under a becoming aspect, an unself-conscious one. If we enter the scene feeling others approve of us, the rest usually follows.

CHAPTER ELEVEN

Monsieur Langlois like most gentlemen of merit was extremely humble about his achievements, very kind and incredibly simple. Instead of consorting with his peers in learning, he preferred the society of his fat, gay wife and also the young, fresh Barbara. Like many of retiring nature, he was intuitive, and divined that she had a charming personality and enough perceptions to become a woman of taste, versus the intelligent strong-minded female so detested by both sexes. Thus it was that on one fine morning in late March of the same year as he sat on the bridge of his barge, smoking a clay pipe and classing some Sassanian hard stone seals, his thoughts suddenly left them and, addressing his wife in the chatty, confidential manner of one who should be working instead of gossiping: "Germaine, that young Barbara is making great progress in my affections; next October, if we do not go to Palmyra, I shall take her to the Bibliothèque Nationale to look at the medals and seals, or do you think she could be made to grasp Byzantine mosaics?"

"My good Langlois," returned his wife, who was writing an article in the tiny sitting-room just inside a little window through which she could just see a brown beard and pipe, "you are too absurd; you take a creature who alone of our acquaintance can clog dance up and down the deck and wish to make her like one of ourselves. Are you mad? It would take centuries to make her notice anything we love; so far she adores the sickly Canova and she told me the other day that Watts 'was a lovely painter'; so sweet, so sugary, enough to make the angels weep! I absolutely forbid it. She is coming this afternoon and you know very well that she will lie on her stomach on the deck and fish for minnows; then she will come in to have mint tea with us in this cabin made deliciously stuffy by the smell of your horrible pipe. By the time her aunt comes for her at six you will have offered her a drop of cherry brandy and we will be listening to her American songs roared from the top of our red eiderdown, for you know how much at home she feels with us. I fancy her aunt thinks us a little Bohemian."

"So we are, my dear," answered her husband placidly. "I hope you have written your article about Scythian art in your nastiest vein. Scythian art! The term makes me laugh; an art that does not exist all built up on a bit of carved bone brought to Catherine the Great by an anonymous traveler. Don't forget to put in something about Glozel; I'm so glad I was right about that fraud. But to return to Barbara, I am a little worried by the behavior of *your* nephew Georges."

"Why *my* nephew Georges? I haven't noticed anything very frightful about him lately, but I know that when he suddenly becomes altogether my relation and not a particle yours, he is on the verge of being disgraceful."

"My dear Germaine, you women are supposed to be so intuitive; you are capable of knowing what other beings are like and put two and two together very nicely, I'm sure. But as to understanding the sentiments and judging them by the rules of geometry, that most beautiful of sciences, no. My poor fat one, here you see your nephew appearing very often on our boring stuffy barge; you see him drop in almost every afternoon to smoke a cigarette with me, and why do you suppose? To see Barbara, or to take the chance of seeing her, and I don't like it."

"But, Edouard," said Germaine mildly, removing a large piece of wood from her French cigarette, "he never speaks to her, he bows curtly, barks a few words at her and disappears with you—not very lover-like conduct."

Monsieur Langlois rolled his eyes up dramatically so that they showed like chocolate drops above his woolly beard: "There again you show no sense; science has dulled your amatory perceptions (fortunately for me); Georges is vain and shy; if he were not at once attracted and terrified of making himself cheap, he would not be so timid and so rude. At any rate he would not go out of his way to be insolent, particularly not before us ... or. ..."

"Besides," interrupted Germaine, "you know Georges would not be attracted by a *jeune fille.*"

"No more he would," retorted her husband suavely. "Barbara is not a *jeune fille;* she is the new hybrid that is so attractive to us stale old Latins; she combines the disarming freshness of youth with the carriage of an experienced woman. The mixture is irresistible to the average French palate unused to innocent freedom. You are now thinking of Georges' numerous adventures with married women, because you have read Maupassant's cocottish literature. My dear Germaine, I declare to you that the number of honest women is surprising; not virtuous, but too frightened, too plain or too much attached to their families to run the risk of a clandestine lover. I read once in an American magazine a very neat summing up of this nonsense: 'If there is anything in the world more lonely and more unsatisfying than the usual illicit love affair, then the world is keeping it hidden.' You may be sure that Georges' conquests so far have been the usual run of mediocre venal ladies who are the saddest side of this melancholy passion."

"Pray when do you find time to read these profound magazines?" asked Germaine dryly; "you seem to know a lot about it; I thought you were an authority on the Sassanians, not a Dresden shepherd. Besides," she added sharply, "he would never marry Barbara. She has no dowry and the vaguest of expectations. Bourgeois families like ours like foreigners but don't marry them. They do not fit into the picture, too extravagant, too good-looking, too lazy."

"Of course," said Monsieur Langlois, "all agree and let's have lunch. Only I have heard of love affairs that never led to anything except pain to at least one of the opponents."

CHAPTER TWELVE

Monsieur and Madame Langlois, never attempt to judge another generation! Georges, your nephew, was not thinking of anything of the sort. He was rather attracted to Barbara and when he met her felt that strange warm thrill that binds you physically to your natural mate. He came oftener to the barge to see her as he enjoyed that feeling, but never with any idea of developing it. Somewhat of a sadist, this young Georges, and apt to punish his own impulses at their birth for the pleasure of feeling superior to them by an easy victory.

At the precise moment of his uncle and aunt's conversation he was thinking that with the proceeds of his last little flutter at the Bourse he might buy himself a Citroen, a bathing suit, and go for the Easter holidays to Spain or the south of France with a few friends of his own type. That is, hard as nails, perfectly soulless and yet very honest. The absence of anything but conventional morality and a total disregard for everyone's feelings, gives the courage to be frank with oneself and others. At any rate there was no trickery in Georges; he extracted the maximum of pleasure from life in general and when it did not hamper him in the least gave very little back in return. With the really selfish there is no room for pretense, and no reason for it, for they cannot be bothered to simulate.

CHAPTER THIRTEEN

Barbara, all unaware of this, went to Etche Berria in a state of great excitement, tempered by a nervous dread of what the Talbot family would be like in their lair and what they would expect of her. She begged Suzanne, with whom she traveled down, to prevent her family from meeting them at the station, and although the Talbots thought this rather ridiculous, they willingly agreed, as the train arrived just after lunch at the delightful hour when well-fed people relax and bask.

From Bayonne, where the big expresses stop, the girls took a tiny local train that wound slowly like a puffing, snorting dragon among the little brown foot-hills of the Pyrenees. The people in the train talked Basque and bad French, also they really wore Basque berets, just as the papers say. Outside the grimy windows, spring appeared everywhere at once in the lavish way known only to that coast; all the trees in leaf, with a wealth of roses, laburnum and wisteria tumbling over walls and gates, while great round lilac bushes stood sentinel at the side of each little black and white house. All the flowers that are reared so gingerly by gardeners in Northern countries grew here generously and without the effort of man: lilies of the valley and big purple flags, anemones and hyacinths, jonquils and tulips. The climate did not feel unbearably southern as the frequent cool rains kept the high grassy slopes as green as Ireland, making it into a grazing country.

"What do you smell?" asked Suzanne as they climbed into a small pony cart at the station, which Barbara promptly filled with immense suitcases full of Miss Goudeau's handiwork.

"I smell a fat, cool delicious scent of cinnamon and vanilla," answered Barbara, sniffing.

"That is our smell," proudly from Suzanne, "you will see." A few minutes' trot brought them to a low, white wooden gate closing a path between two big prairies; on one side the meadows were enclosed by a white fence, on the other by a rounded crumbling stone wall covered by a hanging mass of red roses. As they drove up the path, the meadows changed to a small park wooded in the English manner as a sudden curve in the drive brought them in view of a low bright pink house with square jutting wings, surrounded by a mass of square flower beds full of pansies and forgetmenots, divided by narrow red brick paths.

It was about two in the afternoon, two black and white pointers wagged their tails politely from the big lawn beyond the flower beds while an aged half-blind spaniel rushed up and fussed about them, like a fat old lady, barking in deep bell-like tones most unsuitable to her respectable appearance. A deafening uproar in one of the wings caused Barbara to start nervously. "Come in and be introduced," said Suzanne, flinging the reins carelessly over the pony's shoulders. He broke into an obedient trot and disappeared back of the house, luggage and all, to the stables.

Suzanne walked up three steps and threw open the long shuttered French window whence the noise proceeded. A big, gay room furnished in the 1890 manner was disclosed, with Madame Talbot knitting a striped jersey on a long chair with her husband by her, a pince-nez on the tip of his nose, reading to her in a deep hissing whisper an article in "Le Temps" on English politics. In the middle of the room playing cards were two couples, two healthy, fresh, black-eyed young women, Louise d'Allier and Annette Durtain, and their husbands, all four Basques and like enough to be brothers and sisters. At an upright black piano draped in Japanese silk sat a handsome young man picking out a tune and listening half-heartedly to a short, fat one who bent over and talked to him in impassioned tones about the leading world questions, completely spoiling the beatific effects of his lunch. When the girls came in, the tall youth saw his chance to evade so much earnestness and rushed up to them, reluctantly followed by the stout one still talking earnestly. Suzanne introduced the first as Roger de la Huppe with a Quai d'Orsay reputation as a budding diplomat, and the second as Tiburce Fouquet.

"It is just as well that Barbara did not wish to be met," said Madame Talbot as she embraced both girls; "these savages wished to come for you in Roger's Chrysler, dressed only in their bathing suits, and then go straight on with you both to the Beldune beach, a mere matter of twenty kilometers! I cannot have the feelings of the station master outraged; myself and the servants have become used to your sinful ways but the peasants still respect us and I will not have them shocked."

Suzanne secretly agreed with the bathers and out-wardly with her mother; also she wished to make a good impression on Roger, with whom she had danced a great deal that winter, and thought that the decorous old world note was the right chord where he was concerned. She was a minute too late and noticed with a tiny heart prick that he looked at Barbara with a great deal of approving interest. To her further amazement, Roger placed a monocle in one of his glassy blue eyes and handled the situation in a suave diplomatic manner.

"Could we not, *chère Madame,* conciliate American comfort with Basque prejudice?" said Roger, looking at Barbara for admiration. "Supposing another time we wear our blazers over our bathing suits and a rug over our knees, for the sake of the villagers? We would look like tourists."

Madame Talbot shook her head severely but, suddenly remembering what a good match Roger was, smilingly murmured something about *le progrès, les Américains, idées modernes* and took the girls up to their rooms.

Barbara's was a narrow slip of a place with a wooden balcony covered with wisteria and commanded a lovely view of the distant purple Pyrenees. The walls were instantly a source of delight to her, covered with unframed photographs of the eighties and nineties which formed a close mosaic of the most extravagant type. It had been Tante Sophie's room and collection of photographs; anyone connected with the Talbot family in the late nineteenth century was seen leaning on a velvet chair, spreading a bustle on a sofa, or protecting leg of mutton sleeves under a Japanese sunshade. Of course the family connection was large, extending to cousin's cousins, but when a blank space had to be filled in, Tante Sophie had not hesitated to pin in duplicates. Thus a fat gentleman with long mustachios ending in curled sausages held his head against a fat jeweled paw; his hair was rather long and parted in the middle, his collar ending in points at the ears, leaving the throat bare all but a gigantic satin cravat and large horseshoe tie pin; by him on an equally fat sofa lay a brass helmet, a sword and an open book: Cousin Edmond had retired from the sapper branch of the army early in life to devote himself to poetry, as anyone but Barbara would have guessed from these emblems.

Everyone became very chatty when the girls came down to tea. Still more when two tables were formed for cards, and all sorts of complicated games were played for tiny stakes. In vain Monsieur Talbot (who hated cards) proposed "a little hygienic walk before dinner." Roger de la Huppe was master of ceremonies as always, having decided that the sun shone specially and particularly for himself and all the other members of his distinguished family. He frowned on Monsieur Talbot and Barbara, who cast longing glances on the delicate spring sunset.

"Let the serious Basques play bridge," he cried, "while Fouquet and I will teach Miss Winship to play *belote*."

"Am I allowed to play too?" asked Suzanne, half-hurt, but smiling.

"Of course, my dear Suzanne, but the chivalry of old France must be shown first to our foreign guests." Suzanne did not like this at all, nor did her mother. They both remembered Roger's conversation a few weeks back, when the chivalry of France had been directed more exclusively in her direction.

"In my day," said Monsieur Talbot, "when I was a young soldier, belote was considered a tavern game, not a recreation for young ladies."

"But Monsieur," explained Roger in his best Huppe manner, "the very smartest people like it; only last week at the Chateau de Visy, I taught Madame du Castel de Castelnogaret to play it, the Duchesse de Bilbao raves over it, and my cousin the dowager Baroness de Montvilliers counts up the trumps all night in her sleep. How do I know this?" smiling foolishly, "because her maid sleeps in her dressing-room and complained to our servants about it."

Madame Talbot was mollified by this magnificent array of provincial grandees but her husband, who prided himself on democratic principles (and was accordingly disliked by superiors and underlings alike), said a lot of things about the Republic going to the dogs, the upper classes dragged in the mire and impending hard times all due to belote. No one listened much, and a victorious La Huppe explained this intricate game, which by the way is not unlike bridge, to the girls. Barbara's monkey brains understood much better than the intelligent Suzanne, and she reaped easy laurels for which she was later to pay.

After a lively dinner in which silly gay conversation was at its best, the young people saw what was about to take place. Monsieur Talbot took the nicest fattest armchair, put on a medieval helmet with receivers and prepared to enjoy his radio. After a series of explosions and strange noises the old gentleman found the "Traviata," his favorite opera, given *in extenso* by Barcelona. After looking fiercely around and mutely demanding utter silence, he listened happily and even burst into song when the tune reminded him of a favorite singer.

"Can't you stop him, Maman?" whispered Suzanne frantically.

"No, my dear," answered Maman gloomily, "he very seldom catches a post he wants."

"Can we go and sit on the lawn?"

"No, your father wishes us all around him to-night, particularly as he took his walk alone this afternoon."

The guests sat like stalactites, wished they had not come, wrote themselves imaginary telegrams of recall, and when lemonades and innocuous fruit juices were served at eleven, dared to creak a little in their chairs. Monsieur Talbot beamed at them, wearing the idiotic look of the clairvoyant or the listener to things invisible. "The last duo," he breathed, "nothing more beautiful has been written except 'Samson et Dalila.'" Everyone glared speechlessly at him. "That will be Friday, I think. ..." He rose, stretched himself a little, and said affably: "I am going up to bed before you can get the Savoy band and dance your unimaginable, savage African noises; the thought makes me sick after that seraphic music." He blew them a playful kiss and disappeared.

Something happened to Papa's radio that very evening, although no one knows exactly what took place. Tiburce Fouquet was the last person to leave the room after a series of squawking noises and alarming electric sparks. The next day the village mechanic, who knew all about a wireless, broke two lamps, said he could get them at Bayonne, and was prevented from remembering anything about it by a timely fifty-franc note. A gramophone is a good thing to dance by anyway.

CHAPTER FOURTEEN

Barbara lay in her photograph-lined room with a large but empty tray on her stomach, a pale green and silver landscape through the open window. She had eaten three rolls, two cups of *café au lait,* polished up the jar of honey and was pensively attacking the sugar bowl when Suzanne called out from the next room and asked her whether she would prefer to marry La Huppe or Fouquet. "Don't talk to me, Suzanne," was the answer, "I am thinking." And so she was if a dreamy lethargy could be considered pensive.

First she gazed at Cousin Emile and wondered how he curled his mustachios, then thought of all the men she knew and how they would look with such trimmings: "La Huppe for instance … I wonder what Aunt Virginia will think of him. Why does he always mention people's titles and never speak of those who have none? … I know he likes me better than Suzanne. … I am sure the dances at the Interallied Club are fun … if his sister is nice I will go, he dances very well; although, I may not go; he is so aggravating and cocksure; he knows everything, all the things I don't want to know. Of course I shouldn't have laughed last night at dinner, Suzanne has no sense of humor; but really I could not help it: Monsieur Talbot tells him to go and sit between the two goddesses, Venus and Diana, meaning Louise and Suzanne, and the ass placed himself at Madame Talbot's left, by me. I must lead him on a little, then send him an anonymous letter this summer telling him elderly men should not attempt to improve girls' minds; he must be at least thirty-six. The heroine in that lovely film 'Grace and Disgrace' writes a splendid letter all in capitals. … Perhaps Uncle Georges will help me write mine, only he might think it dishonorable … it is so difficult to know what is dishonorable. Of course, I know what's right and wrong, *that* is quite simple and when in doubt Aunt Virginia can always tell. I wish Goudeau did not make my dresses so big; the pink one is the thing for the picnic to-day and if …" she dropped off to sleep again for about ten minutes and awoke suddenly to find Suzanne all but dressed and looking at her smilingly.

"If you have almost finished your heavy thinking perhaps we might dress together; I hear Fouquet and Papa talking about the next war just under my window. You know Tiburce is General Fouquet's son and really rather nice, although he always wants to fight. Papa says he is his only consolation in the present generation, which does not enjoy its military service and hates the thought of fighting."

"I don't think he dances very well," said Barbara, "but he drives a car all right and he knows all about radio," she added with such a blank, ingenuous look that Suzanne burst into peals of laughter, joined by the innocent one in bed.

CHAPTER FIFTEEN

"George!" said Mrs. Selby to an open door. "George!" her voice rising slightly. "You Gawdge!" in a bellow.

"Yes my dear," answered a smooth whisper just back of her. She turned furiously to face her grinning husband.

"You will worry me into my grave yet; why didn't you say you were here?"

"I did, only you didn't hear me; your voice carries so beautifully, m'dear."

"Anyway, here's a letter for you from Barbara, George. Do read it quickly, I worry so about the child. I hope she is still having a nice time and not bathing in that icy cold Atlantic."

"Oh come, Virginia, not so cold at Saint-Jean-de-Luz."

"Too cold for us tropical flowers," firmly from his wife.

Uncle George slowly sat down, studied the post-mark, commented on the stamp, and taking a penknife from his pocket, carefully slit the envelope.

"George," said Mrs. Selby, "my patience is getting short."

"It's *my* letter," retorted George in a most aggravating, innocent voice, "would you care to read it first, my tropical flower?"

Mrs. Selby burst into tears of rage and left the room, only to return immediately with a perfectly dry eye and the sinister remark that always brought George to her feet: "You will regret this every day of your life, George Selby, when I am gone, worried into a lonely grave in a foreign land. *Then* it will be too late," etc., etc.

George handed her the letter, which read thus:

Darling Uncle George (*'Darling,'* for an uncle by marriage! sniffed Mrs. Selby insultingly), I have much to relate; as you know very well what people do in the country, I will sum it up for you in articles.

1. I eat a light French breakfast (very hungry again by eleven, and lunch is at one).

2. We all play tennis; I don't play very well.

3. We played golf at Saint-Jean-de-Luz on Tuesday; *they* don't play very well.

4. We go to the vegetable garden to see how the fruit is getting on. It isn't getting on; the gardener says there won't be anything to eat, even strawberries, long after we leave. I expect he eats them then.

5. We take lovely walks, each time calling at some farm for eggs, cheese, or butter for the cook. Madame Talbot says a walk without a purpose is like an egg on toast or something of the sort, perhaps an egg without salt. ("Idiot," said Mrs. Selby.) And we always meet the village garbage cart drawn by two beautiful snow white oxen, each one covered with a basque linen table cloth edged with colored stripes; you know what I mean, I think they look very *chic*.

6. We bathe (Mrs. Selby groaned) at a sweet little beach kept by an old man in baggy red flannel trousers, a red beret and some other clothes. Tell Auntie my bathing suit is lovely, I look like the cover of the 'Cosmopolitan,' Suzanne's *was* lovely only her mother made her add a ridiculous ruffle to each leg just clearing the knees.

7. We go to lovely villages high up in the hills where the peasants are nature's gentlemen, polite but proud; they speak Basque and a little French as an accomplishment. Fortunately

the Durtains and the d'Alliers speak their lingo as their families live quite near. Which reminds me that Roger de la Huppe, a most ridiculous old young man who knows everything, took us to tea at the Chateau de la Redoute, a pink barn where some of his relations perch. The lady is an American, married to a Frenchman, or was an American because she is so French she says she has forgotten her English; all but the twang, I must add, for she asked me all sorts of questions about my family, looking down her nose at me, because I am only a Winship and she is Ambro de la Ville-Tanneuse. I tried to remember what Aunt Virginia does on these occasions but nothing came to me. Then Suzanne told her that I was your niece. *That* made no impression. (Mrs. Selby smiled fiercely.) Suzanne added that I was the grand-daughter of a bishop; *that* brought down the Catholic side of the house. Everyone looked shocked and embarrassed, all but Madame A. de la V. T., who relented a little and even quavered a hymn she said Grandfather had composed. It was my turn to be embarrassed, as it sounded hideous! Then we had tea, the kind that brews and brews in a pewter pot, dusty biscuits, and very nice gingerbread. La Huppe and our hostess discussed the genealogy of the countryside whilst the rest of us danced the lancers on a lovely lawn. Tiburce Fouquet knows the lancers very well, a very complicated dance full of the tunes you so often whistle and then we went home and in the evening ... no, I shall have to explain when I see you, about Monsieur Talbot's radio.

8. We often play cards and have such fun; in the evening we go down to the village and buy pink sugar pipes, false noses and licorice spectacles. I am bringing some home as presents to you both.

9. We eat a lot at meals, never between, because it's bad for you (besides there is nothing to eat).

10. Roger de la Huppe is dying to know you both; he is very attentive to me and very boring except when he dances; then he is mercifully silent except for slight pants, he is getting old and winded.

11. And never does Madame Talbot leave us for a second.

12. Suzanne does not like me as much as she did and her mother says I am not a perfect woman of interior, which means that I cannot knit. I am having such a nice time and everyone loves me except the Talbots. I miss you but not unbearably. Kiss Aunt Virginia for me and tell her my clothes are the admiration of the villagers, just what Goudeau wished!

Your very loving niece,

Barbara.

"The little devil," said Aunt Virginia feelingly, "I can read between the lines perfectly. Roger is the ideal match for Suzanne and that minx has been flirting with him; of course he will end by marrying Suzanne but it means a lot of dilly-dallying and bother for the Talbots. No wonder they hate the spoke in their well-greased wheels. It also means that we must find some more intimate friends for the child; I want her to be popular but not to run through a French family every month; no one's visiting list could stand that."

CHAPTER SIXTEEN

Barbara sat in her room, reading an article attractively called "Why Girls Go Wrong," in her favorite magazine. She heard her aunt's short nervous step in the passage, threw the book under the chintz cover of her armchair, picked up "Stones of Venice" and a large book of post-cards illustrating Ruskin's prose, bending studiously over them as her aunt entered the room.

"My poor child, I can't go with you to the *École du Louvre* this afternoon. I feel one of my liver attacks coming on. Do you think you could go without me? Your uncle will take you to the *Opéra-Comique* this evening, and by to-morrow perhaps I will feel well enough to chaperon you to the Bingly-Berry dance. I want you to go most particularly to-morrow night as the most amusing French people and the best looking young Americans will be there; also it is one of the prettiest houses in Paris."

"Oh Auntie," burst out Barbara, "I'm so sorry about your liver; lie down and let me mix your fizzy medicine for you. As you are ill I must confess that I was reading the 'Metropolitan,' not Ruskin, when you came in and I threw the magazine under my chair."

Mrs. Selby struggled hard not to laugh at her blushing niece, and sat down. "I wonder why you should wish to deceive anyone as unsuspecting as your poor old aunt? And you look so guileless!"

"I *am* truthful, Auntie, as a rule, only I hate Ruskin, he is such a prig; he makes me loathe the pictures he likes the best."

"Then, my dear, don't read him any more and go and look at the pictures in the Louvre instead. I don't want you to do anything you hate. I know aunts and parents generally are just old fools and can't guess what passes in you youngsters' minds, but almost everything you learn will come in handy later on. Remember that this is your first season, and that you are living at a very high speed, cramming about three years of pleasure into three short months. Don't you think that some day you may need some of the pictures, books and music that I insist on your assimilating now? You might fall in love with someone really intelligent (Barbara shuddered) and imagine how handy all this learning would be—or you might be shipwrecked and cast on a desert island; after you dressed up in banana leaves for a week you might be glad to remember some nice poems. Of course, my dear, I am only joking, don't take me too seriously, because I realize how tire-some it is to be given a taste for learning, willy-nilly. Only a little mental furniture for your brain is a great pleasure after a while when other things pall …' Mrs. Selby sighed.

"Auntie," said Barbara, "I will never keep anything from you again; only speaking of banana leaves reminds me of something dreadful. I must tell you while I have the courage."

"What is it?" from her aunt, who stiffened suspiciously.

"Nothing much and I wouldn't mention it if I had not received Uncle Charley's check this morning. I can't wear evening dresses made by Miss Goudeau any longer."

"Why my crazy child, I thought that you looked very sweet in the pink chiffon at the Interallied Club dance last week."

"That's just it. I looked sweet. I don't want to look sweet, I want to be dressed like the other girls. Men don't notice clothes very much, although they think they do; anything pink or blue pleases them, but the other girls tell me how original I look and that's a very bad sign. Suzanne, who is very nice to me now she is engaged to Roger, offered to take me to her dress-maker. Could I go, Auntie, I want to so much, I have my check and besides I know that I would then be completely happy, specially living with such a nice aunt and uncle?"

"A fool and his money are soon parted," said Mrs. Selby. "Of course you can do what you like with your own money, only, my little dear, never boast of happiness. As fast as you get your dress tangle straightened out, you will have other desires and dreams to wrestle with. Or perhaps it's my liver that makes me talk so gloomily. Run along to your lecture now; walk one way and take the tram home."

Barbara, rather let down by her easy victory, put on a neat, navy tailor-made, a little felt hat, pinned a large bunch of velvet pansies to the coat and felt very suitably dressed for an erudite afternoon.

She walked briskly to the Louvre and an hour later, having heard everything a good critic could tell her about the Impressionist school, jumped into the yellow tram known as the "Gare-de-Lyon-avenue Henri-Martin," alias the "19." She settled down for a long ride leaning her elbow on the open window sill; she gazed at the beautiful busy quais, the pale green Seine, covered with little tugs and big lazy barges, and the distant Trocadero finished off by two towers which looked like two chubby short arms raised to Heaven, in despair over the rest of the gloomy building. A delicate pink and gray sunset and the silver dust bestowed liberally by Paris itself on all things, cast a poetic glamor over the world in general. A long stop at the *Place de la Concorde,* where the tram broke down as usual, was particularly pleasing. Barbara noticed that this immense square was in a specially becoming mood, with the fountains tossing up feathery sprays of water that glistened like cut glass; the two stone horses at the entrance of the *Champs Elysées* reared up proudly against their background of chestnut trees and the double palaces that faced the Seine were coquettishly outlined against piles of fat white clouds tinged with orange. "On purpose," as Barbara thought. Indeed the whole place looked like an empty stage becomingly laid for an event.

Just then someone who had been sitting by Barbara for some time said: "The view from my apartment is much more beautiful."

Barbara turned round aggressively, to face the grinning Georges Lemoine.

"Oh!" she said flushing, "when did you get on? How do you do?" the last for manners' sake, as she was disappointed at the prospect of sharing *her* tram with Lemoine.

"I was in the car when you jumped in, but you seemed so absorbed I did not dare speak to you before this full stop." He smiled rather rudely to remove any idea of deference to her musing, that Barbara *might* have entertained.

She wisely ignored the smile and was most gracious: "Don't you love Paris at this time of day, the colors are so delicate?"

"Yes; real pastel shades for foreigners. That is what the trippers look for when they come to town. Your brilliant Oscar Wilde preferred decided greens, yellows and browns to these sickly shades."

This was Barbara's chance and she took it.

"Really, you are just too old-fashioned. Can't you think of someone a little newer? I don't pretend to know much, but my uncle and aunt were laughing about it the other evening. They said you Frenchies stuck to Oscar Wilde like grim death, a dead and buried critic of the nineties, as if he were our only classic; whereas it seems he was really a brilliant conversationalist and second-rate author, not a genius. We might as well quote Daudet as your latest talent." All this pretty well memorized, Barbara.

Georges looked as mortified as a big man of twenty-four could, when reproved by an ignorant snip of twenty.

"Who, for instance?" said he sharply.

This was a terrible moment and Mrs. Selby's dark words flashed through Barbara's brain.

"Well," she said slowly, to gain time, "let me think of someone that you might perhaps have heard of in our generation. Do you know Babe Ruth, one of our best critics, or Jefferson Davis, a very brilliant English writer of, er—essays?"

"No," replied Georges, rather surprised. "How do you write their names; I have some American friends who will tell me more about them?"

"I can't spell in the tram," then, hurriedly, "where do you get off?"

"Oh, at the very end; I am going to play tennis at the Racing Club in the Bois, then I must rush home to dress; I want to hear my favorite opera to-night."

"Which is that?"

"Don Juan."

Barbara said nothing for a time. "How are your uncle and aunt? I am going to lunch with them as soon as Monsieur Langlois has finished his lectures."

"I never see them any more."

"What a pity, they are so nice and they think so much of you."

"I am fond of them too, only I have a special reason for not seeing anything of them at present." Georges hoped that Barbara would look curious but she did not. She only wondered how Suzanne could be fascinated by anyone so rude; as if to give the lie to her thoughts, he pursued in a much gentler voice:

"When I went to Italy for Easter, I saw a girl bathing at Portofino who looked very much like you, only not nearly so pretty. Of course she was an American, they are the handsomest women in the world, I think," looking meanwhile with a very solemn face at a most ridiculous, obviously American, old lady who wore a sailor hat fastened under a large bun of gray hair by an elastic. Barbara giggled and fixing with a glassy stare a much mustachioed old French woman in her late eighties, the proud possessor of a single yellow tusk that protruded from her purple lips, said: "No, I prefer the Latin type of beauty." Then, "Heavens, this is where I jump off, goodbye, goodbye."

"Au revoir," answered Georges gravely.

"Adieu forever," said Barbara mentally, waving graciously.

CHAPTER SEVENTEEN

B arbara smiled to herself with pleasure and the feeling of her own importance as she sat in a *baignoire* with Uncle George at the *Opéra-Comique*. She loved *baignoires*: those ground floor boxes which are closed in front by wooden lattice work look very clandestine and mysterious; many others with more guilty consciences than Barbara's have found them so, although they were originally designed for people in deep mourning, who could thus slip in and hear an opera without being seen. Unfortunately Uncle George, who was not romantic, or guilty, or in mourning, spoiled a lot of the fun by pulling up the gratings and treating this *baignoire* (the only seats the Selbys had found at the last moment) just like an ordinary box; he wanted to feel cool in the crowded sultry theater, not furtive.

The music was lovely; Don Juan a handsome, agile barytone; even the clumsy fat chorus could not spoil the magnificence of the party given by Don Juan for his villagers. As Uncle George rather heavily expressed it, though Barbara echoed it perfectly, "the music sounds like a present from an inexhaustibly rich and generous god, who gives freely with a feeling of far more back of all this that we only guess at."

Barbara sat in the box during the entr'actes whilst her uncle sallied forth to smoke a cigarette and look at *les jeunes filles à marier*. She was mystified until he explained that in his day, some twenty years before, the four state theaters, *Français, Odéon, Opéra* and *Opéra-Comique,* were considered the only ones at which young girls could be seen. So that when a marriage of convenience was planned, to avoid giving too much weight to the interview in which the future couple met, a "chance" meeting could be arranged in the *foyer* or theater lobby. Thus one match could be presented to several girls at a time or to a number of unattached young gentlemen and you could not be quite sure which your fate would be. An improvement on the nineteenth century when many of these marriages were arranged at balls or dinners, leaving a much longer, duller chance of making up your mind, for both parties. Twenty years back it had been very smart to select the *Opéra-Comique* for a trysting place (if one may thus express it) but nowadays only the stuffiest of *bourgeois* families still clung to the habit. Uncle George declared the latter were the only respectable looking people left in the world, and he was almost right.

"Well, Uncle," said Barbara, "I understand about this matchmaking, because after all a good deal of this takes place at home, under less formal appearances; Cornelia Deluth's mother took care never to ask a single ineligible man to the house until her daughter was engaged; Cornelia herself told me her mother always said it was as easy to love a rich man as a poor one, so you see it's six of one and half a dozen of the other. I know Anne Thompson's mother said *her* daughter should marry for love, but she picked him out for her and Anne ended by liking her *fiancé* pretty well."

"Of course," said Uncle George in his fat comfortable voice, "people are the same the world over; the same ones give and the same ones grab, only the first kind have most fun. Now I'm going out to have a chuckle at those deluded boys and girls and I'm devilish glad to be out of the marriage mart myself and safely tied up to Virginia."

As they left the box, Barbara pinched her uncle's arm and whispered: "I want to ask something about the *jeunes filles;* why do they go to such improper operas? Don Juan is a wild young man and certainly had designs on Zerlina. Carmen wasn't married to any of the young sports she sings to, I don't see anything very prudish about Faust."

"A most immoral plot," agreed Uncle George, "with virtue in a very sad plight, dying on a straw pallet in great agony; I expect singing makes it all comfortable and poetical, besides, no one is supposed to understand the plot unless they take the trouble and are full of sinful curiosity. Wait for me while I catch a taxi."

Barbara stood in a corner, watching the people fighting their way out, or as they say in novels, "the merry throng surging out." She loved being in a crowd, she was filled with excitement looking at smart ladies covered with enormous jewels and befurred wraps, imagining their lives full of seductive secrets and intrigues, dashing madly from theaters to balls and suppers. The only thing that saddened her magazine dream of bliss was man. The ones she saw were not all of them beautiful, some did not even look like lovers. To her amazement, she saw her uncle return with Lemoine, who bowed very distantly.

"Monsieur Lemoine has his car and will see us home, Barbara. It is very kind of him as the boulevards are full of Russian taxi-drivers who never heard of the Avenue Henri-Martin and don't want to, apparently." Barbara mumbled something and followed them to a dashing, open, yellow roadster, the back seat of which she found most breezy. No conversation with Georges, of course, who drove wildly but well, and as she said good-night, she heard Mr. Selby ask him to come and see them "some evening before the holidays." He said he would, smiled amiably at Barbara and drove off.

Strangely enough, neither Barbara nor Georges had alluded to their meeting in the street-car that afternoon, nor did Lemoine comment on meeting Barbara at the opera.

Barbara insisted on having an impromptu supper of beer, bread and cheese with her uncle in the big, shiny, copper-hung kitchen. Mr. Selby went to bed and "slept like a baby" as he subsequently remarked while Barbara had dreadful nightmares; she rode on a bunch of multicolored toy balloons with Georges Lemoine, rising higher and higher in a sky full of fat white clouds, whilst Uncle George, who clung on to a slender string below, implored them to come down. How Barbara wished that they could! Finally Uncle George exploded the balloons one by one with his lighted cigarette and they dropped to the ground with a terrible thud. To the floor in reality, because that was where Barbara found herself, by the side of her bed, clutching a bit of sheet in both hands; she shivered, snuggled down among the blankets in a sort of nest of her own invention, which looked most untidy in the early light of dawn, and woke late on the morning of the first of June.

CHAPTER EIGHTEEN

The Selbys were a sentimental pair with a taste for making-up. That is, celebrating the anniversaries of their worst scenes by dining out and going afterwards to the *Palais-Royal*. Although this singularly happy and united couple disagreed about everything in general, the one great exception was the *Palais-Royal* theater. Few foreigners bother to see this sweet little theater, all dust and red plush, hidden in an angle of the immense, deserted arcades of the beautiful palace. The Selbys adored it, all, uncomfortable short seats, draughty boxes, rococo curtains looped up by garlands of unimaginably lovely roses and swollen cupids. Even the lady that shows you to your seat, the *ouvreuse,* that most grasping and faded of Parisian flowers, failed to irritate the jolly fat, dowdy audience who came to laugh and split its sides at the most fantastic and improper of vaudevilles—the kind of plays that makes the most stand-offish of neighbors intimate friends and brethren for three hours, a fraternity of conviviality, of seekers after innocent old-fashioned mirth usually caused by adultery, drunkenness or bed-room scenes all accompanied by the most absurd, and fortunately impossible, situations.

Mrs. Selby's family often reproached her with loving vulgar jokes, to which she replied that she and her husband were poets in their way, searchers after the unreal in this grimy sad world. In her franker moments she admitted liking "dirty plays"; that they were, although so innocent that her children's generation did not see anything to laugh at. If the play was too much of a success and ran too long the Selbys had to go to one of the boulevard theaters; this they liked less, and once in a moment of evil curiosity had betaken themselves to the *Grand-Guignol*. A single horror, I think it was "Doctor Tar and Mr. Feather," had led them fainting away to be revived by brandy and water at a friendly café near by, obviously there for the purpose.

To return to the anniversaries, there were a great number: George Washington's birthday, Virginia's and George's birthdays, their wedding day, the 4th of July; not Thanksgiving, Georgians of their generation had little use for it. A very special occasion was the 22d of August, the reconciliation after the Russo-Japanese war, another, the war with Cuba, a third for a terrible row caused by Mr. Selby, who had crossed the immense place de l'Etoile, reading his paper and allowing his second daughter, aged five, to be run over by a bicycle.

Last of all was the first of June, to commemorate a separation which had been all but final. A difference of opinion caused by the celebrated and almost forgotten Dreyfus case. George had said, and stuck to it for months, that a commission of French officers could not make a mistake and that Dreyfus was a miserable fellow and a Jew. Virginia disagreed in torrents of eloquence and floods of tears. When Dreyfus was finally reinstated and pronounced innocent after several trials, George had to apologize handsomely (although he secretly stuck to his opinion) and to take his wife out to dinner and the play forever after on the first of June.

CHAPTER NINETEEN

This year the first of June was an unusually festive event. The Selbys were very fond of their niece, but middle-age is but flesh and blood like the rest of us, and they were a little tired of alternately chaperoning the very young. Also, nothing makes one feel as old and neglected as watching pleasures in which one has no part. Mr. Selby could play bridge and smoke but his wife as she proudly boasted was the only middle-aged woman left in Paris, who neither drank, smoked nor danced and found the company of her peers, *i.e.* ladies with marriageable daughters, highly boring.

This was to be *her* party, with a man who loved and appreciated her. She put on a lavender silk dress rather long in the skirt, added a black straw toque trimmed with violets and a black coat; she waved her own hair and powdered her face; she powdered in the mode of her set twenty-five years ago, rubbing her tiny neat features hard with the puff until she produced a fine polish but left a little snow white powder on the sides of her nose; even thus she was pretty and very youthful looking. Her husband remained as he was except for bedewing his face and hair plentifully with eau de cologne. They sallied forth to dine at a small restaurant near the *Halles*; known only to the very greedy, and to see a vaudeville incredibly entitled (to those who live in Paris) *"Belovèd of his concierge."*

Barbara, feeling very lonely, dined at the big round dining-room table and then set to work with a pack of cards. She had found an old English booklet in which the art of telling your fortune by cards was lucidly explained. She had just discovered that she would have "brilliant love passages with a knavish young man," when the telephone rang, echoing loudly through the empty house. A gruff voice asked for Mr. Selby. "Mr. and Mrs. Selby are both out," said Barbara, "who is speaking? please?"

"Is that Barbara Winship?" replied the same voice much more gently, "this is Georges Lemoine; I wanted to call on your uncle and aunt. I am dining alone quite near you, may I come up for a few minutes?"

"Well", hesitatingly from Barbara, "I would be very glad …"

"Unless of course you consider it improper," in yet another tone of voice smug and bourgeois, reserved for formal occasions.

That settled it for Barbara; she laughed heartily and cried: "Improper! I should think not, come by all means if you aren't afraid of being bored."

"All right," brusquely from Georges as he rang off.

Barbara was filled with jubilation, which surprised her, rather; she hated being alone and welcomed the thought of any young man to talk to; she would even have been pleased to see a female acquaintance, which is saying a good deal for one who did not care much for her own kind.

She rushed to her room, changed her dress, punished her nose by squeezing imaginary spots until it was scarlet and had barely time to rush back to her armchair in the sitting-room and turn over the pages of our best American magazine when the bell rang. Barbara lay back looking haughty and indifferent, but when the bell sounded a second time she realized that the servants had skipped up to their rooms on the sixth floor and that she must answer the door herself.

She did and found Georges standing on the mat; he shook hands without a word, for this youth who was mentally as bold as brass, as hard as nails, and about as sentimental as a lark, suddenly had an attack of stage fright caused by calling on a girl. It was in fact the very first time he had ever wasted a visit on one.

He followed Barbara into the sitting-room while she explained her aunt's absence, declined a drink, accepted a cigarette, paced up and down the floor, peered out of the window as if the Avenue Henri-Martin was a novelty, and suddenly burst out:

"Wouldn't you like to come for a drive with me? I am trying a friend's car, we might go for an hour to Versailles and see how she runs."

Barbara was delighted to do this and went for a wrap while Georges mentally bit his thumbs at appearing so shy; for one dreadful moment, which his vanity could not stand, he fancied the girl might think he was interested in her. He resolved to convey to her that he was not, in some "tactful" manner.

Barbara smiled at him so engagingly when they were seated in a long, narrow, salad-green Talbot that he found it hard to begin the tactful manner at once. When he discovered that she knew all about cars and quite a lot of mechanics, he forgot to be disagreeable at all and they plunged into such a delightful conversation about cleaning carburetors and the many brakes they did not like, that Saint-Cloud lay before them over the bridge before they realized it. On the way to Versailles, bordered by silent sleeping villas, the tall trees stirred slightly, and kindly tried to outsmell the gasolene-and-asphalt combination of the shiny black road. The car turned off the high road and climbed up a narrow diagonal path that Barbara had never noticed before; they drove steadily up through a small wood and reached a small plateau covered with bracken, fern and clumps of bushes, framed by tall trees enclosed in low crumbling white walls.

Barbara gave a little cry of pleasure and surprise: "I can't imagine this scene within ten miles of Paris; where are we?"

"Just above Marly with the woods on either side; no one ever comes to this common but myself." He turned off the headlights and pointed to a little white object. "Look at the rabbit; if we sit quite still we will hear the tree-toads and perhaps a nightingale."

Georges lit a cigarette and enjoyed Barbara's surprise and pleasure; he expanded quite pleasantly. "Do you see that little white house in the woods at the end of that long alley of aspens? That is a lodge, belonging to a game-keeper; I have a room there and come up quite often in the summer for a day or two."

"Alone?" said Barbara with a shiver at the thought.

"Naturally, I come up and do my heavy thinking, I am not very sentimental you know; I am engaged on an important piece of work for my boss and if I succeed it will be very lucky for me." Then ashamed to have said so much to a mere female, he started the car, turning on the lights suddenly and tried to run over a dazzled rabbit.

Barbara was furious. "What a horrid, cruel nature you have, Georges Lemoine! How mean to try and kill anything so sweet, and on such a beautiful evening."

"You Anglo-Saxons are so squeamish! What does it matter? I am glad I didn't run it over because I don't care for rabbit; I would have given it to my uncle Langlois, he adores stews."

They ran down the hill silently.

"A *propos* of stews," said Georges smiling to himself in the dark. "I must tell you about my uncle. While you were away I had a long agitated (agitated on his part) interview with him, about you."

"About me?"

"About you. He told me not to see anything of you. He does not think me 'serious' and warned me of how dreadful it would be if I trifled with your affections. In fact he was so ridiculously solemn that I simply laughed and changed the conversation. I have not been back to the barge for six weeks now as I am too old to take lessons even from uncles."

Barbara was irritated almost to tears. "It is very good of Monsieur Langlois to be interested in my welfare but why tell me about all this?"

"Because I hate lies. I never bother to pretend about anything. I think we could be quite good friends without any sentimental after-thoughts and if we managed to laugh away Tonton Langlois' fears we might have a nice summer comradeship without any misunderstandings. I know you think me brutal," looking at her with one of his rare, lovely smiles.

The poor girl was caught in such a mesh of conflicting feelings that she fumbled blindly for her cue. "I also am frank; I don't know if I like you well enough to be friends with you. That is for you to show."

"I would like to, instead of fighting off imaginary dangers. You see, I am capable of deep friendship but absolutely proof against love. If you leave that disagreeable factor out, you get gaiety (who ever heard of a gay love affair?) and a lot of jolly excursions. Sentiment is not a good summer ingredient; it ruins the holidays."

"So you choose me for a friend?" said Barbara thoughtfully, although the feminine part of her, that is nine-tenths of her composition, was deeply offended.

"Yes, do you agree?"

"Yes," from Barbara, a simple plan flitting through her brain.

"Then leave the rest to me; we will show those old fogies that this generation can do without their sentimental kickshaws and fancies."

They drew up at the Selbys' door. "One thing," said Georges slowly, looking hard at her, "I leave it to you whether to tell your aunt about our drive. They also are full of romance, I can tell from your uncle's mustache; perhaps they had better become accustomed to our friendship gradually. Do as you like about it. I will call again next week."

Barbara nodded, held out her hand which he took ceremoniously and disappeared into the house.

CHAPTER TWENTY

Both of them went to bed in a whirl of agitated feelings; they were perfectly matched, Barbara naturally a flirt and Georges spoilt to death by easy triumphs.

Barbara was enraged at any man proposing to be her friend, and ached to make him change his mind, but she had very little insight into the Latin mind and particularly this very contrary one. Georges on the other hand really believed that he could fence off his feelings by calling them something else, in the manner invented by the ostrich. He was deeply attracted to Barbara, far more so, of course, since his uncle's little talk, but as this was the first girl he had ever noticed, he also did not know how to behave. A most imprudent state of affairs, something like dangling from a precipice by your front teeth.

Barbara's idea of sentiment was to fall in love with someone and marry him as her forebears had done before her; uneasy thoughts about the durability of human affections had crossed her mind occasionally in which a possible divorce occurred as a convenient solution. But, generally, she was convinced that she would be the exception and this point of view was unconsciously encouraged by Mr. and Mrs. Selby's perfect union.

Georges, on the other hand, thought nothing of the sort; his ideal was a reasonable Latin one with the hope of coming out of the fray, which is called life, with as little damage and pain as possible. While he never criticized or asked help of anyone, he expected the same in return; he gave nothing and received nothing, so far. To be a great banker or broker, to work hard and become very rich was his first plan; then to surround himself with beautiful things as the result. He was a real *bourgeois*, he wanted someone else's nice old chateau and park in the country, a small house full of pictures and books in town, a lot of cars and a handsome and very rich wife who would put her money in his business, introduce him to "important" people (the latter somewhat hazy in Georges' mind, but important meant of a kind he had never seen, such as maharajahs, composers, Swiss bankers and a few grand-duchesses) and give amazing parties at which everyone appeared beautiful, intelligent, witty, or of extraordinary eccentricity. As you see Georges was a poet in his way. Any affection except for his aunt, uncle and his old father was out of the question, although he was nice to children and had even decided to have two, a boy first and then a girl. This was how he felt when he met Barbara, perfectly satisfied with himself and life; the inexplicable interest he felt in her upset all his plans and left him puzzled and a little anxious. That was why the "friendship" was invented, rather than give in to his uncle's pleading and run away.

CHAPTER TWENTY-ONE

Barbara did not mention Georges' visit because, as she argued to herself in a Jesuitical manner, Mrs. Selby did not ask her any questions about her evening when she came in. Barbara began the self-deception which is the first sign of falling in love and was not really conscious of having seen Georges three times recently without her aunt's knowledge. Add to this innumerable chance meetings on the barge, which she scarcely remembered, so little had Georges counted for her.

Fate always encourages love affairs in the first stages, especially those that are most unsuitable. A number of cursory meetings at parties were the next events. June is a month of dances and although Georges did not like this form of exercise much, he was socially ambitious and secretly thought that the world of finance, although most magnificent, was not always very gay. He had a leaning to American girls and a wholesome respect for American bankers who never talked business at parties; accordingly he accepted all invitations to their parties.

A week later, quite by chance, Barbara and he sat at a supper table for four with Suzanne and Roger de la Huppe, who were now smugly and happily married. Neither of the la Huppes was capable of any happiness but that which falls to the well-assorted, prosperous and contented, so they prepared to enjoy a long period in which every year would add a jewel for Suzanne, every two years a baby, every six months a car of the latest model.

Suzanne, having conquered the freedom of matrimony, was very coquettish with Georges who rose gallantly to the invitation as any Frenchman would. He treated Barbara with an even brusquer assumption of comradeship than usual on this occasion. Whereupon Roger became "more than polite" to the pretty little thing, as Suzanne remarked on the way home.

Suzanne was full of a party she was about to give in her father-in-law's magnificent house and straightway invited Georges to make an *entrée* with Barbara.

"*Entrée?* What do you mean?" said Georges.

"Oh, I forgot to tell you that my party is fancy dress and that you can come as anything you like provided the material of your costume costs nothing: paper, cotton, rags, cellophane, oilcloth. I have asked all my friends to come in groups of two or four dressed in the same style, it is more fun and gives a better appearance to the rooms" (in case they should be photographed for *Vogue,* she thought to herself).

Georges and Barbara both thought this a splendid idea but were too contrary to express anything but polite indifference. So much so that Suzanne privately told Barbara that if she could think of someone she liked better she could easily work Georges into another group; to which her friend replied "no," she supposed he would do all right.

CHAPTER TWENTY-TWO

Mrs. Selby took to the idea of the fancy dress ball with enthusiasm and straightway decided that Georges and Barbara should go as the king and queen of hearts. She even wanted them to look exactly like playing cards, with the counterpart of their faces and draperies reproduced on the skirts of their costumes. This they kicked at, as being too heavy and as Georges said "too original," but you can imagine them looking like French cards in red, blue and gold. The red was oilcloth hanging in long folds to their feet, with trimmings of bright blue bunting and much gold lace cut out of real tinsel; immense crowns of the same gold adorned their heads. Georges wore long gold-paper hair and a beard; Barbara concealed her hair under a blue veil with the crown over it.

They had a great deal of fun and excitement over their fittings and Mademoiselle Goudeau, although offended at this mockery of kings and courts, did very well. Once she acidly remarked that she was not a bookbinder, after much gluing of tinsel and tinfoil.

At last after six tryings-on and one rehearsal, all was ready.

"Do you think we are going to smell like this at the party?" said Georges to Mrs. Selby, holding his nose. "On a warm evening the combination of glue, metal and oilcloth will be overpowering."

Mrs. Selby roared with laughter. She had a misplaced sense of humor.

"Oh no, my dears; I wondered last night if you would notice it in time. I think if the dresses hang in a draught the smell will evaporate, or perhaps you will get used to it."

"But think of the people at the party!" wailed Barbara.

"Look here," said her aunt rather sharply, "I thought of the costume but naturally there are always petty inconveniences to everything. Why didn't it occur to *you?* Anyway the party is Saturday and this is Monday."

"Hang them up until then, I know they will be all right," from Georges, now thoroughly domesticated and anxious to please Mrs. Selby. "May we go out for a walk to recover?"

"Certainly not; you can have tea here, and think seriously of what you will carry in your hands. I hope you realize that there is nothing in your costumes to show that you are of the heart family. Would you like, each of you to carry a flannel heart, I think you would look mighty sweet?"

"No, indeed," from both together, "no hearts."

Georges pointed out that it was the emblem of a butcher or a surgeon. At which Mrs. Selby stared at him suspiciously and declared: "Very well then, Georges shall brandish a gilt sword and Barbara a large red poppy just as the cards say; and, children, no more arguing this afternoon; I almost wish I had not undertaken the costumes, and it's just possible you may look very ridiculous."

With which consoling thought, she poured out tea for everybody, and as a great favor allowed Georges to dip his toast in his watery brew. He was not an Anglo-Saxon, as she pointed out and could do as he liked. The great English and American tribe must choke down their hard crumbs as they can because they invented table manners.

CHAPTER TWENTY-THREE

The party was a great success for everyone. Old Baron de la Huppe's house in the rue de Lille was a lovely late eighteenth century building, a triumph of symmetry and elegance. The ball made it look far better than ever before because the owner insisted on removing most of the very motley furniture to safety on the first floor. This left the big drawing-rooms on the ground floor bare and beautiful with all their delicate gray woodwork at last visible. Suzanne had insisted on banks of pink and blue hydrangeas; in large empty rooms they looked exactly right. In fact they should never have looked so nice, for Suzanne's taste in all things was horridly conventional.

But what made the la Huppe family burst with pride was the garden; a broad stone terrace and three steps facing the entire length of the house acceded to a big garden running down to the quai and the river Seine. Old la Huppe did not believe in growing flowers in town (a most unnecessary expense) but the big trees and lawns were beautiful.

The young people had great difficulty in preventing him from having a ball after the manner of 1900, a brass band, Venetian lanterns in the trees and a large horseshoe table for supper. In Monsieur de la Huppe's day and provincial set, supper at little tables was distinctly improper. Suzanne aptly pointed out that he must have known very disgusting people if they could not even be trusted to sit down and sup by twos and fours; but the old man said that he knew what he meant, which is more than anyone else did. He naturally disapproved of everything after that: the Hawaiian band made him melancholy, the very good jazz from Montmartre was noise, not music—the champagne was so dry that most of the guests would contract diseases of the stomach— he knew that many of the costumes would be improper and that he, la Huppe, the head of his family would politely request the objectionable ones to leave his party. His grumbling was hideous and quite groundless for if there were immodest ones, even his well trained eye did not discover them.

No one could have considered Georges and Barbara's disguise improper. They looked very handsome as they walked slowly in their long stiff robes, and quite unlike anyone else. Lots of Pierrettes, Indians and gentlemen who had draped themselves in their mother's dining-room table covers wished that they had taken a little more trouble and produced the applause that greeted the Winship-Lemoine couple.

Of course the costumes were heavy, hot and difficult to dance in. Then as Barbara pointed out sotto voce to Georges, as the evening waxed merrier, the linoleum awakened and smelt strongly. Georges suggested the garden, led Barbara there, sat with her on a stone bench for a minute, then stifling an imaginary yawn, left her. She was speedily joined by a gorgeous Doge in red brocade who admired her extravagantly and told her so. The jealous Georges, as soon as he saw Barbara so pleasantly engaged, returned in the most tactless manner and succeeded with black looks in driving away the Doge. Barbara was beginning to feel flattered at this rivalry but when Georges disappeared a second time, she became incensed by this dog-in-the-manger attitude.

She slipped back to the house and explained matters to Suzanne; she straightway introduced Georges to the tall bony daughter of a well-known banker whom he could not offend. "That settles him for half an hour," quoth Suzanne triumphantly,

"Mimi Lindenberg is difficult to work off on anyone because she *will* talk about the soul. Berry Johnson has been looking for you ever since he came and for supper you shall sit with Tiburce, 'melancholy' Martin the humorist, and Jeanne Simon. Georges shall not lay eyes on you again until the surprise scene."

Barbara forgot about him and by the time she sat down to supper, and had enjoyed two helpings of lobster mayonnaise, began to feel the most important and best looking girl in the world. She refused champagne but drank deeply of what she thought was cider cup with fruit floating in it. It was in reality a diabolical old-fashioned mixture called Bischoff composed of iced sweet white wine, liqueurs and fruit—none more intoxicating. She found Tiburce most amusing for the first time, also very handsome and told him so. The cup having worked its magic effect on him also, he was not at all surprised.

Berry Johnson, a handsome American of thirty, watched her with amusement and whispered: "You are having a much better time than your partner in hearts. Look at him."

Barbara looked and saw Georges gloomily sitting at what is politely called an "older people's table," flanked by the banker's daughter, still earnest and dreadfully sober.

"One of the saddest things in the world," remarked Barbara dreamily, "is to have a nasty disposition; the next saddest thing is to be the only tipsy one or the only sober one at a party."

All agreed.

"I also have had an idea," cried Tiburce.

"Really?" from the others roaring at their own wit and the profundity of their repartee.

"Yes," very solemnly, "I have noticed that the one that talks of being tipsy is the only one remembered as such, whereas the ones that drink and say nothing are considered sober by the others."

All agreed again and then agreed again and again about the splendor of this party, the happiest moment of their lives. Just as Tiburce began asking Barbara with passionate interest about the healths of Mister her uncle and Madame her aunt, a hollow drum was beaten around the tables by a Negro wearing a terrifying wooden mask, a bead and feather costume and a lot of white paint. The erudite said he was a medicine man and perhaps they were right, although on most days he was an honest dweller of the rue de Lille and an excellent butler.

The drum summoned the guests to the ball room where they found Suzanne and Roger in fresh costumes. Suzanne as Venus in pink satin and pearls reclined in a white satin shell looking as always, a perfect *femme du monde*. Roger was completely changed by a short yellow curly wig, buskins, a skimpy tunic and a harplet. (He must have been Apollo.) Back of Suzanne was a curtain on which hung two or three beautifully painted Greek masks, and through one of these presently issued the seraphic voice of one of the oldest denizens of the *Comédie-Française*. This happy institution not only teaches the young how to bellow verse, but it preserves as ingenues and Lotharios, the oldest men and women in France.

However, to return to the party, the guests were informed with much pomp and eloquence that they had all been closely observed since their arrival and that the gods in a fit of benevolence would distribute three prizes. The first for the best group of costumes, the second for the best dancers and the third for the most virtuous pair.

The last prize called forth much ribald giggling until the names of Monsieur and Madame de Neuville were announced by the drummer as having won this coveted tribute. An embarrassed old couple stood up to receive a bulky parcel from Suzanne (which they refused to unwrap for fear of more jokes).

"You have chaperoned five girls to this party, oh Neuvilles," boomed the masked voice, "their unworthy parents are now asleep in bed, worn out by two months of night vigils. You alone have stood the test of a Parisian season to the very last. ..." Loud clapping from the guests drowned the rest of a speech which might have been much longer.

The second prize was given to a rag picker and her mate, a dreadful looking beggar almost too good to be true; they had danced well and continuously, never once leaving the floor for the garden or another partner.

After great applause the drummer announced the first prize, won as the Comédie-Française said, "by the king and queen of hearts, Monsieur Veensheep and Mademoiselle Lemoine." Barbara could hardly believe it, her first thought being her aunt's joy. She straightened her crown firmly over her veil advanced to meet Georges whom she seized by the hand and stood in front of Venus who smirked and handed her a small parcel containing a lacquer and gold vanity case with a red heart in the corner. Georges received a cigarette case in the same design, also with a heart on it—"so that I can never use it," he reflected bitterly.

Barbara insisted on going home with the virtue prize, Mrs. Selby having seen her to the la Huppes' door, had returned home and to sleep these many hours.

CHAPTER TWENTY-FOUR

The next day was Sunday. Georges after a few hours' sleep due to much supper and sheer exhaustion, awoke about ten, hating the world, very cross with himself and all mankind. He lived in the Ile Saint-Louis at the very top of an old house built on the southern point of the island. Above the trees that bind the quais in a rustling garland, he could see most of Paris, Notre-Dame quite close, and all the domes and monuments that lie wrapped in different colored mists on the horizon.

Georges looked from his Empire bed at his room, usually tidy and severe but now littered with preparations for the ball and the remains of his costume. Through an arch facing his bed he could see his nice long sitting-room, panelled in eighteenth-century oak and amusingly furnished with unpretentious modern leather armchairs and a few toys such as a gramophone, portfolios of prints, and a large electric train with a station house, and an elaborate system of rails and switches to change the track when one circuit became monotonous. In one of the windows hung a large wicker cage with a dove in it, perpetually watched by a small black cat.

He rang for breakfast, then flung out of bed and marched into the kitchen to find a note from his aged maid (a gift of his mother) to the effect that as he had given her leave for Sunday she had prepared his tray, but that he must heat his café au lait and not leave the gas burning all day. This added fuel to his wrath as he had hoped to vent some of it in acid remarks on the poor old soul, in case she spoke to him. The telephone by the bed rang and the jolly voice of Jean Collignon asked him to go boating with him on the Marne and bathe in the afternoon. Georges refused rudely, jumped out of bed again, kicked his costume to the ceiling and threw his gold crown out of the window. He felt better after his bath and even whistled as he drank his coffee, although he stopped suddenly when he recollected how angry he was with Barbara. He even thought of writing her a note to tell her so, when reason told him how ridiculous that would be. In moments of sanity, when he had not seen too much of her, he confessed to himself that she did not encourage or even appear to notice his now violent inclination for her. He thought of her continually and as the idea of affection made him scoff, imagined it was merely a physical attraction. "One nail drives out another" said he aloud and naturally in French "I will take that little *mannequin* out for the day; we can have lunch in one of the big trees at *Robinson's* and as she is very pretty I won't have a chance to think of that beastly girl." This plan was carried out at once and Mademoiselle Rénée Laprune, *mannequin* at Worth's wished that she were dead by the time she had finished lunch with the morose Georges and had worn out his headache by walking about all the afternoon in the densely populated woods.

Incidentally she struck him off her list of companions for the summer months when her grand-fatherly protector took the waters at Vichy.

CHAPTER TWENTY-FIVE

"Auntie," said Barbara about a week later, as she sewed a pink voile dress briskly, "when are we going to Andrésy?"

"I will open the house next Saturday, and your uncle can bring you down Sunday morning. We always manage to get to Andrésy for the fourteenth of July because we love the village parade with the six firemen, and in the evening a surprise from the entire population in the shape of a torchlight procession; you never saw anything so funny in your life. If all goes well when we are settled I will also produce a surprise."

"Why do you say 'if all goes well'?" from Barbara, struck by a new dramatic note in her aunt's voice.

"Well ... because of things that girls should not worry about."

"Is it money?" inquired her niece, who like most orphans, knew a good deal about it.

"Just so. I think I will talk about my troubles a little, selfish though it is. You know Barbara, that your good kind uncle, who never hurt a fly and is the sweetest creature that breathes, has one dreadful failing that has kept me awake at night (off and on, of course) for the last twenty-six years."

"Oh Auntie," cried Barbara thrilling to the mystery, "does he drink or run after girls?"

"Barbara! How can you! You coarse, vulgar, unfeeling girl! Of course not, he speculates. The poor dear loves it and all his life has wanted me to be a millionairess. When we married we were very well off even for America. Yet in spite of repeated legacies we get poorer every year. His English blood prevents him from discussing his money troubles (or joys either) even with me. But I haven't lived with him all these years without knowing when the market is bad. It always goes to pieces when he buys a stock. He has a bull nature."

"What's that?" from her entranced confidant.

"Well, you know the bulls and the bears on the Stock Exchange or must I tell you? I thought every fool in America knew that; the bears paw the market down and the bulls throw it up on their horns. Your uncle buys when the stocks are bullish and thinks they are going higher. In fact he always thinks things are going to be all right. Deliver me from optimists and those ticking machines in banks that reel out bad news and make so many men rush and blow their brains out. Anyway George talks about Linseed in his sleep and Jews. And he went off this morning looking very cheery, so I fear the worst. However, he'll be back in an hour or so. Just hand me 'The Sorrows of Satan,' will you, my dear, and I will try and forget my troubles."

Barbara bent over and kissed her aunt most lovingly; Mrs. Selby, always shy where exterior signs of affection were forthcoming, patted her niece's arm awkwardly and snuggled down on her sofa with a tattered yellow volume.

Barbara went on sewing, thinking hard; she was rather disappointed by her aunt's confession as she was apt, in the Southern manner, to think lightly of such things. She came of a family that lost its money in cotton and rice, as a matter of course, and somehow did not connect this hazardous form of pleasure with anything dramatic. The French atmosphere which she was slowly absorbing was still very foreign to her. She heard a great deal amongst her French friends about money for your children, money for your old age, and again money befitting your walk in life, and now suddenly Uncle George seemed a breath of

Savannah; there gentlemen made and lost their money at all ages and did not bother very much about what they could leave their children. Then she had visions of supporting both Aunt Virginia and Uncle George by sewing or maybe by giving French lessons. She looked up at this unbearable thought and beheld her aunt peacefully sleeping; she rose to pick up "The Sorrows of Satan" now sprawling on the floor. Just then her aunt opened one gray eye and said in a perfectly matter of fact voice:

"If you ever breathe a word of what I told you, Barbara Winship, I'll shake you by the shoulders until your teeth rattle down your throat."

Then she went back to sleep; this amazed Barbara, used as she was to casual Southern ways and threats.

CHAPTER TWENTY-SIX

The house at Andrésy was opened on the succeeding Saturday, so nothing very dreadful had happened. On the contrary, the Selbys bustled about in their best form; both were delighted to be back in the little village on the Seine where they spent the best part of every summer. It was near enough to Paris for Mr. Selby to reach it morning and evening in a wheezy, gasping train that always rushed into each station belching forth vast volumes of black smoke. It departed in the same style, slowing down directly it was out of the station-master's sight, and repeating the performance twelve or thirteen times before arriving at the Gare St. Lazare. Needless to say this train connection with a beautiful country twenty miles west of Paris was so slow that only people with large properties and cars, or plenty of patience and spare time lived at Andrésy.

The country was pleasing and gay with a very busy Seine covered with barges and tugs, to say nothing of a few islands, meandering down to Havre in a valley between rows of gentle hills that changed perpetually as to size and aspect all the way down to the sea.

The Selbys' house was a low cream colored building of the early nineteenth century; the ground floor composed of a few very large, low-ceilinged rooms and countless small, misshapen ones on the other two stories. An enormous garden with fruit trees bordering broad walks and a lot of coarse meadow grass called lawns by the gardeners, sloped down in a terrace high above the white road that escorted the Seine all the way to the Poissy lock, four miles distant.

After about a week of great calm, Barbara began to be restless. She had arranged her tiny room, worried the maids until all her dresses were ironed. Her nails were manicured to perfection, her hair curled in a new and fancy manner, and she had read all the light literature to which she would be entitled for the whole summer. Her aunt insisted on her taking down with her thirty-six volumes: twelve foolish novels, twelve classics and twelve innocent French romances. The "heavy" books were Mrs. Selby's choice, and the French ones bought from a list sent by Madame de Malassis in a firm sloping hand. Barbara wondered which were the most horrible.

Here is Mrs. Selby's list: "Trench on Words," "The Tempest," "Travels with a Donkey," "Essays of Elia," "Esmond," "Martin Chuzzlewit," "Comus," "The House of the Seven Gables," "Emerson's Essays," "Queen Victoria," by Strachey, "Napoleon" by Ludwig. The complete works of Lord Tennyson. A very nice choice of books if somewhat heterogeneous, but Barbara suspected a deep-laid trap for improving her mind, and mistrusted those volumes. Madame de Malassis sent an idiotic list of books. It is shameful to think how much teaching atrophies the mind and renders all communication with the young impossible.

That morning Barbara roamed about the cool living rooms and "fixed the flowers for Auntie"; she pinched the apricots on the trees in front of the house to see if they were ripe, and walked to the vegetable garden in the hope that something would be ripe. The gardener was at one end spraying a vine with a nasty blue liquid; she managed by bending over a row of bushes to secure a pound or two of raspberries before he noticed her. Then she went back to the house where her aunt was darting to and fro like a sandfly. Mrs. Selby had a sheath of telegrams in her hand. "What is it, Barbara?" she enquired a trifle wearily.

"I feel a little faint, Auntie, I must be hungry, could I have a little rum and milk with an egg in it? I might lie down in the garden and admire nature."

Mrs. Selby handed her "The House of the Seven Gables" without losing a minute. "I advise you to take this with you, you might like it. You aren't going to be ill, I hope, you have been so quiet lately. ..."

"No indeed, Auntie," very perkily; "wouldn't these be lovely rooms for a party, so little furniture and a lot of space for dancing?"

"Give a party, what do you mean?" said her aunt reddening.

"Why nothing, I was just thinking that people give all their dances in town where they live in small flats and when they have plenty of room in the country, nothing happens much."

"Ass," said Mrs. Selby. She called Barbara back. "I want to lunch early because immediately after, François will drive you over to the Langlois' barge. They expect to be at the Poissy lock by two o'clock and they want so much to see you. I think they might take you away for a little trip provided, of course, that you can bear to leave us!"

"Auntie, I love you both a great deal more than you think." Which was quite true.

Unfortunately there was one person she loved a great deal more and that was Georges Lemoine.

Barbara knew it now and was in despair. Georges had called to say goodbye to her aunt, never looked at her and ostentatiously said very loudly: "Au revoir, Madame, I hope to see you again in October." *In October,* and he hoped to see Mrs. Selby, not Barbara. It was too dreadful to be despised. Most saddening of all was the fact that he had insisted on knowing her, and just as she was beginning to like him … no, ceasing to hate him and getting to love him … it was unbearable. She gulped down her egg-nog with tears in her eyes and obediently took the Hawthorne with her into the garden. To her surprise she liked the gloomy New England novel very much, and was tempted to say so, only she feared to encourage her aunt too much on her literary campaign.

CHAPTER TWENTY-SEVEN

Anyone who has been to Andrésy knows François. He drives the only carriage in the place, "a victoria by the hour," as he eloquently terms it, hitched to a mare with funny knees and traces of much usage. François' family had always been coachmen and now that so few of the gentry needed his broken down vehicle, he practiced a variety of trades, particularly broaching casks, and bottling the acid white wine of the country. When Mrs. Selby sent for him, which was frequent on a summer afternoon, François would add an old red waistcoat to his dirty clothes, take down his grandfather's chimney pot hat of white linoleum and behold, a coachman.

Mrs. Selby was fond of jogging to Poissy by the Seine road, an hour's drive each way if Coquette, the mare, felt in good form. François nodded most of the way, leaping on his box with an agonized shriek when Mrs. Selby prodded him in the kidneys with her sunshade and asked news of the countryside. Once safely at Poissy ("where Saint Louis was baptized, my dear") François repaired to his favorite café and had a *vermouth-cassis,* a *Chambéry-fraise* or some other mixed drink which is the French workman's form of cocktail. *Chambéry-fraise* is a thin white wine with a dash of strawberry syrup, the effects mild, lasting and pleasant. If Mrs. Selby were a long time cheapening antiques such as pewter and crazy old chairs, François would talk politics with his acquaintances while the *patron* wiped glasses and stared at them out of glazed black eyes. Poincaré was too hard on the rate-payers.

Briand was weak when dealing with other nationalities and the Chamber of Deputies a band of clever people who were elected by the people and then made François pay them each sixty thousand francs a year to represent his grievances. The *patron* was superior and disapproving; like all the other *patrons* in the world he staunchly supported the government and hoped it would last long enough for him to make a large fortune in five years, then he could retire for ever to loll in peace.

Then François and Mrs. Selby met in the shade of five o'clock and drove happily back to Andrésy, one full of new ideas to startle the village bar, the other with armfuls of old junk.

On this day, the fifteenth of July, François drove Barbara to the Poissy lock. He hated driving her anywhere because she hurried him, always asked pointedly when Coquette was going to die, and why he didn't cut his long frizzled mustache like Charlie Chaplin. This time however she was quite silent and thanked him politely when they got to the lock, telling him to come back for her at seven.

The river was peaceful and still, with the *Stéphane-Mallarmé* moored a few hundred yards from the lock. Remains of the glorious fourteenth of July in the shape of old crackers, defunct Catherine wheels and burnt patches showed on the grassy bank; otherwise all was lovely; the poplars shimmered in the heat and the lock keeper slept on the path, his yellow dog by his side keeping one red eye open for tramps.

The Langlois wore their country clothes, Edouard a panama, and gray alpaca coat, Germaine a black and white gingham dress and her amber beads. They were delighted to see Barbara and fell into broken, familiar conversation with her although they had not met for two months, owing to Monsieur Langlois' conferences. The poor girl was dying to talk about Georges, but he was the last person they wanted to mention as he had not been near them since Oncle Edouard's paternal conversation. They gave her all their news and finally wrung a little out of Barbara, who told them of her parties. After refreshments in the shape of grenadine syrup and biscuits they went for a stroll and the Langlois asked her to join them on their trip down the river to Havre. It would take about two weeks and they could either be tugged back the same way or she might return to Andrésy from Havre by train, leaving the Langlois to glide into one of the numerous canals that furrow France.

"You might find a young man with a Rolls-Royce cabriolet to motor you back from Havre," said Monsieur Langlois with a twinkle.

Barbara blushed and said she knew of no young man interested enough in her to do this but she would tell her aunt of their invitation and indeed she was most anxious to come. Then after playing some time with the big Afghan dogs, François appeared on the road and drove her home in a great bustle for his dinner.

CHAPTER TWENTY-EIGHT

Several cars were lined up in the High street at the back of the Selby villa also a large pale blue char-a-banc, with "Alfred's limousine" written in one corner, the signature followed by a huge green four-leaved clover. Barbara smiled and wondered what it was doing there as she had often seen it in Passy used chiefly for the weddings of the poor. Too poor to afford victorias and too proud to walk arm in arm to the church.

She crossed the little flagged court with the bored feeling of one about to dine without much pleasure and then to bed without much sleep. Marianne the housemaid met her in the hall and told her Mrs. Selby desired her to go straight up to her room and read the note on her mantelpiece. Barbara bounded up full of misgivings, wondering what she had done or what catastrophe had taken place. She instantly thought of Uncle George the speculator, especially as she heard many voices below and the scurrying of feet, which might mean an accident. Then she heard excited, cackling laughter from her aunt.

She found a note which said "Put on what you find on your bed and come right straight down." She looked and beheld the very strangest garments imaginable. She rubbed her eyes and took in the details: a pair of long boned stays, white silk stockings, an immense white taffeta dress and a wig of golden hair, elaborately waved with a jug-handle knot on the top of the pompadour effect. Barbara grinned and recognized her uncle's favorite period, 1895-1900. A sepulchral voice outside the door briefly said: "Hurry up, step on it, or you'll be late." Barbara rushed to see who it was but a distant rustle of silk down the coal black passage was her only reward.

She forgot her troubles as she struggled into the corsets and found herself the proud possessor of an hourglass waist. In her dressing-room instead of her own rather subdued paints she found raspberry colored rouge and dead white powder. These she applied liberally and found they matched her peroxided wig perfectly; the white taffeta dress billowed around her feet and fortunately the long princess body fastened at the side for she struggled into it without apoplexy. Then seizing a pair of long white gloves she went down very nervously, not knowing what to expect.

The hall looked normal and quiet, just as when she went up, but on the living-room door was pinned a card with "Barbara's party" written in capitals. She entered feeling most self-conscious as about thirty people turned and smiled at her; a small woman in mauve satin and yellow guipure, the top of her head a mass of curls, gave a shriek which paralysed her: "Barbara put on your gloves!" A stoutish man in a very strange dinner coat, fancy waistcoat, gardenia buttonhole and heavy plunging black mustaches, smiled and kissed her after the manner of Uncle George.

She gazed from one to the other, unable to recognize anyone else. A mass of palms partly hid the piano, which was draped in the most absurd way; big standard lamps with fussy tulle shades stood in the corners while the mantelpiece proudly bore a mixed flower piece arranged in a floppy artistic manner; the recipe had evidently been, one sweet pea, one lily, one hydrangea, one bluebell, etc., regardless of size.

Barbara was about to speak when at a sign from her aunt, a party of red-coated tziganes sprang from behind the piano with their violins under their arms and attacked a slow waltz called *"Quand l'amour meurt."* A delightful piece of music with much pathetic wailing in the high notes and sudden significant pauses. Mr. and Mrs. Selby arose and sailed into the middle of the room dancing the Boston in a complicated, dizzy manner; round and round they whirled, reversing and pausing, one foot lifted and waiting, only to begin again with much majesty.

The other members of the party composed of Mrs. Selby's and Barbara's intimates, were delighted. The only old lady present, an Englishwoman in a fascinating plaid bicycling costume, had to be suppressed because she said the Selbys reversed too much and that Queen Victoria never allowed it at Court. By and by several Edwardian couples joined in, looking like frigates as they circled, light as thistledown, their trains delicately looped up. The young people hesitated to dance anything so complex, and Berry Johnson confided to Barbara that "those red devils frightened him."

Barbara recognized her friends one by one and finally spied Georges dressed in striped gray flannels with a stiff high white collar and hard shirt, a country costume for the late nineties, it seems. He was clean-shaven as usual, but his hair was curled into a roach in front of the most ludicrous effect and the poor benighted girl thought he looked very nice in spite of this handicap. As the dance ended, he joined her with a radiant face; he could not for the life of him conceal his joy at seeing her again.

"Isn't this a nice surprise and weren't you completely taken in, Barbara?"

"Indeed I was. But pray where did the clothes come from?"

"Lots of them were your aunt's, who apparently never throws anything away. My costume was my father's and the Talbots have unexpected treasures. Of course there were not enough evening clothes to go round, but I insisted on your having the white dress; it is the one I like the best."

Barbara was so pleased. "Don't you think I look ridiculous?"

"You look lovely; your uncle says you are a regular Gibson girl, whatever that may be. But no time for talking now; your family has arranged a most complete set of rejoicings. The first is a dinner-supper to begin at once; I'm hungry, aren't you? It is nine-thirty."

The meal was most informal, Mrs. Selby telling the guests to sit by whom they chose. The bicycling gentlewoman insisted on placing herself on Barbara's right but as Georges sat on the other side, she didn't mind at all. They fell into conversation that was mostly heavy pauses and looks; once Barbara fancied that Georges touched her arm and she felt a dull thudding pain in her stomach, as if she had been winded. For a few minutes she was so completely happy that she realized it and wanted to tell everyone. Instead she chose to impart this information to Georges who shook his head rather sadly but smiled.

All this time the red coats circled around the long table playing waltzes, and when the spirit moved them, suddenly sounded caterwauling noises or very high notes indeed in the ear of the chosen one.

Mrs. Selby knew how to entertain; after supper the guests found that one of the sitting-rooms had been arranged as a theater; they rustled in, the stage curtains parted, and a series of ridiculous *tableaux vivants* were disclosed all in the period of the party. Mrs. Selby and her husband did the last: a copy of a celebrated gold medalled *salon* picture called *"Vertige"*: the scene represents the corner of a very palmy, curly legged ballroom; a splendid lady is sitting on a sofa while a courtly gentleman in very long wrinkled trousers bends over the back of it and kisses her passionately. Barbara thought she would die laughing, especially as Mr. Selby waved a white gloved hand at the audience and his wife lifted her skirt a few inches and showed a black patent leather boot. It was altogether lovely.

They all trooped out into the garden which was very black, and suddenly from an island in the Seine a perfect shower of stars and rockets shot up, the beginning of the fireworks. Georges stood by Barbara and watched her face as it showed up from time to time in the lurid flashes of comets and Catherine wheels. The last picture was a triumph, BARBARA written in big letters of all colors with a frame of blinking stars. She turned away with a sigh of pleasure. In the last month more had been done to make her feel grown up and important than in all the twenty years of her patchwork, pillar-to-post existence.

"Let's go and learn the two-step," she cried, hoping this evening would never end; her aunt was in favor of a Virginia reel, which was easy and great fun. Then the cotillion led by a very handsome pair; during one of the most complicated figures, Georges managed to draw Barbara, as they danced through an open door leading into the pantry.

They both looked frightened and guilty as they parted but walked hand in hand through a passage that was a short cut to the vegetable garden. A wisp of a moon had arisen and showed the broad, box-bordered walks and squares of vegetables in a bluish light. The center of the garden was marked by a round stone cistern, the water shining like a moonstone.

Barbara sat on the stone edge and looked at Georges. He remarked in a very still voice: "If I push my hair back, will you take off your wig? It is Barbara that I want to talk to."

Barbara took off her wig but remained silent, her face very set; she felt for an instant that she was frightened.

"Barbara," said Georges in the matter of fact voice of tragedy, "will you belong to me?"

For a moment she thought that this was an old-fashioned proposal, but immediately after, her brain registered exactly what he meant. She looked blindly at him with a smile of agony as if her features had not understood in time what her mind had grasped.

He waited for a little while and then went on: "You are surprised and hurt, I know, Barbara. I hate myself for saying this to you but I cannot pretend to anything else. I cannot and will not marry you, because you would be wretched with me; I am inconstant and bad tempered. But I love you and I know that you love me. If you would consent to a love affair I think we could both be happy. I will not conceal from you that my aim is to get rid of this obsession, which is making us both miserable, as soon as possible. I don't want to influence you and I will never come near you again unless you say so. It is for you to choose."

"But, Georges," said Barbara timidly, "don't you think this is a little hard on me?"

"Only hard on you if you lack character. It is no more immoral to belong to a man that you love for a year than to pretend for a lifetime to like another. Think of women who out of laziness and softness go on living all their lives, tied to one man and intriguing with several others, lying respectably to themselves and the world. They are not married women, they are merely hypocritical snares."

"But couldn't we marry and be happy forever?"

"I am not sure of being faithful to you forever; if I could think that, I would marry you in a minute. Of course there is divorce; but that is a very cheap way of showing everyone you have made a mistake."

Georges was horribly moved and quite sincere; he never hid or pretended anything. He did his best in a situation that he had wickedly brought about, not to talk sentimentally or to sway Barbara by any endearment. He sat a few paces away from her, outwardly serene, with his heart in his mouth.

Barbara braced herself up, looked at her reflection in the well, put back her wig and said drearily: "All right. Georges, I think we have nothing more to say to each other. One comfort is that I know how you feel; you don't know how much it hurts. Stay here for a few minutes, because I don't want to say goodbye to you in public."

"Oh Barbara," said Georges, opening his arms to her and then dropping them to his sides, "you don't know how much simpler it would be to marry you and lie; don't forget that I am yours and waiting for you."

She had disappeared into the house and although her face was a little chalky, the tired guests noticed nothing forced in her manner as she waved them into their bus and cars.

CHAPTER TWENTY-NINE

After a great shock, the animal body does all the work it is accustomed to without help from the brain. Barbara washed, folded her clothes neatly on the usual chair, put on her nightgown and slipped into bed. Then her grief broke out and she cried like a puppy, sobbing at first, letting great warm tears run down her cheeks and form round crystals on the pillow before they turned to water. She even stopped for a moment to watch them; when she realized why she was crying, she began sobbing again. She tried to say her prayers to drive away her grief but she could only whisper over and over: "Don't let it be true, don't let it be true." She turned off her little pink lamp and the darkness seemed friendly and cool.

"Last night, when I went to bed it was bad enough, but I didn't know all this; perhaps it is not true; perhaps Georges was joking (he didn't look as if he were joking though, answered her brain), perhaps he was only trying me." So she tossed and turned until sleep suddenly took her into heavy, still, dreamless regions and then as suddenly released her at dawn.

She awoke with a start to see a large empty, ugly, gray and white sky, forlorn, without sun and color. A thousand birds and little beasts awoke too and prepared with squeaks and chirps for a long, delicious, useless summer day. The crazy village clock struck a few strokes and Barbara remembered her misery. As Georges had talked to her in the garden, an hour had struck too. Every single word he had said came back to her, she saw his face clearly, and instinctively closed her eyes and put her fingers in her ears to ward off the scene.

He said it wasn't wrong, but somehow she knew that anything she could not tell her aunt was dreadful. Somewhere in her tired brain an awful voice belonging to a street preacher to whom she had once stopped to listen, echoed solemnly: "The wages of sin is death." Was it sin when every pulsation, every fiber belonged to Georges? The thought of his name gave her a little pain in her heart. "That's why hearts mean love," she thought, battling with confused sensations. The clock struck something else, the birds grew shriller and the sky very pink. "It's going to be fine again to-day," she murmured, draping off to sleep again.

CHAPTER THIRTY

When Marianne brought in her breakfast, Barbara lay exhausted and empty of all feeling, almost indifferent. She sat up in bed to put the tray on her knees; catching sight of the costume which the maid bore away on her arm, everything came back to her and she began crying again, but weakly, like an invalid recovering from a long illness. In her long, broken night, nothing had occurred to her, no thought of the future, only the idea that this horror would go on forever.

She dragged herself wearily up, feeling a thousand years old, dressed and walked downstairs on tired, shaking legs. "Why does this happen to me? Why me? Why not someone else who wouldn't care so much?" She almost cried again.

Her uncle and aunt were sitting in the garden at a round table, reading and talking, very much pleased with themselves, their party and things in general. Barbara greeted them quietly and sat down just back of her aunt.

"Did you have a nice time, child?" said Mrs. Selby briskly. "I had a delightful evening. I kept thinking, however, that perhaps I was giving a party that amused me more than a young thing like you. You looked so sweet, I declare I felt proud of you."

Barbara tried to say something but a squeaking sound like a mouse was the only result. Her aunt turned round sharply and looked at her. The poor wretch tried to smile and failed miserably.

"Barbara, what is the matter with you? Your face is like putty, deep rings under your eyes and you look as if you had been drawn through a key-hole. What is it, Miss?"

No answer.

Uncle George, who was reading his paper and had noticed nothing, said jovially without looking up: "She's tired, or perhaps she's like me, suffering from unrequited affection."

At this, Barbara put her head down on the table and howled. The Selbys looked at each other horrified. Uncle George patted her hand and whispered:

"Don't you cry, my pretty one; has anyone been mean to you? Have I hurt your feelings?"

Mrs. Selby said nothing but looked very worried; finally, when Barbara could only burst into an occasional sob, she raised her up very gently and took her to her own enormous bed-room, closed the shutters, gave her some aspirin and made her lie down.

"Don't you move until lunch time, lovey-dove, and try and sleep; you have had too much excitement lately, you're worn out."

Barbara appeared at lunch, still very pale but quite calm. She did not speak much, nor did the Selbys talk to her. They merely told each other their funniest jokes, delighted when a wan smile flitted over their niece's face.

She went out for a walk in the afternoon, looked better at dinner, and played rummy with them until an early bed time.

CHAPTER THIRTY-ONE

"George," said Virginia two or three days later, "why does Barbara read the telephone directory all day?"

"You don't mean to say so?" answered her husband absently. "Perhaps she is writing a novel and looking for striking names."

"Nonsense, but I will be relieved when the Langlois are ready for that trip. It will be a change for her; that child seems to live on excitement. Have you noticed that the moment it gets quiet here she begins to mope?"

"No, my dear, but then I'm a silly old fellow, I don't notice anything much. Never could understand girls anyway."

"I sometimes find you a great comfort," said his wife serenely. "*My* family is so spirited, altogether too high-strung and sensitive; it's a great relief to live with someone stolid."

"Thank you, darling, for those slippery words," answered George calmly; he had just returned from Paris and was enjoying the delightful quiet of Andrésy after a stifling day in town. As usual he had a paper in his hand. "May I read my evening paper? I see a new cabinet is being formed, and I want you to know that France will go to the dogs if they include a single rascally Jew. I hate those fellows."

"Do you?" said his wife, very suspiciously this time. She kissed the top of his innocent black head and ran into the house to find Barbara, another very deep character.

CHAPTER THIRTY-TWO

As is ever the case, Barbara's physical side came to her rescue. Within three days she looked very well and fairly cheerful, although anyone but a close relation would have noticed that she lived as a sleep-walker. All the while her brain was racing wildly, struggling to get the right angle of the quandary she had been forced into. A voice, promptly silenced by her heart, said at intervals: "You know it's not right, you know very well there is no choice, so why even discuss it, Barbara?" The voice grew fainter and fainter, less and less frequent as it was snubbed by Barbara, who sided with her heart.

The latter found plenty of poor excuses which satisfied the girl at once: "You may never love anyone else, when he knows you better he will become so attached to you that you will never be parted—after all it is a great compliment to be loved by such a handsome boy; you are the first person he has ever loved. No, he did not say so, but I know it." The very laborers as they slouched home to supper, their loads slung over one shoulder, roared of love, and how wrong it was to neglect its call.

Barbara had not become attached to her pain. It tore her unceasingly. A dozen times a day she would open the directory and read the following item as if it were a startling piece of news: Lemoine, Georges, 2 Quai Bourbon, *Gobelins 45-45.* Then she would close the book and imagine she had telephoned and that he would arrange it all. She even went so far as to take down the receiver but the sound of her uncle whistling "Waltz me round again, Willie," in the next room stopped her. The same old pain attacked her night after night; she longed to be rid of it, of all memory of Georges, yet she hugged her grief closely to her by fighting it.

On the morning of the sixth day after the party, Barbara looked at herself fixedly in her glass. She stared and stared, finally remarking aloud to her room: "I can't stand this another minute; I shall go mad and I suppose that's what everybody wants. Everybody wants! I must be crazy already! Georges would not ask me to do anything that was not perfectly natural. I expect that most people are like Georges only I never knew it; he probably thinks me a prig for even hesitating. Anything will be better than this pain."

She sat down at a small table and wrote:

Dear Georges:

    I would rather be yours than do anything else in the world.

    I am sending this letter off quickly before things can stop me.

                               Your Barbara.

She ran downstairs and met her aunt who absently kissed her.

"I am going out to mail some letters, Auntie; do you want anything?"

"Not a thing, child; don't stay out too long, the sun is very hot to-day."

Barbara drew the first easy breath of many hours as she thrust the letter into the box outside the village post office. Then she sat on a bench opposite it for half an hour until she saw the postman appear with a big black leather bag on his shoulder, mount his bicycle whistling and disappear in the direction of the station.

CHAPTER THIRTY-THREE

Forty-eight hours after, Marianne brought the answer up with Barbara's breakfast tray. A letter in a bold, square handwriting.

Dear Barbara:

I hear that you are going down the Seine with my uncle and aunt. I am motoring next week and will join you at Rouen for a few minutes. What lovely weather! I hope that you are not feeling the heat too much.

With respectful remembrances to Mr. and Mrs. Selby, yours ever,

Georges Lemoine.

Anyone but an infatuated Barbara would have found this rather a casual acceptance of all she had to give, but she thought differently. She almost burst with joy and considered it a masterpiece of diplomacy; and how beautifully worded. Anyone could read such a letter and not catch its cryptic meaning. She buried her head in the pillow to conceal her smiles, even from herself.

There is a fallacy about guilty consciences not knowing a happy moment; this one did. Barbara forgot remorse and pain in the thought that she was going to see Georges again. Another four days flew by before Mrs. Selby and François drove her to the lock.

CHAPTER THIRTY-FOUR

The *Stéphane Mallarmé* drifted down the Seine very slowly, with considerable pauses; in spite of the fact that the country between Rouen and Paris is a hackneyed theme, it was to all three travellers a most varied trip. The Langlois were anything but smart, but everything they did was like themselves, kindly and comfortable.

When Barbara awoke in the early morning, the barge had begun the day without waiting for her, and from the little window alongside of her bed she could see the water slowly parting in little waves to let the clumsy black boat go by. A mirror on the opposite side of the cabin reflected the bank and fragments of the slowly changing scenery. Barbara lay in bed quite late sometimes reading the Langlois' books, which would certainly not have been included on one of Madame de Malassis' lists; as she occasionally raised her eyes, she saw reflected in the looking glass, a little white village, two brown horses jingling in front of a pedlar's cart, perhaps nothing but distant green and brown hills or a confused mass of poplars.

She felt no emotion whatsoever except that Georges would turn up at Rouen, although she wondered how he knew exactly when to expect them. She thought of him always and gradually transformed him into something very much like herself. Georges in the spirit was present at lunch which they always had at some little village on the way, in the summer house of the only inn. Monsieur Langlois had a perfect passion for eating out of doors and his instinct always took him to the right spot. (Usually one that looked as if Richard the Lion Hearted had been the last guest or perhaps in modern times, Washington Irving.) Monsieur Langlois adored village churches; although they all looked very much alike to Barbara. After lunch the village vehicle took them to one, if not quite near, for it was very hot and the daily walk was something to be undertaken between five and seven to get up an appetite for dinner.

Barbara was very proud of the dinner because she and the bearded cabin boy, Jean, fished a little every morning when the barge was moored to the bank. Jean was an expert and they always caught enough gudgeons and minnows for a dish obtained by the simple expedient of frying brown and covering with coarse gray salt. Madame Langlois made muddy Turkish coffee of the most delectable and deadly sort; her husband prided himself on scrambling eggs better than anyone else in the world, so accordingly all agreed it was the one dish of which one never tires. Barbara made them some fudge once and although they loved it and devoured it warm from the pan, even Jean had nightmares and Edouard said his liver felt sore to the touch and ready for a bad attack.

After much dallying on the way they reached Rouen in six days and took a whole day off for sight-seeing. The riverside port was animated and ugly, but the town with its jumble of hideous modern and beautiful old architecture was a great novelty for Barbara, particularly as she expected to see Georges at any turn of the street.

CHAPTER THIRTY-FIVE

And so she did. They had had lunch at a restaurant on the old market place, the sad site of Joan of Arc's funeral pyre; Monsieur Langlois was congratulating the cook on the lobsters of which he had inordinately eaten, when Georges drove up, greeting them amiably but casually. The Langlois' prided themselves on not showing any resentment for two months' neglect, especially with the reason for it standing in canary colored tussur by their side.

"We are just off to the cathedral," said Germaine pleasantly. "How strange to meet you here."

"I am driving to Granville for the races," answered her sardonic nephew, "and I thought I would cheer myself up with a good lunch on the way. Where is the barge?"

"Waiting for us in the canal," from Monsieur Langlois rather snappily, "do you think it follows us on a lead?"

"Don't go to the cathedral, Oncle Edouard, let me take you to a much nicer church a little beyond it. *My* church, or rather chapel, is too Gothic for words."

"I know it very well," said his uncle crossly, "was taken there by a clever young Frenchman like yourself before you were born. However, Barbara has not seen it, so we might go and take in the cathedral on our way back."

Germaine and Georges led the way followed by Barbara and Edouard, still rather red in the face from an unaccustomed glass of apple brandy. Occasionally the party went single file through doorways and odoriferous alleys and suddenly it happened that Barbara and Georges walked together.

"We may not get another chance," he said in a cool voice hardly raised above a whisper; "quick, what are your plans?"

"I leave your uncle and aunt at Havre next Friday and return to Andrésy in the train, changing at Mantes."

"Splendid, write to Mrs. Selby telling her you will be two days longer than you expected on the barge. Leave on Friday, my uncle will put you into the train at Havre, just behave quite naturally, get in, but for Heaven's sake jump off at the next stop which is Motteville. I will meet you there with the car, we can have a little tour for two days, then I will take you back to Mantes and you can arrive at Andrésy at the time you said. Remember. ..."

"Barbara, look at these lovely plates," said the firm compelling voice of Madame Langlois who had stopped in front of a dusty, cheerless shop full of antiques.

"Lovely," said Barbara, "may I buy one for my aunt? I think the shaving cup with the edge hollowed out for the chin is just the thing for Uncle George."

After that they walked to the church. Georges managing one more whisper.

"Remember, insist on taking the four o'clock train from Havre."

"Do you love me?" said Barbara in a wistful bleat.

"Yes, the four o'clock train, now mind."

The church was a triumph of ogival gothic with as much carving and general ornateness as could be spent on one small chapel. Barbara laid a little bunch of flowers, given to her by the waiter at lunch, before a shrine to the Madonna and thought in her timid Episcopal heart: "These flowers aren't very nice, but I would like you to have them. And I hope everything is going to be all right; you never had a wicked thought they say, but you understand me, don't you?"

She turned away quickly, but the others were deep in conversation with the learned sexton about some photographs he had taken of the carved altar stalls and saw nothing.

They parted from Georges, who had not yet tasted food and was ravenous. As they walked silently to the cathedral, Barbara suddenly felt a prisoner, a prisoner of her own devising and she longed not only to be out of Rouen but away from the whole world. There was something so dreadful and precise in her guilt now. Deceiving her aunt, deceiving the Langlois, and the great romantic moment of her life, running away with a handsome young man, hedged in by a network of trains.

CHAPTER THIRTY-SIX

By four o'clock on Friday, Barbara was in a perfect frenzy of excitement, with a dull cold feeling in the stomach, and clammy hands. She tried hard to be natural and vivacious but only succeeded in appearing delighted to leave them. A dim suspicion of something unnatural flitted through Monsieur Langlois' mind as he saw her red, shiny face, but a minute after he thought she was homesick for her aunt and anxious to see her again.

"I wonder why you insist on taking that suffocating four o'clock train," he remarked gently after lunch. Barbara mumbled that she had telegraphed her aunt to meet that one, that the Andrésy train coincided with it exactly at Mantes.

"My poor child, I feel sorry for you on a day like this! Do you know that it stops at every single hamlet from here to Paris?"

Barbara felt so hypocritical, knowing that she was to jump out at the very first village, that she could not answer.

Finally with Jean bearing her bags, they staggered to the ugliest, dirtiest and smelliest station in France, that of Havre, or as it used to be called Le Hâvre-de-Grâce. Monsieur Langlois wore his handkerchief inside his sailor hat like an Arab and remarked that it was much cooler at Aden. The train set forth with a series of jerks and whistles as if reluctant to take Barbara, the guilty one, with it. She leaned out of the window and waved at kindly, simple Edouard; he drew one leg behind the other, holding one trouser pocket out like a skirt and curtsied low, oblivious of the delighted people on the quai. Barbara was too horrified at herself to laugh heartily because as the hour of the appointment drew near, she found everyone around her affectionate, innocent, and gay while she, by comparison, was a monster of deceit and guilt. What perplexed her most was the simplicity of the path she trod; everything ran so smoothly, fitted in so perfectly. All her life she had been told:

> "Oh what a tangled web we weave,
> When first we practise to deceive."

She was struck by the words "when first"; what would it be later on if so easy at the very start? The train shrieked again, this time like a dying pig and pulled up at Motteville. Barbara took her bags down and descended with her ticket in her mouth. She glanced around and saw Georges looking at her with a lovely, expectant look. He was leaning outside the palings which separated the station-master's cabbages from the road.

She staggered out and they shook hands in the usual Winship-Lemoine manner, without a word. Georges put her bags in the spider, already half-full of his own and they started off as quickly as a good roadster, painted pale yellow, can take you. After about three miles, they turned off into a shady lane and stopped.

"We are not in such a hurry," said Georges, "but I was afraid of meeting someone we know. The whole world is loose in Normandy at present. I did not even dare to wait for you in the station at Motteville or help you with your bags."

"I know," said Barbara; she was about to pour out her fears, guilt, tremors, etc., but stopped herself. "How did you know where to find us at Rouen and what day?"

"I did my military service with Jean the cabin boy and he telegraphed me where you were. I told him I wanted to make it up with my uncle, also I presented him with fifty francs."

"I am so glad to be with you," from Barbara.

"So am I," from the business-like Georges, kissing her hand and drawing his arm around her waist; "but I am still very much frightened of you."

"Of me?" rather amazed.

"Yes, I can't understand you—such a mixture of candour and sophistication. I never expected to hear from you again, and now you appear so unconcerned about it all."

"Are you trying to frighten me?" said Barbara, laughing.

"No, but when I look at you I have the horrible sensation that I have met my match," said the ardent lover in a burst of frankness. "Also I do not think that you resisted me enough; it is most disconcerting."

"What a contrary being you are," whispered Barbara fondly, after a few reciprocated blandishments. "Would you rather that I had not come?"

"Yes and no; now don't be offended until I explain. I am glad because I love you, no, no, because I am attracted to you; but I am sorry because I do not know just what place you will occupy in my life."

Barbara was confounded. "Do you mean to say that you are still thinking of yourself and your future? What about me? I never think about mine."

"You ought to," said Georges, driving off slowly; "you should. The future is most important, and I, for one, would never want to hamper you from making other plans."

"I have never heard of such a thing in my life; here you are young and happy, with me to love you, thinking and scheming for the future, and what for? To have all sorts of pleasures when you are old, ugly and ill (perhaps). I can't enjoy things with lucid thoughts at the back of my brain. I believe you are an old fogey at heart, and when you go to parties you try and fascinate bankers."

"Think anything you like," said Georges sharply, "only let's decide where to dine; this aimless road and conversation does not take us anywhere."

Barbara looked at his profile, pinched his arm until he winced and said, "Let's go to Mantes and have lobster for dinner and cherry tart with cream, only hurry up; it's a good three hours' drive from here."

They reached the Deauville road and drove in trails of dust and curses from other travellers, at top speed; no time for anything but an occasional smile and a cigarette. But plenty of food for reflection for both of them. Barbara realized that she did not have anything in common but love with Georges, and that it is very little for an excursion into life. They were both very proud of each other's looks, but Georges felt at times that he had done something very silly—just what he had boasted he would never do: exchange freedom for love. Who can ever boast of being friends with a girl? And this one seemed very spirited and not to be bullied.

Barbara had an affectionate nature, and Georges just the reverse; *that* ought to appear very clearly in the pages of this narrative, although neither of them realized it sharply. Thus they were doomed to fight it out unless fate stepped in, or rather justice, because a helping hand was needed for Barbara.

Just before they reached Mantes, a strange throbbing noise and equally peculiar smell struck them both. They bent down and listened.

"It can't be," said Georges firmly; "this is a new car, unless I ..."

"Forgot to put in enough oil," from Barbara. "Georges, it cannot be."

"It sounds like it," answered Georges gloomily. "I can tow slowly in to Mantes, there is a good garage by the station, I remember; only, if it's the connecting-rod bearing, as we fear, it's an eight-day repair."

The garage was a few steps from the station. Georges, now very fretful, said, "Wait here until I get the mechanic. The damned thing won't run another yard; or rather, don't wait here, go for a little walk like a good girl."

"I don't want to go for a walk in this heat," said Barbara, very nettled. "I want to wait here with you."

"I don't want you to, darling. Women are a nuisance on these occasions. Please do as I say."

Barbara was very angry at this heavy dictatorial manner, assumed, it must be confessed, to cloak Georges' irritation at his own stupidity.

He walked off to the garage, leaving the car in front of the station, and Barbara looked hard at his receding figure. Then she jumped down in the hot dusk, picked her bags out of the spider with the strength of furious, hurt pride and ran into the station. A weary porter told her the Paris train was expected in four minutes. She got a ticket, flew down the platform, and climbed into the boiling compartment of the very train she had left at Motteville three hours and a half ago.

"This is too heavenly," she thought, bursting into hot angry tears. "Spend two days with that cross lunatic! Yes, of course I love him, but I would rather die of spite than let any man order me about."

She cooled down a little, and a horrible thought struck her; she had taken the Paris train, she had written to her aunt to expect her two days later, and she remembered thirty-nine francs and forty-five centimes in her purse. What was she to do, and where was she to spend the next forty-eight hours?

Dizzy with horror, she thought of the tangled web; that was it, that was where the meaning came in. It failed to relieve her long.

She was in such a stupor that she allowed a friendly little fellow of three, very dirty and sticky, to stand on both her feet and attempt to paint her face with a grimy banana. When she realized it, she pinched him surreptitiously with a fixed agreeable smile on her face in case his parents were within eyesight, and fell to counting her money again, in the hopes of finding a stray banknote.

The more she meditated on her folly, the more she felt that she would have to tell Mrs. Selby, a most unbearable thought. When she arrived in Paris, she could drive home to the Avenue Henri-Martin, but the concierge would be sure to tell her aunt, through the servants. "Oh, how awful," exclaimed Barbara aloud, and in English to the taxi-driver as she gave Mrs. Selby's address; she felt tragic and hungry. Visions of the delighted janitor telling the servants how Miss Barbara had arrived in August, without a key, to spend two days in a deserted flat, filled her brain.

She opened the glass window that separated her from the driver and told him to put her down at the *"Brasserie du Coq"* on the Place du Trocadéro. This he did with a certain amount of jaded surprise only equalled by that of the waiter who presided over the tables outside the *café*. Young French ladies do not go to *cafés* for drinks at any time, but particularly not at ten o'clock of an August evening with a dressing-bag and suit-case. However, he advanced wearing the national expression of waiters, eyes looking everywhere but at the client, and the puzzled, absent air of the somnambulist.

Barbara entered this respectable and deserted establishment, a stone's throw from Mrs. Selby's flat, and sat on one of the oil-cloth and horsehair benches that lined the walls. She ordered a strawberry and vanilla ice and ate it ravenously, regarding the nodding lady at the desk with the beautifully waved hair, the long zinc bar with rows of gaily coloured bottles, running spigots of water and piles of sugar in a princely German silver bowl.

She read all the labels on the bottles with an air of passionate interest but, strangely enough, her heart was not in it. Her tired body refused to obey her mind and worry about the near future. She felt a little less hungry and ordered another ice, gazing at the palms in hideous glazed pots, most expensive to break, the partitions of glass engraved in the likeness of billowing curtains which hid a party of languid chess-players.

Could she telephone, she enquired presently. Yes, she could; this way, please. Barbara shut herself up in a greasy booth and asked for the la Huppes' number, thinking she could frame up some cock and bull story for Suzanne. Again and again the wire burred. softly, with Barbara listening feverishly in the *café*. Suzanne was of course away.

Barbara stared at a sign urging everyone to drink Dubonnet for the sake of health and prosperity, frightened to death, wondering what to do and whom to confide in. For one wild moment she thought of the Salvation Army, to which her uncle subscribed generously, an absurd idea considering the questions that would certainly be asked. Her brain next suggested Berry Johnson timidly; she waved the plan away, as he was not an intimate friend, but with the idea that she would presently after a decent struggle call him. "I must make up my mind that he is away or out, and then perhaps I can get hold of him," she murmured, picking up the receiver. Berry Johnson suddenly became the most important person in the world to her with his pink, weather-beaten face, hard deep-set blue eyes and curly yellow hair. After two or three rings his voice answered,

"Yes, who is it?"

"Barbara Winship."

"Why, Barbara, how nice of you to call me up. Wasn't that a nice party? How is Andrésy, and how is your aunt? Don't forget I am dining with you all next week."

"Yes, I know, Berry; my aunt is very well. Listen, will you do something for me now?"

"Of course; can it keep until next week, or is it very urgent?"

"It is a matter of life and death. Will you jump into a taxi at once and join me at a *café* on the corner of the avenue Kléber and the place du Trocadéro?"

"Why, Barbara, this sounds like a movie; is it a treasure hunt?"

"Berry, don't waste a minute. Do come now, I am waiting for you."

"You aren't going to propose to me?" said Berry's voice, laughing inordinately.

"I never felt less like it, to you or to any other man."

"Well, thank you kindly, ma'am. I'll be over to your mysterious rendezvous in ten minutes."

Barbara paid the bill and sat down outside the *café*. She watched the cars circling around the big square, lit up by occasional blue electric sparks from the trolley and the red lamps of the métro station. From the dark circle of trees and flowers in the centre of the square, dismal, muffled sounds issued into the night. A military band was playing variations on "Faust" for a crowd of gaping shopkeepers.

Berry's jolly, kind face peered out of his taxi and he jumped out to greet Barbara and her bags.

"You ought to be wearing a floating black veil and a false nose as a disguise," he remarked genially; "where do we go with your bags?"

"Well, Berry, I don't know—anywhere."

"All right; anywhere," he repeated to the driver, then, as an after-thought, "the Gare de Lyon; that's as far off as anywhere in the world."

He helped Barbara in; she was much relieved to be treated in this casual manner and said immediately with a trembling upper lip, "Now, Berry, do you mind if I tell you everything?"

"Certainly, by all means," he replied with a grin; "I am used to being the guardian angel of young ladies in tussore dresses and green scarves; they are the only ones that I ever help."

"Berry, don't you dare joke with me; I am in a corner, and you've got to advise me. First I must explain all, but promise not to tell a soul."

"I promise; I may tell my grandfather, but he lives in Narragansett, so he won't hear the news immediately. Now hurry up and tell me why you got me out of my nice cool apartment to drive to the Gare de Lyon, and in this weather too!"

After much hemming and hawing and "I hope you understand," and "No, I forgot something important," Barbara plunged into a long and complicated tale. Berry seized the gist of it, and buried his face in his hands to prevent his grins from being too apparent.

Barbara waited anxiously for an answer; it came in muffled tones from behind the hands, "The wages of sin is death."

"I know that," said the poor girl tearfully, "I have thought of it a lot, but I'm so hungry and so tired. What do you suggest apart from that?"

"Well, first of all you must write Georges a letter of apology for taking French leave and abandoning him with a broken-down car. Then you shall have supper at the most magnificent restaurant in the world. Honestly, Barbara, you never saw so much gold and such handsome caryatides in your life as at the buffet of the Gare de Lyon; and such palm-trees, they will remind you of Florida. Perhaps you would prefer to write to Georges after dinner? Anyway, you can think it over."

Berry ordered some beer for himself and smoked a cigarette; he did not dare laugh, much as he longed to, while she ate a large meal with an occasional tear welling up in her tired eyes. When he thought the proper time had come, and she had finished her cherry tart, (she had not resisted it, in spite of her sorrow) he began solemnly:

"Look here, Barbara, of course I was joking about writing to Georges, but I don't think your uncle and aunt would understand about this little escapade; besides, they might be hurt at such cunning concealment. Yes, yes, I know, girls will be girls; but I adore Mrs. Selby, and she would worry about a small matter such as you have just poured out to me. Of course Georges behaved in a very foolish way, he has no worldly experience, but then you aided and abetted him, didn't you?" Barbara nodded miserably. "He isn't a bad boy at heart, but a trifle selfish, and he probably didn't get you. He thinks he did, but my mother was French, so I have an inkling of the way both your brains work. What we must do is to find a place for you to sleep and spend two days. After which, I will take you back to Andrésy in some manner that has not yet occurred to me, and no one will know a thing about it; only in future fight shy of the Georges type. They aren't your brand."

He smoked thoughtfully for a few seconds and went on, "My grandfather from Narragansett always stops at a little hotel in the rue Vaneau. The people who keep it know me, and I will introduce you as my cousin just arrived from America; only you must park there for Saturday and most of Sunday, and don't you dare leave your room. You can be ill all day (cancer is a good incurable disease), and to-morrow evening when the shadows draw around us and all is guilt and deceit, I will prowl in and take you out to dinner at some low dive."

"Oh, Berry, I am so glad I asked you to help me."

"So am I—imagine your explanations to Suzanne, she would not have understood at all. Remember that you have been so deceitful that, no matter what comes up, you must stick to one story which we will concoct together. Now allow me to take you to the Guardian Angel hotel; nothing could be more appropriate for such an innocent young thing as yourself."

"Don't rub it in, Berry; I feel very sorry for myself to-night."

"I'm not joking. I feel very sorry for you too, but the only way to take such a sad tale is to smile; and you must admit, my poor dear, that parts of your story do bear a gentle smirk."

CHAPTER THIRTY-SEVEN

The *Hôtel de l'Ange Guardien* was a clean, comfortable place, very much like the Brevoort in New York, on a tiny scale. After Barbara had slept for twelve hours she felt the shock of the past fortnight very keenly. Her sharp pangs settled down into a dull, gnawing pain, and to live with this kind of sorrow is quite possible—only it neatly removes any reason for existing. None of the minor pleasures count for the lovelorn lady; getting up in the morning to a day of little excitements and amusements, enjoying the country or the town, had little meaning for Barbara during several long weeks.

In the meantime, Berry took her out to dinner and cheered her up on the Saturday night as best he could. He described her sentiments so accurately that Barbara was appalled and shrank from him.

"Ha, ha," he jeered diabolically, "I suppose you think that you are the only one that was ever crossed in love. My poor girl, it happens to me at least once a year, and look at me: merry and gay, slaving away at the Vendôme Trust in August and managing to feel very cheerful. No, Barbara, believe me. You will feel like this for a month, then for another six weeks, because you won't want to forget your grief too early; widows cling to their weeds for the same reason for an extra six months, or at any rate lots of them do. Then some morning you will wake up feeling very gay, your breakfast will be delicious and everyone kind and good. You will wonder what has come over the world until you suddenly clap your hands and yell, 'I know, I'm not in love. I don't care for anyone, hurray!' Then shortly afterwards you will begin all over again, only this time you may have better luck."

Barbara did not believe a single word this jolly cynic uttered, but she was most grateful to him for getting her out of the scrape. After much discussion on Sunday evening they took the train to Andrésy. Berry hurried to the Selbys to engage them in conversation and make them late for the Hâvre train. Two minutes after that impossible train had puffed out, all three arrived at the station to find Barbara waiting on the platform, with a sickly grin on her face.

She behaved very naturally—in fact she was so glad to see her relations that no acting was necessary. Berry pinched her and whispered, "Register surprise for me," and she did. Of course the Selbys asked him to dinner and that bridged over the first evening at home most successfully.

CHAPTER THIRTY-EIGHT

Life at Andrésy flowed on very smoothly for the next two months. Mrs. Selby did her duty by her niece, and invited friends from Friday to Tuesday each week; during the interval she recovered. Berry came often, the la Huppes once and some amusing French couples: an occasional bachelor for Barbara and, artfully mixed in, some of the Selbys' personal friends. Barbara said to herself every morning that her heart was dead, but boating, dancing, tennis and picnics served to pass the time away very pleasantly.

Incidentally, seeing people at close quarters was excellent for her. Cynics consider that travelling is a severe trial, but the country even for a few days is a very good test. She learned from her aunt that the guests must be amused and not pestered to death with attentions and violent exercise. Mrs. Selbys' only other rule was that the differences in age of the invited ones should not make wretched pariahs of the "older people". So a good deal of general conversation and many comfortable excursions in the woods and down the river proved to Barbara that even men and women of forty are human and larky. In Savannah the lines were more rigidly drawn, and society split into infinitesimal sets comprising débutantes, older girls, young matrons, matrons, etc., etc. Being a nimble-witted creature she assimilated much of her aunt's excellent manner and the art of making each guest feel the centre of the universe.

Barbara stayed a week with Suzanne at her husband's large place in Touraine; she went there in late September for the shooting, which is the gayest time of the year in that part of the world. All the neighbouring châteaux were filled with guests both Parisian and Provincial, and she had the opportunity of seeing even more mysterious types of French people than ever before. She liked and appreciated them more and more.

"Monplaisir" proved a large square house of no particular style, with a small park and tennis courts, the centre of the la Huppe estates. The latter were composed of five large farms, owned by the family and let to peasants who cultivated the land and divided the profits with the landowner, a favourite arrangement in France. As the land contained several small woods, chestnut groves, ponds and warrens, it was not valuable enough to lose its picturesque qualities, but provided good shooting. The proceeds from the five farms just paid for the upkeep of "Monplaisir "and enough good, sparkling white wine for town and country consumption.

The la Huppes, even the old Baron, were at their best in the country on their own place. Roger was no longer supercilious, but a delightful and hospitable host. Backed by Suzanne and her Basque servants, many improvements transformed the dreary old rooms. For instance, the departed Baronne de la Huppe's collection of stuffed birds, erstwhile distributed all over the house, Suzanne declared worthy of a museum; so she arranged them all in a small room which her father-in-law duly showed to visitors.

When Barbara arrived she found a motley collection of friends assembled.

"I will tell you the worst at once," confided Suzanne. "You see, both Roger and I have relations that never come to Paris, but that pay visits all summer, returning to their manors and châteaux in the autumn. Some are nice and others a little eccentric, but we try and jumble them all together so that the bad pass with the good. I asked Georges Lemoine to come down for a few days, as I suspect him of a little leaning towards you, but he writes that he is going to New York to study banking in ten days; he said to be sure and tell you how much he regrets missing you. So you will have to annex one of Roger's friends. To go back to the guests now staying here, first in order of importance is Tante Sarah Lamotte. She has fits, just nervous fits, and makes faces; you must not look at her too much, it excites her. She has a companion who removes her when she begins to stammer and beat on the floor with her foot."

"I promise not to laugh," said Barbara.

"Laugh, I should think not! Then we have a cousin of Roger's whom I do not like very much. He will probably never marry, so we are his heirs and get both land and money when he dies; as he is fifty and very hearty, I can look forward to at least forty more visits from him at the rate of one a year."

"What is he like," asked Barbara curiously, "a monster?"

"Not at all; he is tall and handsome with curly, iron-grey hair like astrakhan and thin hawklike features. He shoots and hunts all day during the season, the rest of the year he sits hermetically sealed up in his gloomy red mansion, smoking a smelly pipe and reading. So far he does not sound so bad, but his manners! Always very polite, but managing to convey a sarcastic meaning you can't possibly overlook. He gets his facts quite correctly, and then spends hours trying to trip you up and make you out both a fool and a liar. He even makes Roger feel silly, and you know how clever he is. I could talk about Cousin Charles for hours, I loathe him so. He wears night-shirts and ..."

"That isn't a very malicious habit," interrupted Barbara, now thoroughly interested.

"No, but wait a minute. If he sees you leaving the room with a book, no matter what it is, he will ask to look at it for a second and then calmly walk up to bed with it. One of the maids brought his breakfast yesterday morning and found him standing in his night-shirt, both elbows on the mantelpiece; he was still reading my book borrowed at eleven o'clock on the previous evening. I can only suppose that he had begun reading it as he undressed and then forgot to go to bed at all."

"What on earth was the book?"

"Larousse's medical dictionary; I wanted to look up Tante Sarah's fits." Both girls laughed immoderately, while Suzanne continued,

"Now about the nice ones: Jacqueline Maurice and her husband, you know them, so I don't have to explain, two of Roger's friends. One, Yvon Pasquier, loves Americans and is attached to the ministry of foreign affairs in the service for propagating French thought in various parts of the world; his department is America."

"Goodness," said Barbara, "I hope he won't ask me any questions. I never seem to know anything about America when I am asked, and I can't translate an English word or vice versa. The result is that Americans don't believe I understand French and foreigners are convinced I don't know English. I hope he won't be too inquisitive."

"Of course not; he is very polite. My favourite is Jacques Laborderie; he is younger than Pasquier, and wants to become a publisher; he knows all the modern writers and imitates them beautifully; he talks scandal to perfection and gets on far too well with Tante Sarah; he haunts her in the hopes of seeing her in a fit; I must say she is much worse since he arrived. It's very mean of him; think how dreadful it would be for us if anything happened to her while she was staying here. That was what I wanted to look up in the dictionary."

"All this sounds great fun," solemnly from Barbara. "Do you dress much here?"

"Not in the day-time, but a good deal in the evening; I hope you brought some good dresses. Remember I wrote you to bring a garden-party model? You know, the floppy English kind with plenty of bows, sashes and knots. We are driving out to a big afternoon party given by the old Duchesse de Vernon and I want you to look very nice; so does Roger. The old lady belongs to a very fast set, and, my dear, her son wears pink hair, pink socks, old rose shirts and a handkerchief to match; he sounds very shady but he only does it to annoy his mother; Roger says it is very funny, but I can't help thinking if it were someone less important, he would find it dreadful."

"Are we taking Tante Sarah?" asked her morbid friend.

"No, and not a word before her, please; my father-in-law is going but not the detestable Charles, so we can enjoy ourselves."

Barbara went down to dinner, looking as old as she could in a black taffeta dress and a frenzy of expectation; to her great disappointment, Tante Sarah sat in a corner, a quiet old lady, very well dressed in pale gray, her only eccentricity a large black lace hat tied under the chin with ribbons.

She found the others as Suzanne described them and liked Jacques Laborderie at once for his light-hearted, amusing gossip. Every time he sidled up to Tante Sarah, Suzanne cleverly circumvented him and forced him back into other groups. She also darted up when Cousin Charles entered the room and introduced him to Barbara adding: "She is an American, but not descended from a light lady and a convict as I know you will try to insinuate."

"I know all about America and its charming inhabitants," answered Charles suavely. "Roger tells me you are from the Southern States, Mademoiselle."

"… Nor from a slave driver," threw in Suzanne nimbly, marshalling everyone in to dinner before he could say more.

After dinner various groups were formed after the manner of house-parties since the middle-ages, and Jacques approached Tante Sarah once more. Suzanne was arranging a bridge table and was powerless to check him, but Barbara joined him eagerly.

The old lady was sitting in a far corner of the immense drawing-room quite near a tapestried door. She looked up at them with a faint gleam in her apathetic eyes. Jacques drew up a chair in a winning manner and asked if he could smoke. "Not a cigar," said Tante Sarah firmly, "only bankers smoke cigars."

"Speaking of bankers, Madame, do you know the Morgenthals who have just taken Clairfontaine, near Chambord?"

"I knew the former owners," she answered dully, "the son threw himself out of a window in 1890 and broke his neck. No one but I knows the truth about it."

The companion hovered nearer, making desperate signs to Jacques which he pretended not to see.

"Do tell us," begged Barbara, thinking the conversation was going splendidly.

"It's not a proper story for young girls to hear, and Mademoiselle Claire is looking at me," said Tante Sarah with a cunning smile.

"Please tell us," pleaded Jacques. "I am writing a book on the period; all this information is of great value to me; remember I told you all sorts of amusing things about Paris the other day."

"Yes," from the nervous one, "that's true; Mademoiselle Claire says you excite me, but the truth shall be told for once. Well, to put it briefly, this young man took a fancy to a very pretty housemaid and had obtained a rendezvous in her room that night, the night of his tragic death; and why did he throw himself out of the window?" her voice rising nervously and picking madly at her dress, "because Philippe de Lamire, when he tiptoed up to the girl's room, entered and closed the door, found it empty. Presently Zola crawled from under the bed, President Sadi-Carnot from one curtain and General Boulanger from the other."

Tante Sarah rose in her chair. "General Boulanger," she shrilled as her companion closed in upon her, "and he said 'either write me a letter of apology in algebra or throw yourself out of the window'; you see he was in uniform so Philippe did not hesitate." She moved calmly enough as Mademoiselle Claire urged her to the tapestried door, but added in a terrible earnest whisper: "Poor Philippe could neither read nor write and Boulanger knew that and besides ... I know the end ..." she trailed out.

Barbara was faint with fright and even Jacques looked staggered and remarked: "Then it is true after all that she was in love with Boulanger and never recovered from his meteoric career and sad end. I hope the La Huppes did not hear all this." But they had, and disapproved vastly. Jacques had to promise not to badger poor old Sarah any further, particularly as it seems that he looked a little like Boulanger, only, of course, beardless.

The rest of the evening was comparatively tame, spent in dancing and in playing Polish Bank, at which pastime Barbara lost most of Mrs. Selby's money. She hoped like all born gamblers to make it up the next evening but she departed owing Suzanne a small sum, plus the servants' tips and her railway fare to Paris.

Shooting, for those who do not shoot, means trudging about ploughed fields, scrambling through hedges, eating hurried lunches and beginning all over again in the afternoon. There were occasional stops for Suzanne and Barbara for a short nap in a shady grove, but they kept as much as possible with the bulk of the guns. Not so much for love of them as to avoid Cousin Charles, who was a sharpshooter; he found his own game and shot it alone. He was an excellent rifle, only, like the cross-eyed man, he did not look where he shot and caused the only casualties of the season. So far they amounted to a pair of velveteen trousers and a couple of ducks, but he was considered dangerous.

Charles, to give Suzanne the lie, was extremely nice to Barbara and on Sunday morning when the others had gone to Mass, took her for a walk along the Loire, that now all but vacant bed of yellow sand. She gazed at the pale blue sky, the green-gray flat wooded scenery shading delicately down to warm beige tints as it met the gigantic river bed; over it all floated the misty subdued golden light peculiar to that kindly country in September. Charles told her all about the historical *châteaux* and explained that the river used to be very deep and that the immense castles that look down upon it were built of stone that had been brought all the way from Nantes in barges. He described the way the Valois kings of France used to travel slowly up the river in beautiful flat boats shaded with gorgeous silks and followed by ships full of musicians and courtiers; how Catherine de Médicis, that agile plotter, did a great deal of her business on her barge with a few trusty poisoners. Barbara said that it sounded to her just like Shakespeare; Charles agreed with her which elated the lady considerably.

Suzanne, a matchmaker like most married women, urged Barbara to marry him and become her cousin, forfeiting, as she remarked, millions. But her friend only grinned and told her not to be so funny.

CHAPTER THIRTY-NINE

Barbara went straight to Paris, feeling much better as to the heart, although she still thought a good deal of Georges and worried about all the girls he might fall in love with in New York.

Returning to Paris was an event, and the avenue Henri-Martin looked lovely, with a few rusty golden leaves still fluttering from the chestnut trees in the fresh air. Aunt Virginia said her husband looked tired and worried but his niece found him his usual affable self. He gave Barbara quite a big check to "get ready for the winter campaign, my dear," and she planned many gay doings in which her clothes would be pure triumphs of taste and color. Suzanne promised to take her to some of the great dressmakers, so Barbara waited for her arrival.

Meanwhile she had a shock. Her friend Cornelia Deluth, now Mrs. McGehee, announced a grand tour of Europe, staying for a week in Paris. The girls saw a great deal of each other while Mrs. Selby cornered the tall silent Walter McGehee and prodded him for Savannah news. She was disappointed by what she heard, even though he warned her that Savannah was growing up and society not what it used to be. He dimly knew her set and introduced her to some new names which made her very angry. At every mention of a stranger she compressed her lips icily and exclaimed: "The Baxters! Why, her grandfather used to deliver my mother's milk. What, the Tempests going to parties and meeting your wife when their great-grandfather was a cracker and kept a store on Bull Street. You can't tell me about

Savannah, Walter, I wonder Cornelia's mother can sleep in her bed at night." Walter said she didn't mind much, that Savannah kept up with the times, but Mrs. Selby was indignant. She who was broadminded and intelligent as far as Paris was concerned, became a provincial snob about Savannah society.

Meanwhile her niece battled with Cornelia, who either cried and said Barbara had changed to her, or bridled when she admitted that she loved Paris.

"My mother says the Latin races ought to be wiped off the face of the earth," said Cornelia once. Barbara had never noticed before what a flat, toneless voice she had.

"I bet she never saw a real one; anyway I notice we all liked the Nouettes, the Legris, the Bonnards, and they were French a hundred and fifty years ago."

"Yes, but look at the immorality in Paris."

"Kept up specially for you to see, dearie," said Barbara, surprised at her own warmth; "besides, you needn't hand me any of that old-fashioned stuff. Look at the things that happen in New York and Chicago. Three-quarters of my French friends, thank goodness, never even heard of them, and they won't from me."

"Yes, but that's up north."

"Nonsense; Auntie says Memphis passed for the wickedest place on God's earth in her time and Savannah. ... You don't know the half of it, as Mister Gallagher says. Neither did I, until I came over, because I was just a kid, but my aunt tells me things about my own family that would make your hair curl. Why, my great uncle John—you know the nice old judge? Well, he kept two families, his wife's and another. Every time I had a cousin, an illegitimate one appeared too. Now that's deceit for you, and besides it's disgusting to be married twice at the same time."

"I never heard about that," said Cornelia crossly. "Of course if you rake up old scandals ..."

"You know very well that I'm only taking that instance because it is in my own family and that Uncle John is dead and buried, but you may be sure that we are not the only ones."

An interminable discussion made them hot and angry. Barbara, who had looked forward so much to seeing Cornelia, now hated her and wished that she did not wear dark blue satin and gun-metal stockings.

Barbara's perceptions, although confused by mixing with too many people, were rapidly expanding. Also she liked Walter and tried to fascinate him, just to keep her hand in. She found him amenable in a mild way, which Cornelia also cherished against her.

Cornelia returned home "after a perfectly lovely time in Europe. And Paris! Too marvelous, every minute there perfect, the shops would fascinate you girls and those lovely, lovely picture galleries (she never saw the inside of one), when I close my eyes and see those pictures in the Louvre. ... I ramble in memory through each of those rooms filled with gems. Yes, I saw a good deal of Barbara Winship; I was so disappointed in her, she looks old and hard and disagreed with everything I said. She is very stuck up and has lost all of that sweet girlishness that was her only charm, back in Savannah. She loves the French—they are too attractive—but I don't believe she can speak a word of their language, although she does gabble at taxi-drivers. They are too fascinating for words with their rough manners and whiskers and they talk so fast. No, I didn't go to the Morgue, I couldn't find it and of course that smarty Barbara didn't know where it was," and so forth and so on; that is the way journeys are told.

CHAPTER FORTY

After a breathless Indian summer, October turned rainy, then cold and windy. Mr. Selby looked worse and his wife watched him anxiously, with bursts of affection. His face grew ashen and drawn, from taciturn he became quite silent, although still smiling. Even Barbara at last noticed that something was wrong and at once bought him a present, a duck pie, his favorite dish. He hardly touched it and when they played cribbage in the evening sighed in the most alarming manner: "Nothing, it's my liver, I expect it is time for my calomel," he explained in a burst of theatrical frankness which deceived no one.

Finally, one day he let himself into the house at three, walked into the sitting-room, dropped into his armchair and groaned loudly. The answer would have been "What on earth is it, George?" if his wife had been in earshot, but she was out. When she returned, two hours later, she found him still sitting with his paper in his hand and a very red face. He muttered: "Market very bad, Mr. Crosby, please get me my slippers, Virginia is out and I'm getting old and broken; ask that damned Adler to give me three days more, I'll get the money, everything's going to be all right. I don't want my wife to know anything about it. I'll crawl out somehow." He stared at her hard. "Why, Virginia, I thought you were Crosby; mighty hot in here, how y'getting on?" He collapsed, breathing hard.

Mrs. Selby clapped her hands to her head and screamed loudly two or three times; then she recovered her nerve and never lost it again during the weeks that followed.

When George was in bed, still gabbling, and the doctor had seen him, she telephoned to Mr. Crosby, the invaluable secretary and confidential man of the Carolina King Cotton Company, presided over in Paris by Mr. Selby.

"Mr. Crosby, my husband is very ill, the doctor says he has pneumonia and," here the tears blinded her, "has very little chance of pulling through; will you come up to see me at once, please? Thank you." She hung up the receiver and glared at Barbara: "Don't you dare to cry, Miss, he's going to live, because I'm going to make him live. Go and sit with him while I talk to Mr. Crosby; don't let him jump out of bed, he is light-headed, and see that the fire behaves like a gentleman."

Mr. Crosby came in, looking very important and concerned. He was devoted to his boss and disliked the idea of talking to his wife about his business. When I tell you that Mr. Crosby's favorite axiom was "the hand that rocks the cradle rules the world," you will guess him to be a little old-fashioned as far as the ladies are concerned.

He shook hands with Mrs. Selby in a mournful manner, as if George had already departed. "What can I do for you, Mrs. Selby?" he murmured, professionally.

"Do for me?" she answered briskly. "You can save my husband's life if you will only speak the truth and not hum and haw in the usual manly manner. Who is Adler and how much money does my husband owe him?"

Mr. Crosby was winded: "Adler?" feebly.

"Yes, Adler; now hurry, I may be able to do something."

"Well, he is Mr. Selby's private broker; you see, stocks have been low lately and Mr. Selby bought largely about three months ago when the market was firmer. Early in October he bought some more rubber shares on credit from Adler, expecting a rise that would have compensated everything. Instead Wall Street went down lower than ever before and ..."

"Go on," feverishly.

"But this is confidential information Mr. Selby gave me this morning; I don't know whether he would like me to tell even his wife."

"Like you to tell me!" roared Mrs. Selby, stamping her foot. "Really, my patience is at an end. If you don't tell me this minute you will be no better than a murderer because now I can still do something; or would you rather convince yourself it is serious by hearing the poor man in the next room?" She opened the door slightly and Mr. Selby's hoarse voice was heard drowning timid soothing remarks from Barbara.

"Leave me alone, the fellow has a heart; Adler, just give me a chance; my wife doesn't know a thing about it and I can easily raise twenty thousand dollars, but it will take a few days. Adler, listen to the song I made up for you in the office:

I wear my pink pajamas in the summer when it's hot,
I wear my flannel nightgown in the winter when it's not,
But sometimes in the springtime and sometimes in the fall,
I slips just in between the sheets with nothing on at all.

It's a fine song (not quite sure whether I invented it or not but that dirty Jew would not know) and Adler, you can sing it to two tunes: 'John Brown's Body,' or the 'Merry Widow Waltz' ..."

"Now do you believe me?" whispered Virginia.

"Well, it won't do any good, but Adler wrote this morning and said that if the twenty thousand dollars were not at his office by twelve to-morrow, he would write to the President of the King Cotton Company in Charleston. Adler has known Mr. Selby for years but he is scared because the market is so bad and it means quite a large sum to him. Anyway the President doesn't like his representatives to gamble and this is a serious matter."

"I should think so, it is exactly two years' salary; thank you, Mr. Crosby. I'll ring you up to-morrow morning and could you take the money to Adler? Tell him he almost killed the goose with the golden eggs this time."

Mr. Crosby gaped slowly: "Do you think you can get the money?"

"Naturally, if my husband's life is at stake. Goodbye," she added pushing him out firmly but with a polite smile on her pale lips.

She opened George's door and beckoned to Barbara: "My poor child, we have a hard time ahead of us; I can't ask my own daughters for much help, with all those tiny children. Never mind, sit with your uncle, change his bandages if you can when they dry and don't talk to him. I am going out."

She jammed a hat down on her head and walked out having telephoned to several strange people, including an Episcopal bishop who happened to be in Paris.

Meanwhile Barbara sat behind Mr. Selby's big pillows; by the light of the log fire she could just see his hands playing the piano on his sheets; most of the time he hummed and talked persuasively to Adler. She was terrified and felt she could never smile again if Uncle George disappeared. She did not say the word "died" even in her thoughts. All his kind, endearing habits came back to her, also his tiresome trick of covering everything with newspapers. The chattering red-faced lunatic in the bed was a caricature she did not associate with him. "It will never be the same if I don't see Uncle George reading the *New York Herald* in his chair when I come in—and he gave me that big check too." She hadn't cashed it.

Her aunt came in at about nine o'clock looking very white but composed.

"Is he just the same?" she asked faintly.

"Well, Auntie, he is much quieter."

Mrs. Selby felt his pulse and shook her head. "Ring up the doctor, Barbara." When she returned, her aunt was looking over some checks, curiously as if she did not know what they meant.

"I think that's about twenty thousand dollars," she said dully, "count them up my dear; I got eight thousand from Mamie Fairchild for my diamond rings and the pearls; I knew she would pay what I asked for them; what a mercy I saw her name in the paper this morning; here is all of Evelyn and Margaret's spare cash. They are coming over early to-morrow morning to help us. Bishop Page, gave me, gave me, mind you, not lent me, two thousand; the rest is old Mr. Havemeyer's, the banker, a friend of my father's."

The doctor refused to be optimistic and the two women took turns all night at watching the invalid and the fire. In the morning, Barbara for the sake of the airing, took the money to Mr. Crosby and the Jew was silenced.

Mr. Selby settled down into a terrible pulseless apathy; the doctor at last told his wife the truth. His heart was very bad and had evidently given up the struggle. "If he does not want to live he will ..."

"Die," completed Virginia, "no, he won't, he can't die."

She dismissed the doctor in her usual masterful manner. Then she bent over a table littered with medicines and prepared an injection of camphorated oil. She paused a minute and nodded to an uncommonly good idea. A bottle of Bourbon whisky contributed a small drink and armed with glass and syringe she bent over her husband's bed. George had the strangely intent look of the very ill, withdrawn into regions that the healthy do not penetrate. At the same time he appeared on the watch for something that he knew all about, but without curiosity or impatience.

After the oil had been injected, his pulse grew a little stronger and a resentful flicker came into his eyes as much as to say: "Why do you bother me? Leave me alone, I am thinking of something interesting."

Mrs. Selby grasped his hand and said loudly: "George, do you hear me?" He pressed her hand feebly still with the absent look on his averted face. "George, listen to me, darling, I have some good news for you, Adler says it's all right." His eyelids fluttered. "He will wait as long as you like." George's mask looked vaguely interested. "Now drink this and let me fix you up nicely." The whisky worked wonders, George whispered: "Did you say Adler?"

"Yes, Adler says not to worry, just pay him when you get better. Now you have got to get well quick; you wouldn't have me spend the rest of my life working to pay off a miserable Jew would you?" Mr. Selby pressed her hand again a little more firmly and fell into a light fitful slumber.

With terrible ups and downs, after three days he was pronounced out of danger by the doctor, who knowing nothing of the skirmish with Israel, was much surprised at the turn for the better. Mrs. Selby wagged her head to herself, said "you don't know me, my dears" to an imaginary audience, took down the telephone receiver and proceeded to sleep all the afternoon. She left the reviving George to his niece with strict injunctions not to talk to him and not to give him any of the new medicines the doctor had so kindly prescribed.

A week later he sat up in his chair and his wife read the papers to him: the Gumps, the interesting crime about the lonely old lady discovered in a parcel cut up into forty pieces of exactly the same size. "That fellow's an artist," said George admiringly. He held out his hand timidly to his wife and said: "Virginia, the white horse* almost got me that time."

"I know he did; oh George, how could you let yourself drift off like that, I thought I would never get you back."

"I didn't want to go, but I was so tired I had to give up."

"All this because you wouldn't tell your poor old wife your troubles."

"I must say," piped up Barbara from the sofa where she reclined looking as tired as her uncle, "anybody who buys Auntie for a fool will want their money back."

The Selbys smiled fondly at her. George said he wanted all his children around him for lunch next Sunday, this patriarchal display of feeling being one that he always possessed even when in rude health. He began choosing the meal carefully and fell into a baby's sleep as he finished off "Sally Lunn and jam, fruit, coffee, liqueurs, cigarettes and a nap."

---

* Death

CHAPTER FORTY-ONE

Pneumonia, mercifully, comes and goes quickly, so Mr. Selby was up and out in a jiffy. When the tiresome news about the money was explained, he seemed immensely pleased and planned paying it off in installments beginning with the banker.

"Of course it may cramp our style for a long time," he remarked to his wife.

"About three years; that means three thousand a year to pay off, as the jewellery brought in eight thousand and Bishop Page gave me two more. I would much rather owe that much less and not have those big Brazil diamonds, I don't care for them anyway. I shall replace them with enormous amethysts and yards of pink pearls from the 'Galeries Lafayette.' I love cheap jewels and flashy stones."

Virginia really meant this, and adored the shops in the rue de Rivoli with their tempting glass pendants and rings.

Then it was that Barbara unfolded her idea to her aunt on the very day that Uncle George went back to his office.

"I think I ought to do something for my living," she blurted out suddenly; "now that Uncle George is better, couldn't you help me to find a job?"

"Well Barbara," laughing heartily, "we can still manage to keep a sparrow like you, in spite of coming down in the world. We won't feel those three thousand dollars at all between you and me, because I have hopes of an old cotton claim being paid;

it is not very much but I think it will wipe out the first loan easily; so you see you needn't worry."

"You aren't trying to discourage me? I have been thinking of it ever since Uncle George fell ill."

"Of course I am not; but people like you and me come up to the scratch in a crisis but need plenty of rest in between times and lots of amusements."

"It must be so interesting to have your own money," said Barbara, then flushing she explained, "I know I am welcome to yours, Auntie, but think of the feeling that you can do something people are willing to pay you for. It seems impossible that anyone should pay me!"

"It does sound funny," agreed her aunt placidly, "but stranger things have come to pass; of course I shall help you but I warn you solemnly that no one can save you from the boredom of routine and that's what is called a job. Now let me see, what would you like to do?"

"I would not like to work in an office."

"Most offices would not like it much either," answered her inflexible aunt. "You don't know typing or shorthand."

"I could learn."

"So you could; but I see clearly that you don't want an all-day job of any sort. You want to start out at about ten o'clock in a taxi, drop in at your office and sign a few important letters and checks; or stroll down town in perfect weather and see how much your beauty parlor earned for you yesterday. That is not it at all."

Barbara laughed pleasantly: "It does sound nice. You know I like drawing, do you think I could work for *Vogue* or *Harper's Bazar?*"

"I am afraid you will have to begin a little lower in the magazine scale; remember self-made women always begin by licking the letter flaps and sweeping the floors; you write very nice letters; what about articles on fashions with sketches; you are fond of clothes, it might amuse you. But first catch your hare, then cook him, as the old recipe book says. I know very little about it but I am sure that I can find you a little position; only it takes a stout heart to go out into the world and work, even with an aunt to back you."

"Why so doleful, Auntie? I am dying to begin."

"Well, the back stairs aren't as pretty as the front ones, and it takes a lot of grit to tear a little money from this hard world."

"I'm going to tear a lot of money from it," said Barbara confidently.

Mrs. Selby was a lucky woman; everything she attempted looked easy and came out successfully, probably because she was intelligent and did not attack the impossible. This time, she did not exert herself much, because she thought her niece much too young to work. After enquiries at the chamber of commerce she learned that many dozens of trade papers, technical or professional, existed, each one with a correspondent in Paris at least, or a large staff. Her head reeled when she was told that one paper was published every day. She had made no headway at all when her husband came home and mentioned casually that he had met an old fellow at a business lunch, whose wife was retiring from journalism; she wrote for trade papers and it might be the thing for Barbara. The man had said there were a lot of them, that they did not pay very well, but that his wife would be very pleased to see Barbara.

Barbara went and reported that the lady was an invalid who had not left her room for twenty years and wrote the fashions entirely from imagination and faithful descriptions of her friends' clothes. "She gave me a lot of her stuff to read and is writing to the 'The Upholsterer,' 'The Provincial Haberdasher,' and 'Hats and Chapeaux' to recommend me as her successor. The first two papers are English and the third Canadian. Isn't it nice of her?" dancing about and hugging a huge parcel of papers.

"Perfect strangers often do more for you than your own flesh and blood," said Mrs. Selby sententiously, holding out her hand for a paper. "Barbara, do you really think you can write for an English paper; how I wish you had studied 'Trench on Words' this summer!

"I don't write very correctly but I am such a monkey that if I steep myself in the lady's style perhaps I can imitate it."

Mrs. Selby approved; they both sat down on the sofa with one of the papers and this is what they read:

Paris, October 15th, 1929. Although the whirlwind existence of the *élégante Parisienne* is by no means complete without a sojourn at her *Château* in the country, yet a few of our smartest *mondaines* have returned to the *salons* of the *élite* among *couturières*. The preparations for winter styles appear to be largely a question of tassels, frills and laces with of course a great deal of fur; the latter is almost always black or the favorite brown, etc.

"Tassels! *Elégantes mondaines!*" repeated Mrs. Selby in amazement. "I don't think poor old Trench would do you much good here."

The other articles were written in much the same arch, playful style colored by an invalid's powerful imagination. Barbara was accepted for a trial by all three papers but after several attempts to imitate her predecessor's style gave up and dashed off an article to each with a tincture of truth and a rattling schoolgirlish sparkle. Mrs. Selby begged her to be guided by her, and not to be so jocular, but her niece refused to listen to reason.

Both awaited results with anxiety and in a very short time two dignified letters appeared from the "Upholsterer" and the "Haberdasher" respectively. Both papers declined any dealings with Barbara. The "Haberdasher" was especially indignant and wrote as follows:

Dear Madame:

As recommended per our esteemed correspondent, Mrs. Stevens, we consented to try you as our reporter on Parisian styles.

We are sorry to say that your trial article was a great disappointment and does not suit us in any respect. Our paper is a conservative provincial organ distinguished in tone and *clientèle*. Might we say that the tenor of your article is both flippant and trivial? Expressions such as "top-dog" stockings and "gold-digger's" suits are incomprehensible, nor do we favor facetious phrases such as "lingering with the lingerie." They are quite incompatible with a British publication of high standing.

We remain, etc.

The "Upholsterer" was equally furious. Barbara feared the worst from Canada but after a month received a breezy letter from "Hats and Chapeaux" congratulating her on her excellent, lively style and hoping to keep her as their correspondent for many years.

As the first taste of blood to a tigress, so thrilled the heart of Barbara to her first check from Canada. One article a month left her with plenty of time on her hands and she took up her very pleasant worldly life where she had left it in June.

Then "Hats and Chapeaux" wrote late in December announcing the creation of a dry goods review with a modest but weekly place reserved to Paris fashions. Would she accept this post with rather poor but steady pay? To Barbara it sounded magnificent and when she realized it meant attending all the press openings of the collections at big dressmakers and choosing models to be reproduced as sketches, her joy knew no bounds. She chafed and fretted waiting for this important minute in her life to begin. She told all her friends and the news was received with envious approbation.

CHAPTER FORTY-TWO

It had become very smart in Paris te be an independent woman with a check book. Whether they needed it or not, married or single, everyone in that town in 1929 did something. The more old-fashioned painted on porcelain or made artificial flowers, but the bolder ones sold anything. Duchesses bartered their connections and worldly experiences for highly paid articles in fashion papers. Spanish grandees sold doubtful antiques; ladies dropped into their shops every afternoon, worried the saleswomen, pored over the books and were nuisances. Every form of scandalous memoirs, chiefly those involving the living, were an instant success. Needy gentlewomen had no hesitancy whatever in unfolding the dull scenes of their childhood or the more exciting events raked out of their parent's past. The upper middle-classes, ever conservative, merely lay in bed in the morning and did a little brokerage on their own account. Every tea-party was a mart for grand-ducal jewellery appearing magically out of respectable hand-bags and the number of middle- men or rather middle-women increased enormously. The conscience, reputation and professional ability of everyone in command was gauged for advertising purposes and publicity to an unsurpassed degree. You bullied or persuaded a queen to sign a testimonial about a car or a cold cream and received a limousine or a fat check in return. Life became an exciting and always remunerative gamble. Professional go-betweens were out of a job and honest men, hedged in by a net work of intriguing beauties, hesitated to go out to dinner.

The tax collector, so vigilant and so hard on the honest mediocre rate-payer watched, in powerless rage, most of the money in the country go into commissions which left no traces; the amateur has no patent and keeps no books. In fact, that is sometimes their weak point from a business man's point of view. This riotous trading was an unending chain, as the very lady who passed her dressmaker on to you with a ten per cent commission on every rag you bought, had to buy from your jeweller in return.

All this was fun, but the cleverest of the restless ones accepted jobs with salaries and very short office hours. So Barbara joined the Vanity Fair and was most amused by the bartering and chaffering around her.

CHAPTER FORTY-THREE

On the twenty-eighth of January, Barbara went to her first fashion opening, which took on the face of an evening party with all the press, the buyers and most of the designers' friends. The Selbys took her there and retrieved her at eleven-thirty, very happy and genuinely pleased with the three hundred odd models she had seen in a cloud of Abdulla cigarettes and champagne.

The next afternoon she saw another collection which she also liked, the next day, two more collections; after that two or three a day for a fortnight. By the evening of the fifth day she was ready to scream for fatigue, nervousness and boredom. Even the presence of a buyer in a short leopard skin coat and top hat failed to soothe her. She looked over her notes feverishly, tried to get a clear idea of the coming fashions and finally cried one afternoon at Worth's because a photograph was refused her.

Her aunt failed her for once and insisted on her continuing. It was very cold outside, stifling in the show rooms of the dressmakers, overcrowded with jabbering buyers and exhausted saleswomen. By the middle of February, she had salted down her notes with her tears and written some fairly clear articles. By the end of the month she took to her bed and stayed there for two days, dead to work or pleasure.

Uncle George was deeply concerned and wanted her to give up this horrid pastime, but his wife said, no, Barbara wanted to work and this was an easy occupation except for August and

February, the first named month being an even worse repetition of her experience.

The succeeding weeks were child's play, Barbara took to the articles and wrote them very well; her peculiar child-like angle of the fashion jargon was a success and she even had imitators who brought out their Paris letters in baby talk, thereby moving the English language one link onwards in its American transfiguration.

CHAPTER FORTY-FOUR

B erry Johnson looked around his hideously furnished flat. The walls were covered with sapphire blue blotting paper with gold spots, the furniture, composed of shabby divans and dome-shaped black velvet chairs like so many ghoulish thimbles.

"I don't care," he sang, "I don't care, I'm going home."

He went on packing; the simple method for trunks and suitcases alike consisted in flinging armsful of clothing in, then sitting and jumping until the lids locked.

A pleasant looking young man sat on one of the thimbles and looked very disapproving.

"What does it matter?" said Berry. "That's what they are going to look like anyway, when the customs officials are through with them in New York. Besides they, the officers, I mean, will be so disappointed at not being able to plough through a neat gentlemanly trunk and tear its liver out."

His friend rose and walked all around the adjoining rooms and passage.

"Berry, are you really lending me this flat?"

"Yes, my boy, I am, for six months; you can do what you like with it until I return. Of course the gift entails obligations, but more about that anon."

"Anon?"

"Anon, my good bully frog, means later; wait until I persuade these bottles into my socks."

"Berry," said the youth, "before you go, tell me the truth; are you going to see your grandfather in Narragansett?"

"My grand ... why bless your fresh young heart, Michel, he doesn't exist; he is a figure of speech, a way out of difficulties, an excuse. Now that I am going home, he's dead, gone home too. But now for a few solemn words. I am lending you this handsome flat, my new electric shaving mirror (broken glass means seven years' bad luck or I would try and crowd it in with the rest) my lovely cook, wig and all, and the unlimited use of my bath and shower. You think I am doing all this because I love you?"

Michel nodded agreeably: "Of course you love me."

"Well I don't; I have a sincere regard for you and I am very sorry you have to live with your parents at the age of twenty-eight. So I am doing everything for you, but you, too, have duties to fulfill unto Berry."

Michel looked frightened. "Don't look like a terrified hare with your ears back. Listen, I am leaving my girls in your charge and you must love, honor and obey them."

"But what about my own obligations?"

"Nothing to do with me; either you take on my cherished ones and my flat or you go back to live in a small room in your mother's house."

"How many are there?" said Michel faintly.

"There are three, all dangerous unless properly handled," said Berry, lighting a cigarette and flinging the match on the divan where it burned a large hole in the velvet and caused a pungent smell; he watched it fascinated for a moment and continued:

"But observe, the first two don't have to be kept for me, I just want you to let them down gently and keep my memory green." He placed a large dirty hand on his heart. "Just can't stand scenes, make me feel so weak, so small." He broke into his dance and song once more all about going home.

"I think," said Michel, "I would rather not have the flat."

"Ah, please, you aren't going to desert poor Berry-Berry in an hour of need are you? Remember I'm coming back and I want to find things all calm and quiet for me when I return. I'm an old man, two whole years older than you and my poor heart won't stand much more sorrow."

"Berry," said Michel in a menacing voice, "stop this and tell me about those girls."

"I knew you would do it," answered Berry cheerfully; "to put it briefly there are two awful ones and a charmer. In the first class, we place Mrs. Baxter. She told the whole of Montparnasse and a half a million Americans, all living in Paris, that I was in love with her last year. The result is that we are asked everywhere together and how that woman plays up to it! I have to go and sit in her would-be salon (which is far more like a saloon than a drawing-room) every second Saturday; not a pleasant occupation for me, I like football. All the geniuses from the cafés for a mile around, come and look profound. When they talk, I can't understand a word they say, they are so infernally deep. If I hazard a remark, the kind that passes between lowbrows like you and me, what happens? Shrugs and silence. Honestly my feelings would be hurt if I weren't so bored. Then they leave me alone with Eleanor Baxter and she gives me a list of errands to run when I'm not chained in at the bank; how I hate her!"

"But why do you stand it?"

"Why? Because her husband is the manager of my bank and I want to live in Paris; you don't suppose I would otherwise. I tell you, love wouldn't bind me to such a horrible situation."

"Must I take your place?"

"Bless you once more, of course not. You couldn't," from the fatuous Berry, "but I did mention that you would call from time to time and that your Mamma would let her look at your grandfather's pictures. She won't like you; you're dark and not beautiful like myself. All you do is to make things polite and pleasant so that when I return to France, Mr. Baxter won't be unkind to me and transfer me to the baggage department. Oh thank you, thank you. Now about Georgette. I really did like Georgette once upon a time; she is a distinguished French lady of affectionate morals, very pretty, you know her, she used to be the pride of the big candy shop on the Faubourg Saint Honoré. Well, my boy, I liked Georgette quite a lot, even though she took all my salary from me, until she lost her best lover, a cheese and butter magnate and transferred her affections to me." Berry wiped his face and was astonished at the looks of his handkerchief, which he showed mutely to his friend. Michel looked disgusted. Berry went on with his low narrative:

"Now I am a trifle tired of her because she cries and tells me all about the sorrows of her father the taxi-driver (never be hard on one again, Michel, it may be one of her relations) and her mother who excels in the confection of bead funeral wreaths. Now don't get your feelings hurt, I love and respect the great French institution of bead funeral wreaths, they look their best in the rain and outlive the memory of the poor corpse.

"I can't stand tears; they depress me and make me wish that I were dead. She wants to know always and ever if I think of her in my bank and if my father would approve of her as a daughter-in-law. You know about America being a republic full of half-naked savages, no social laws exist there for Georgette. That would be all right, only she threatens to kill herself with a solution of sulphur matches if I don't take her out to dinner. Once she ate a whole tube of aspirin, and you think perhaps she died? Not at all, she slept all around the clock and lost her job. Merely do this for me, soothe her down, make a little discreet love to her to bridge over the first weeks of absence; discreet love I said, for Heaven's sake don't let her get to the tearful stage with you and she will meet the romance of her life in a month's time from now and forget us both; only I don't wish her to drink a bottle of kerosene and blow up just to aggravate me as I step on board my beloved boat which is taking me home. Because I am breaking the news to her by letter."

Michel was becoming very gloomy. "Bring out the third," he commanded.

"The third," said Berry, starting nervously, "oh what a fright you gave me; why, the third isn't a love, she's a girl, a friend. It's Barbara Winship, perhaps you have heard of her?"

Michel shook his head.

"Well, I want you to know that Barbara is a very nice American girl of twenty-one or two, very gay and my sacred charge, first because I love her aunt and next because she dances beautifully."

"But I don't like American girls."

"You don't like American girls?" said Berry advancing like a panther, "you don't like American girls? Then I'm afraid I must knock you down for insolence." He pushed Michel over suddenly and threw him on the divan. "And now I'm going to Desdemona you for daring to speak ill of nature's best and purest handiwork, the American maiden." He busily covered Michel with cushions saying meanwhile, "Do you promise to take Barbara out to dinner on the anniversaries and be nice to her?"

"Yes," said the dying one, "and what are the anniversaries?"

Berry explained the Selbys briefly and their anniversaries. "Of course they can't enjoy themselves with their niece moping at home, so I have charge of her on those events and take her out to dinner; afterwards we go to a movie or for a long walk along the Seine. But if you want to change the order of the rejoicings you can, because that girl added to her other failings is the weakest, most amenable human being that ever I did view."

"Do you mean to say that the Selbys are going to send their niece out to dinner with a stranger?" said Michel sitting up and smoothing down his curls.

"How crude you are! They don't even know of your existence; but they will in a minute or two because after my bath, I will take you there to call."

"I have thought everything over; I refuse your flat definitely and forever, all its goods and the infernal tasks that go with it; you Americans are a nasty commercial race, not a generous bone in your bodies."

"My temper is getting short," said the irritating Berry, "and I won't take a bath, I'll just wash my face and hands; I shall take you at once to Mrs. Selby, you ungrateful, boneless fool. It's a cocktail party, not a formal call; you see if you don't like it very much. You'll get what the governor of North Carolina always offers the governor of South Carolina when he calls. Never mind, it's a joke; and when you get there don't say to Miss Winship in your fatuous way 'I'm going to take you out to dinner at least twenty-four times a year' because she wouldn't understand, never having heard of you and Mr. Selby would have to knock you down and possibly kick you downstairs; leave the dining out to me."

CHAPTER FORTY-FIVE

Michel Saint-Amant was such a nice young man that no description fits him; when he went anywhere, which was seldom, as he was both retiring and busy, the wickedest people instinctively made the best of themselves and tried to appear as sympathetic and sweet as they felt him to be. With it all a total unconsciousness of his charm. Michel had his faults; his absent blue eyes were too far apart and his black hair would curl when he forgot to put on his South American hair glue. He was the prey of bullies like Berry and easily softened, which explained that his mother by tears and prayers had kept him with her until Berry's offer of the apartment.

Michel had written a slim book of sonnets which he was now ashamed of, although they were excellent, and a very poor but earnest play of which he was extremely proud. Earnest is a mild way of putting it, for it contained several murders, the best to be performed on the stage. Berry thought it would make a splendid movie and had annoyed several managers with it, but most actors objected to hanging by their feet, even for a minute, from a chandelier. In the meantime, Michel read books for publishers, wrote very brilliant articles of criticism and was only waiting, as he bitterly remarked, to be old and idiotic before he was appointed to a good paper as a reviewer. Years before twenty-five both for work and pleasure are like the hours before midnight for sleep, they count double, only all the old gentlemen in the world have forgotten it.

Madame Saint-Amant, a widow both rich and generous, could be considered a perfect mother who spoiled everything by a passionate curiosity for all things regarding her son. The reaction on Michel was to make him as secretive and deceptive as possible as far as his mother was concerned. He had been to Oxford for two terms and there met the irrepressible Berry, who gravely assured him he was learning English; this was meant as a joke but was not so much of one as either boy supposed. Berry improved Michel and gave him self-confidence and Michel unconsciously softened Berry although that exuberant creature would never have admitted it.

They had seen very little of each other in the last three years as Paris separates most lives very successfully. Berry's idea in offering his apartment was a friendly one but also came from a spiteful desire to checkmate Madame Saint-Amant in her maternal efforts to retain her son for life. His plan concerning Barbara was to amuse both parties, but he suited his purposes a little too generously when he threw Mrs. Baxter and Georgette in too; in fact it was diabolical of him, a practical joker would sacrifice his nearest and dearest for the sake of a good jest.

CHAPTER FORTY-SIX

The Selbys were at home occasionally in the late afternoon to a few friends; they did not serve cocktails, as George said they ruined his palate for wines. Instead they helped their guests generously to large mint juleps. Incredible as it may sound they grew the mint all the year round: in the summer at Andrésy, in the winter in a complicated glass frame which disfigured the bathroom and fostered some very mangy spearmint, the object of constant watering and quarreling.

Berry, like everyone else in the world, was very fond of juleps and although they made him tipsy and liverish, always accepted and even clamored for a Selby invitation.

When he entered the sitting-room with his hand crooked under Michel's elbow to prevent flight, Mr. Selby was remarking to a very red-faced gentleman that the tinkling of ice in a glass was the prettiest sound in the world.

"No matter what time of year," agreed the apoplectic one enthusiastically as he held out an empty glass.

His glass was replenished and George turned to another guest whose snow-white hair contrasted with a mahogany colored countenance: "How are they off for liquor in your part of Virginia, Ellis? What do they do in Prince William, it's pretty near Washington, ain't it?"

Ellis nodded sadly: "Poorest county for spirits in Virginia; we make a little parsnip wine but it isn't very satisfactory. Why, sir," he cried warming up at the memory, "it's terrible tasting stuff and you have to drink it lying down."

Much commiseration was expressed by the other two, made keener by the thought that Charleston and Savannah were much safer and nearer the coast.

Michel after introductions all around, instantly fell in love with Barbara and sat down to talk with Mrs. Selby. His gentle voice was a pleasure to the latter especially as he seldom raised it, and let her hold forth. He gazed, fascinated, at Barbara, who had so far merely smiled amiably at him and thought him nice looking; Barbara always thought that of tall young men whose faces were not positively repulsive.

She sat in an armchair, with a watery julep in her hand talking to Berry who held a very dark brown glass. They were conversing most seriously about something and Barbara nodded her head solemnly several times. Everytime she did it, the light caught her hair and the little curls at the back glistened like metal.

Mrs. Selby called her and told her to mix a drink for Monsieur Saint-Amant; this she did and brought it presently. Her aunt rose and joined Berry. Barbara, like a well conducted Miss, sat down by him. She stared at him for a moment.

"What's the matter?" said he (his first words to the love of his life).

"I'm looking well at you to see how you look before and after, that is if you aren't used to juleps," (her first words to her new young man).

"I have drunk whisky in England," quoth he proudly.

"But this is much stronger, it's the mint that does it."

Michel drank his julep and the effects were speedy; he turned a trifle pink and asked Barbara a great many questions about herself, a thing he would not have dreamed of at other moments. She answered politely and asked him about his work, a few very

stereotyped remarks, which he considered beautiful and beautifully worded.

He was obviously in love with her in the most artless manner and tried to please her, instead of biting his thumbs and rag-
ing as Georges had done. Forgetting all the reticence due to a
short acquaintance he asked her to come and see his mother's
pictures with Berry one day soon, to-morrow, for instance, as
Berry was leaving in forty-eight hours. In spite of the julep and
dawning love, his brain warned him of the folly of this invitation and the miserable life his mother would lead him in conse-
quence. "Which is worse," thought he as Barbara thanked him
and accepted, "to tell *Maman* that I met her to-day and brought
her to see her the next, or to pretend I have known her for some
time and get the 'concealment scene'?"

CHAPTER FORTY-SEVEN

When Berry and Michel left the Selbys the air struck them both as unusually fresh and bracing. Michel was most enthusiastic about the whole family.

"I told you so," said Berry, "but aren't you getting your cues mixed? I said Mrs. Baxter, not Barbara, for the pictures and now I've got to see those blasted Nattiers again and waste my last afternoon with you."

Michel pretended to be much surprised at his mistake and tried to carry if off by giving a boisterous stage laugh. Berry was not deceived and said meanly:

"Being kindness itself, I tried hard to arrange with Barbara about the occasional dinners, but she refused."

Michel looked miserable. "You asked her too soon, on purpose. How could she accept when she scarcely knows me; you might give me a chance, you're so mean. I asked Mrs. Selby if I might come back some day without you and everything was going on so nicely, now you've spoiled it all."

"April fool, April fool," danced Berry in the deserted avenue, "don't get into a tipsy rage with me, Barbara said nothing and neither did I. And you needn't think you can poison my last hours in town by talking about her all the evening."

Madame Saint-Amant was very nice the next day; she fortunately took it for granted that Barbara was Berry's *fiancée* and no one cared to undeceive her for sheer terror of the cascades of questions that would inevitably have followed.

Barbara was her usual gay but silent self, a difficult but not unheard of combination; she radiated health and vitality but wasted little effort on conversation, beyond the demands of exacting French politeness. She had great difficulty to refrain from giggling when she saw a new French Berry instead of her breezy compatriot; his French blood came out strongly in certain atmospheres, and the well-ordered stately rooms decorated in the profusely gilt manner of the late eighteenth century struck awe to his soul.

Madame Saint-Amant looked about twenty-five, dressed very youthfully and was the typical, vivacious witty French woman dear to yellow-backed novels. Berry bent over her hand and kissed it in a courtly manner, then talked to her of various acquaintances while Michel tried to draw Barbara out. All four looked at several rooms full of Nattiers and minor French masters, who smirked icily from the brocaded walls. Barbara liked them but thought privately there were too many, too many valuable little tables covered with gold knick-knacks, too many imposing circles of gilt and tapes-tried armchairs drawn up in uninviting chains around empty hearths. She noticed too, that there were no flowers and that all the windows were closed, although it was April and very warm. Of all the houses she had seen in Paris, none had been more magnificent and crowded, yet deserted and forlorn. She compared it with her aunt's apartment, full of books, shabby furniture and flowers; she preferred the latter, but then her taste was anything but perfect.

She was touched by the sweet gentle manner of Michel and felt his charm but it never occurred to her to fall in love with him. Strangely enough, there was a certain ethereal quality in him that made her feel very material and raw although she was not particularly earth-bound.

Berry unexpectedly begged her to see him off the next day and Michel was so pleased when she consented. A lot of other people were at the station bent on the same errand for the cheerful are ever popular, but Berry clung to Barbara and Michel in a burst of affection, besought them to write to him and looked wretched as he stepped into his compartment at least ten minutes too soon. He pulled down a window. Barbara was quite moved and said: "Berry, what am I going to do without you? No one to take me out to dinner, it isn't done in respectable French circles; must I wait six months before I see the inside of a tavern again?"

Michel looked at Berry appealingly; the latter pretended not to see him.

"The girl plainly has a taste for low life," answered Berry, "you don't suppose anyone can replace me? Cheer up I'll be back in November. Ask Saint-Amant to get you a taxi, I can't bear to think of you all alone in this dangerous part of Paris, when I'm gone." He sobbed. "The worst murders are committed right around here in broad daylight. Goodbye, goodbye perhaps forever." He blew kisses to them and horrified all the groups on the platform, both French and native.

They waved to him, the train moved out slowly leaving those on the quai with the usual dejected and abandoned feeling of being left behind, balanced by the elated impression of the travelers. Why is leaving everything behind one of the nicest sensations in the world?

Michel turned to Barbara. After a few banal sentences in which they pronounced the eulogy of the departed, he said: "Would you like a taxi?"

"Well," hesitatingly from Barbara "the traffic is so impossible in these parts at lunch time, the *métro* would be best, I think. You know there is a line that goes directly from here to the avenue Henri-Martin."

"I will take you there, if I may?"

Barbara acquiesced and they walked to the underground without a word.

Michel, who lived miles away on the left bank, was delighted to take the stuffy *métro*, quite out of his way, rather than leave her. Such is the power of love to make us do the most uncomfortable tasks unsolicited; that is one of the reasons it is a strange and much talked of passion.

Conversation in the *métro* was as usual a series of shouts and jerks. They both gave it up. Barbara fell on an old man's lap and he cursed her under audible cover of his paper. Michel could not understand him. When they reached the station *rue de la Pompe*, he walked down part of her avenue with her and in a fit of shyness left her a few steps from her aunt's door. He stood waiting for a taxi when the sound of running made him turn his head. There stood Barbara smiling and out of breath: "I forgot to tell you that my aunt wishes to call on your mother to thank her for her courtesy to me, showing me those beautiful pictures."

Heavens, poor Michel realized that ten minutes' conversation between the two ladies would expose the fact that Barbara was not engaged to Berry, that he hardly knew her. What possessed him to invite her?

"I am so sorry," he answered hurriedly, "but my mother is in mourning."

Barbara, full of memories of yesterday when Madame Saint-Amant had worn a flame colored satin dress began: "In mourning!" Then she pulled herself up "Of course in that case, it is out of the question."

"Well, not exactly in mourning," said Michel also recollecting the pink frock, "only we expect to be in a few days."

Barbara looked very sympathetic. "If I had only known, I would not have intruded on her yesterday."

Michel struggled in an ocean of lies. "Just an old man, a distant relation, a grandfather I think."

Barbara was rather shocked at his off-hand manner. He blushed furiously and said: "Might I come to see you some afternoon, perhaps I could explain better?"

"Please do," Barbara answered in an important voice, "only let me know, because you see, I have my work and that takes up a great deal of my time."

"Oh, you must tell me about it," cried the enraptured Michel, grasping at a topic of conversation, "I will come very soon."

Barbara nodded and smiled and under the majestic impression of her own importance, she, a busy girl with articles to write, turned away and wagged herself down the avenue.

CHAPTER FORTY-EIGHT

Mrs. Baxter sits conversing with the wretched Michel two weeks after Berry's departure. She telephoned asking him to come to an informal party at about six "as I want to make your acquaintance before my other friends arrive." She did not care so much about replacing Berry, for she had the whole of the bank to choose from, but was suddenly fired with a desire to meet a real Frenchman, an unknown factor in her set. There were some mild French clerks at the Vendôme Trust but somehow they slipped through her fingers when it came to errands, and she was tired of their smiling, silent presence at her deep, vinous parties. What a triumph it would be to acquire a Parisian man of letters; of course he would fall in love with her and languish for years; she would enrapture him occasionally with a smile, give him nothing else, naturally, she was a very virtuous woman, and take him to all the cafés in Montparnasse; there all her friends congregated of an afternoon and evening, very busy seeing life under its dirtiest and shoddiest aspects.

Eleanor had lived in Paris about three years and must have imbibed the strangest ideas on all subjects; even Mrs. Selby, used as she was to oddities of this sort, would have been surprised at some of the things that Eleanor knew "for a fact" or "my husband was told at the bank." Her imperfect French, learned from servants, gave Berry many a good guffaw and he was careful never to correct her unfortunate and literal translations from the English.

Added to all this she was perfectly beautiful, came from a town in Iowa that was just forty-one years of age, and fondly showed postcards of the "old Methodist church where my parents were married." Morally and mentally she was as facetted as a cut glass stopper, with about as much personality. Eleanor was a liar, inside and out, a real liar that told falsehoods, and an unconscious one that perpetually acted a part. Sometimes she was her own idea of a great lady from the Faubourg Saint-Germain, sometimes a prairie flower with a shy but hearty smile. Other impersonations were the bluff stern woman of business, worried about the stock exchange, the young girl miserably married to a wealthy banker, the fascinating snake that no man can resist, and last of all, the intelligent woman of the world from New York.

That was her favorite rôle which she had just learned, quite alone and it really did her credit as far as imagination was concerned. She resolved to come out in that act for Michel, read a few passages of Ezra Pound, remembered some new words and rehearsed a novel and irresistible way of toying with a chain. Then she ordered some flowers, stood them in baskets on the floor and pinned some cards on them, from imaginary admirers.

Her studio sitting-room was a sad case of undigested modern art, carried out in cheap materials. Black tables with the enamel nicked off supported dusty muslin arum lilies in iridescent glass vases, aluminium chairs and fur cushions were reflected in mirrored walls, where the glass was not painted in enormous Negroes and Indians. Because a lady with excellent taste had a small pearl gray boudoir, Mrs. Baxter showed cubic armchairs covered with battleship gray vegetable silk satin. Altogether one of the meanest, cheapest efforts in decoration possible. Mrs. Baxter thought it beautiful.

Mr. Baxter also thought it beautiful; he loved and admired his imitation wife in all her moods, though he secretly fancied a more home-like room to relax in after banking hours. At the parties, he mixed the drinks, handed sandwiches and relapsed into canine adoration of Eleanor.

The bell rang at six and was answered by a slip-shod Annamite, a coolie in his own country, who ushered Michel in with a black *betel* smile. Michel gazed curiously at the room, looking very well dressed and wholesome in this artistic center. Meanwhile Mrs. Baxter let him wait while she gave a few touches to her striking costume. Finally, she put on a hat made of silk crochet and gold stars, ran down the passage, burst open the studio door and stood there for a minute before she advanced to greet him. She panted softly, breathed:

"Monsieur Saint-Amant, how splendid of you to come early, I was afraid of missing you and ran all the way home. Just been spending the whole afternoon with Gertrude Heffeldinger, you know, the great Picasso collector."

Michel kissed her hand: "I have met Miss Heffeldinger, she has beautiful pictures."

Mrs. Baxter tore off her hat. "Forgive me, I can't help relaxing a minute after those intense minutes of artistic pleasure. Really Gert is just too wonderful." Then remembering the New York attitude she sat down severely in an armchair, motioned him to another a long way off, rattled her chain, put on a monocle and said with an intelligent appreciative air:

"Tell me, Monsieur Saint-Amant, what do you think of our intelligentsia?"

Michel, fumbling a little, said he liked them very much.

"I want you to be truthful; it is such a comfort to meet a really cultured Latin, whose senses have been whittled down to needle point sensitiveness. Do you not think that we Americans are just a wee bit crude?"

Michel answered quite truthfully that he liked them very much.

"Oh I know, we have brains of course, talents, even genius (for Oswald Smith *is* a genius you know) also we have, forgive me for being so brutal, money. But don't you think we lack background, just the subtle halo that surrounds one's personality making the ego less perceptible?"

Michel although he knew English, only caught the word money and said that it was a very nice thing to have.

"Oh well, of course, we can do fine things with money but cannot we attain our ideal without it? Is there anything in the world worth while bartering the brightness of our souls for?"

Michel looked dizzy, as though hanging into space from a great height, and entirely agreed with her.

Eleanor gave him a soul-mate look and crossed the room slowly to sit on the back of his armchair. "Excuse me," she said in a husky tear-veiled voice, a new accomplishment, "I had to come, it's your aura," with a sweeping gesture around his head.

He smoothed his hair hastily and said: "I can't help it, it won't stay down properly."

She continued: "Your aura reminds me of dear Allan Dupont's, the same clear pale blue with gold flecks, it hurts so to feel him so far away."

"Is he in America?" asked Michel, wishing she would leave his chair before anyone came in.

"No," with averted head and clenched white hand, "he has passed out from the finite to the infinite, into the cosmos which absorbs all things. Cholera morbus," she added, "in a few hours, just a simple tragedy, only the heart remembers and bleeds.

Forgive me, Monsieur Saint-Amant, somehow I feel I have met you before, perhaps in a previous incarnation."

"Allow me not to think so, Madame," said Michel firmly, "I am a Catholic."

The door opened and wholesome Mr. Baxter walked in.

"Oh, Harold, meet Monsieur Saint-Amant; he is a friend of Berry Johnson's. Monsieur Saint-Amant has just been telling me the most interesting thing; he is a Catholic."

"I have met some very good men among Roman Catholics," said Mr. Baxter in the solemn manner he felt proper for foreigners. "Do you reside in this city?"

Michel said he did and began talking to him about Berry, hoping to slip out when some more people came. Sure enough they arrived in a body, a motley crew of honest men dressed amazingly to suit the artistic needs of their quarter, and some women to match.

Mrs. Baxter as Michel said goodbye, gave him an arch smile and impatient gesture. "But we have not spoken of dear Berry; I have something very important to tell you about him. Will you promise to call me up to-morrow morning?" Michel promised that he would. She looked the part of shy young love and simpered: "If you don't I will, goodbye." She smiled fondly once more and when the door closed on him became a westerner again to enjoy her cocktail.

CHAPTER FORTY-NINE

Michel held his sides when he was safely downstairs; he tried to remember the conversation. To think that poor old Berry had stood it for two years. He smiled, planning to ask Barbara the meanings of all those long words. He was not going there again, to Mrs. Baxter's, and he knotted his handkerchief carefully to remind himself to answer the telephone in a disguised voice every morning until Mrs. Baxter forgot him. Then he thought of Berry's future and promised himself to go to Mrs. Baxter's once more, but unexpectedly, and drop a card.

Michel knew Montparnasse very slightly although he had once spent an hour with a literary friend in the cloakroom of one of the largest cafés, there spelling out rude limericks, scrawled on the walls, some of them witty and all of them improper.

As he rounded the corner of the rue Campagne-Première, where the Baxters lived, and turned into the boulevard Montparnasse he ran into that very friend, a jovial youth, called Tristan Lemerre, bearing an immense leather satchel full of manuscripts under one arm and a small picture under the other.

"Michel," he said solemnly, "this is fate, allow me to make your fortune for you, shall I begin?"

Michel seized him by the elbow and they seated themselves at a large, crowded café; the waiter regarded them with suspicion when he heard them speaking French and shook his head gloomily at their order, a bottle of Vichy water. Lemerre smiled at the waiter and explained: "You see I do most of my business at cafés; if I drank your fizzy drinks all day, I would most likely explode every evening; meanwhile thanks to your good offices, I take care of my liver and thus, by drinking Vichy, even when I become very rich I will not go to Carlsbad."

The waiter brightened at the word Carlsbad for he was a German and it was the only sound he had understood of Lemerre's harangue.

Michel said impatiently: "Don't waste so much time explaining your insides to the waiter; what are you going to do for me?"

"Well, briefly, everything; you know that the great Heuzot the literary critic of *Le temps et l'Espace* died a week ago and there is no one to replace him, or rather a great many but no one that will exactly satisfy the French middle classes. For years it has been a mutual admiration society between them, the *bourgeois* buys what Heuzot likes and he only recommends nice safe literature, not too upsetting, or sad, or improper; above all no new ideas and if possible, no ideas of any sort, but a good clear style and a wholesome love of the classics. Now with his sudden demise the paper is helpless and will lose a hundred thousand subscriptions in the provinces if they choose the wrong successor."

"You're so long-winded," said Michel, "do you want me to replace the old beast? If such is your idea I am about to call a taxi and take you far, far away to a nice little place in the country where a kind doctor will keep you locked up."

"I must be patient, even if I try and benefit him; no that's not quite it, but I heard to-day that the paper is about to try Labique, the man who digs up literary souvenirs and unearths authentic historical documents. He has written himself out anyway and his post will be given to the first critic who can furnish something new. Now, my boy, you are going to be Labique's successor; you have the style and the taste and I will see that you get the job. Furthermore, I will provide you with an untapped source of reliable information in the shape of an old Polish gentleman who sits in this very café from nine to twelve every evening. I will introduce you and he will tell you extraordinary things about every event of importance that took place between 1865 and 1929."

Michel was dazzled: "Why doesn't he write himself?"

"Because Polish noblemen of his school do not write for newspapers and also he is very rich. He has arrived at the age when he must impart his recollections or burst; and mind you, every word he says is true and he possesses band-boxes full of letters and manuscripts. All of this will be yours if you sit here two or three times a week and listen to him. Incidentally, it is an amusing task for in spite of his seventy-five summers he is alert and witty, not merely garrulous."

"But why don't you undertake this fascinating work yourself?"

"Because I write a novel on tramps all day and in the evening I contribute the theatrical news for the 'Morning Star,' so occasionally I have to go to a play or a review. Just say the word, I'll furnish the old gentleman and you can begin to-morrow evening. Will you?"

"Will I! It is the very thing I wanted; I will be the only young man who writes for *Le temps et l'Espace*. It shall be graven on my cards and, as late as possible, on my tombstone."

They arranged to see the Pole on the next evening together and Michel's first article would be submitted to a table full of graybeards, twenty-four hours after.

Michel was so excited at this opportunity for glory that he decided to walk home and go straight to bed; he even forgot Barbara for about ten minutes, although afterwards he had a long mental conversation with her in which he told her of his brilliant future and asked her if she loved him a little.

The concièrge handed him a letter on orange paper with rough edges intended to suggest medieval times, which used no note-paper. The writing was immense and many passages were underlined in purple ink. Michel read that Monsieur Berry had often spoken of him, that the writer was sad and neurasthenic, in fact had not eaten since Monsieur Berry's departure. Could she see him, or rather would he call on her in her modest retreat; she could no longer leave her bed but hoped to live until he came. Signed with distinguished sentiments Mademoiselle Georgette Leblond, 127 rue d'Au-teuil, pavilion to the left, if *Meman* is not in, the key is under the mat.

Michel had forgotten about her. His life was becoming too full for one young man. First Lemerre's splendid opportunity, then Barbara. He had been to see her twice since Berry's departure and felt that things were going slowly but smoothly. Mrs. Selby was charming to him, most interested in books and the trend of modern thought, although she stoutly defended Marie Corelli.

Barbara was nice to him. Michel's best asset was his conversation and, not very much of a gossip himself, had the gift of making others talk and put them at their ease. Barbara felt positively brilliant in his presence and never had so many ideas as when stimulated by him. In fact, he was a great favorite both with the Selbys and Barbara and had he only known it stood on the brink of an invitation to dinner. After which Mrs. Selby would have probably asked him to spend the evening with her niece. The second of May, anniversary of their first motor accident, was fast approaching and the new play at the Palais-Royal sounded entrancing.

But coming events in this fiction do not cast their shadows ahead, any more than they do in real life; everyone was still happy, including Uncle George, who inherited a dozen silver forks and a diamond ring from old Cousin Bartlett of Augusta; Mrs. Selby persuaded him to sell the diamond and keep the money as a party fund.

CHAPTER FIFTY

Michel slept for hours and hours and awoke much elated; the events of last evening came back to him slowly. He spied the orange letter on the mantelpiece and sighed; he would go to see Georgette at once and get her off his mind. Berry's apartment was an expensive purchase. First Mrs. Baxter, who was much worse than he expected, then this Georgette. He dressed slowly and without enthusiasm while the cook flicked a duster gayly and swept around the furniture. Berry's flat looked dreadful now, for Michel had brought his books and stacked them on the floor in heaps, then masses of papers, files and indexes, also on the ground. Berry's small but complete library consisted of two shelves filled with the best detective stories.

"When I get rid of Berry's girls, I'll buy some bookcases," thought Michel.

Auteuil used to be a hamlet near Paris and now forms a complete village just within the town. A great many Parisians live there on the principle that cities move west, but it will be a great many years before they wake up and find themselves the shopping center. In 1929 it looked strangely quiet and pretty; the big boulevards bordered with trees and hideous apartment houses were crossed by village lanes where large gardens and small villas lay fast asleep, ten yards from an underground station.

Michel climbed the steps of one and found himself in the rue d'Auteuil, the high street of the village; he passed all sorts of old and new buildings, musty shops and brand new groceries before he came to a small square marked "127"; the three sides of the square were lined with pretty little houses, each with a triangular front and little stoop, very much in disrepair. The center of the square was a mass of lilac trees and cats.

Concièrge du square said a sign with a pointing finger on the first house. Michel knocked at a glass partitioned door and two very dirty ladies inside looked up angrily. One harpy, the *concièrge*, was having her fortune told by the second harpy (her favorite tenant) with a filthy pack of cards.

"Mademoiselle Leblond?" said Michel.

The *concièrge* looked at him for a long time with as much insolence as she could, knowing she had him at her mercy. "Oh, you mean Georgette, third house to the left." She shuffled to the door, leaving Jezebel the second to glare at him and shouted:

"M'ame Leblond, M'ame Leblond, someone to see your daughter."

When Michel arrived at the third house, a voice was roaring through the closed front door: "Come in, come in, come in." He entered and was suffocated by a smell of bird-seed and washing, the favorite smell of the Parisian working classes; a handsome but enormous woman was threading purple beads on fine wire and making them rapidly into flowers. Michel remembered the funeral wreaths.

"Mademoiselle Georgette Leblond?" very politely.

"That is my daughter, she is ill."

"I know, I am a friend of Mr. Johnson's, I mean Mr. Berry's, and I received a letter from her yesterday."

"Oh, I know, the poor girl's heart is broken; between ourselves Mr. Berry should not have departed and left my daughter in that condition and without resources. She gave up her place in despair over his absence."

"What condition?" asked Michel, his heart fainting within him.

"The doctor says anemia caused by sorrow and now she has lost her place and, my good sir, what are we to do?"

"May I see her?" asked Michel, greatly relieved.

"Certainly, I cannot move because of my legs; I caught a hot and cold from sitting in a draught and it has caused a swelling in my calves; go up the stairs and knock on the door, there is only one."

"What picturesque diseases this family indulges in," thought Michel as he climbed the stairs. "I must ask a doctor about this hot and cold business."

He knocked and a feeble voice told him to enter. It was a charming room, all white muslin, rosebud wallpaper and a gigantic bed of the throne persuasion, for one acceded by graded steps. The sheets and pillows were of a dazzling white, threaded with pink ribbons, and Georgette, the picture of pink and white health, her golden hair arranged in careful confusion, lay swooning on this couch with her eyes closed.

Michel thought he had never seen such a pretty girl and was properly taken in, as he should have been, by the setting.

"Is it my dear Berry?" said the patient in a coarse raucous voice, very much like that of the *concièrge*.

"No, I am Saint-Amant, a friend of Berry's; I came to see if you needed anything."

Georgette opened her eyes, shot an appraising glance at him and closed them wearily again.

"Nothing, what should an invalid need?"

"Some invalids have requirements; your mother says you are anemic, perhaps the country for a little while would agree with you."

"Leave my interior and *maman*, never; the country is too noisy, the animals and birds call to each other all night." (She must have been thinking of the jungle.) "I like the suburbs of Paris better, but only for the evening. That might do me good." Georgette opened her eyes wide and added coyly: "In Berry's letter he said a friend of his would bring me a little souvenir, and as he gave me your name and address, I wonder if you are perhaps that friend. Nothing much, of course, for we both had ever a horror of mixing sentiment with money. Are you the friend?"

"I don't think so." Michael remembered that she absorbed all of Berry's earnings. At random he added: "He said that he had arranged everything in his letter."

"But next to nothing, a mouthful of bread. Americans do not know how to treat ladies; I prefer my countrymen, they at least understand etiquette between civilized, refined human beings."

Her countryman bowed, wondering what was coming next in the way of embarrassing pitfalls.

"I was thinking of what you said about the country, perhaps a little drive in your car some evening would do me good."

Michel blushed: "I have no car, alas."

"No car?" Georgette drew her breath sharply and realized she was wasting all her charm on a pauper. Then with a shade of condescension: "What is your profession? I am sure that you are about to buy a Rolls-Royce."

"I am a man of letters."

"Do you write novels? I adore love stories. I read a beautiful serial in the *Journal* every morning, 'The Proud Bastard,' it is superb, and full of delicate sentiments."

"So far I only write articles," said the modest Michel.

"Ah, that is a different matter." Georgette was no longer condescending, she was patronizing. "Let me give you some advice; I am a woman of the world and have seen many artists; they never succeed and they never keep a car. You should write an operetta or some comic monologues, everyone appreciates that."

"Oh come," said Michel, forgetting never to argue with the sick, "lots of people write good articles and take taxis."

"But we should all look prosperous; look at me, dying of misery; I have a car, a beautiful five horse-power Renault. It gives me prestige, I can drive out to nice restaurants, lost in the dead of the country, twenty kilometers from Paris."

An idea struck her; if Berry chose meanly to send her impecunious youths, at least she could extract a dinner or two for her pains. He was well-dressed too. To be seen with a nice-looking youth was good for her prestige, as she expressed it, and impressed her new "serious" lover, a ripe haberdasher; besides it kept him properly jealous.

She held out a limp hand. "I know this is the beginning of a long acquaintance, you shall take me out to dinner, I will drive you and you can read your articles to me, I will tell you when there is anything to change."

"But I am very busy at present."

"I know, of course, everybody is; this is Friday, I will certainly be better by Tuesday, we can drive out to the Pavillion Henri-Quatre and you shall read something to me then. I will fetch you in Fifi at eight. No, I insist; it will help me to recover. Oh, my heart, a spasm!"

She grasped the region around that organ and winced in a brave manner.

"Well, with pleasure," said her victim, looking most doleful.

As he walked downstairs, he hated Berry; the Pavillion Henri-Quatre is a most expensive restaurant and his mother went there very often in summer.

CHAPTER FIFTY-ONE

Everything went miraculously for Michel. The Polish gentleman took a fancy to him and Lemerre's mad scheme succeeded in its smallest details. A most amusing series of articles appeared in *Le temps et l'Espace* on frauds, literary, political and financial; each fraud furnished with suitable documents. A large public of serious French people was amused and shocked, which comes to the same thing. An article once a week explained sundry matters to them, why their fathers had lost their money in Panama and other mysterious affairs, why seemingly incapable cabinets had braved public opinion for years, why certain great authors had occasionally brought out idiotic books. And nothing scurrilous either, at least nothing more dreadful than the truth. The people who had perpetrated these horrors were dead or ashamed, so this was a simply arranged matter.

Psychologists noted at this period that many of the higher moral reflexes to which past generations had obediently responded, if without enthusiasm, were in abeyance. What would have been libel ten years before were now merely witty allusions to one's past. Everybody liked being in the public eye (except Mrs. Selby who was quite safe) and newspapers were besieged with applicants for publicity of any sort. Elderly authors pouted when their publishers stopped advertising them for a week.

To return to Michel, his very real talent lay before the public and he attained a post of importance with little or no trouble; of course as life is full of "ifs" you will think that it was not all luck, that he was a young man of parts and attainments. So he was, but there are thousands of such in Paris, waiting for fortune to beckon with her crooked Jewish finger.

The Selbys enjoyed his articles, especially Uncle George, who banged on the table and roared: "That's capital, sir! I declare that part about the anarchist who blew himself up with his only bomb in 1905 is first-rate. He stumbled and fell up the stairs of my favorite restaurant; well, even at the time it struck me as being a mighty queer accident." He shook with laughter. "And now this letter proving the police had stretched a string across the middle step ... capital, capital, a splendid way of disposing of him. ..."

Barbara was not so interested; naturally things that happened just before her birth could not thrill her, and she preferred talking about her own articles; she once read Michel one on hats, which he listened to attentively with the glazed eyes and stiffening muscles of utter boredom. Also as he drew her out with skill and love, she had ideas; she took to having them all the time and he applauded them as only the enamored could, for most of them were idiotic.

Things were going delightfully for Michel; he had been asked to dinner and, in spite of the strange fare, he was never happier; they had okra soup, fried chicken with rice and some very chalky sweet potatoes. Then an American salad full of nuts and dressing which shocked his French soul, followed by ice-cream and cake. He wondered what his mother would think if she could see this strange foreign fare, but he liked it or would have enjoyed it if Mr. Selby, in a burst of cordiality brought on by the article on anarchists, had not sprinkled all his food with red pepper. A small innocent bush grown at Andrésy (who says you can't grow tropical flora in France?) produced enough peppers to last the winter and agreed with Uncle George's cast-iron stomach;

his guests suffered great agonies, particularly the servilely polite ones like Michel.

Another great joy for Michel was that he had disposed of Georgette; the dinner at the Pavillion Henri-Quatre passed very successfully, his mother was not there. Georgette chose everything that was expensive and drank champagne à la russe, that is, in great quantities and beginning with the soup. Then she insisted on another dinner at Fontainebleau, to read dear Berry's letters to him and as a farewell. That was all the astute young lady extracted from Michel and she abandoned him for more profitable quarry in the shape of a cigar-colored Brazilian who only drank green Chartreuse; apart from this alarming tendency he paid for everything and never said a word: the ideal protector.

Michel, emboldened by the dinner, asked Barbara to go walking in the Bois some morning and to his surprise she accepted, as she always did everything, at once. Barbara's best point was her willingness to agree.

They walked down the avenue Henri-Martin which led them straight to the Bois and Michel knew the way to the left of the big lake where this civilized park becomes almost wild; they pranced down several bridle paths, crossed chains of little lakes and streams and came to a mass of bracken, blackberry bushes, small shrubs and trees much stunted by undergrowth. They were delighted with the world and extremely gay. An elderly gentleman in pale blue shorts was the only sign of man. Michel explained: "That is Colonel Macduff; he runs here every morning to get his stomach down, then when he's very hungry has a huge lunch at Voisin's and begins all over again the next day." Barbara said she was glad she did not have a large stomach, in a fat, priggish voice, little knowing, poor girl, that it is the easiest thing in the world to grow and the hardest to get rid of.

They left Macduff on the right and continued straight through the thin springy grass; presently they came to a dell half masked by bushes. Michel sat on a fallen tree trunk, invited Barbara to join him and whispered, "Look"; at first she saw nothing and then about twenty yards away, sitting or ambling about the bushes, were the deer. There is a large family of them in the Bois, but they choose their friends and are not very tame unless properly approached. The fawns were there, jumping at the lower tender branches of the trees, two young bucks fiercely rubbed their horns against the bark of an oak, very coquettish does, dressed in their new pale buff furs, lay in self-conscious groups, quite aware of their charms. A stag with a respectable beard looked suspiciously at Michel and Barbara as much as to say: "Just you say one word and off my family goes." It was a complete picture of domestic life except that none of the animals read the papers, as Barbara whispered to her companion. He smiled but did not answer. As they remained quite still, the deer grew more familiar and allowed them to see all their best antics such as fighting, courting, gymnastics and very spectacular performances consisting in stamping on the ground with one hoof after the other and then listening to nothing for a long time.

Presently, Barbara whispered that she had several ideas, so they had to go. Michel tried to stave them off by remarking with as much sentiment as he dared that he had known her for six weeks. This did not impress the minx much; she powdered her nose and said:

"Saint-Amant, listen to me: you know the motto of the French Republic is 'Liberty, equality, fraternity'?" Michel said yes. "Well," she continued triumphantly, "you must write an article and say that they are not true to it. Take equality; why do old ladies push in and take my seat in the bus? Why do the papers say Monsieur Poincaré, Monsieur Doumergue, and simply call murderers Duval, Baratoux, without any mister; that's not equality. I ought to read: 'Monsieur Duval has been sentenced to ten years' hard labor,' or simply, 'Briand is the new head of the cabinet.' Then another thing, why are Frenchmen considered talkative? I have known several quite well and they hardly say a word. Then another idea, why are mothers here always shorter than their daughters? Then ..."

"Certainly all this is quite true," said Michel thoughtfully, "it would make a good original article; I suppose in America that the press always calls burglars mister. If it is a typical French lack of courtesy, I must draw attention to it at once."

Barbara grew scarlet, then burst out laughing: "Well, I must say that was rather foolish of me, but I thought it over in my bath this morning. I wanted to help you. I thought you would be so pleased."

Michel seized her arm in his excitement and called her Barbara for the first time: "Of course I'm pleased, how sweet of you to think of me in your bath."

"I do a great deal of thinking in my bath, or else I practice my singing. There is a beautiful echo. On good days when Aunt Virginia forgets to get me out, I sing almost the whole of 'Funny Face.'"

"Do you," said Michel intently, "but what do you think of me?"

"Of you? Well, nothing much, just vaguely, you know."

"Don't you think anything more precise?" asked the insistent Michel.

"Oh, well, I sometimes wonder if you are always as serious as you sound when you talk to Uncle George, if your conversation with other girls is as deep (!), and if you tell your mother that you come to see us foreigners. By the way, how is your grandfather?"

"My grandfather, why he's all ... oh, you mean my grandfather who was so ill, well ..." Michel wondered whether to kill him or cure him and decided for the latter solution. "He recovered miraculously, he had a hot and cold."

"Oh I see," said Barbara, who had never heard of this complaint and suspected something fishy, as well she might; "I am so glad, now my aunt can call on your mother."

"I am so sorry she has gone to Biarritz for six months." He thought in his foolish lover's brain: "I can't bring her back until I propose to Barbara."

Michel then had a brilliant thought, not to be compared to Barbara's idiotic brain waves.

"Would you like to go to the big fair with me some evening; your aunt won't mind your going out with me?"

"Well, I would like to but," very primly, "she doesn't let me go out alone with men."

"But I'm not men, I'm Berry's friend, and I like you all so much, I feel as if you were my family."

This brought no responding note, so he tried again: "You know the fair is at Vincennes, there are lots of new merry-go-rounds and airplanes, and prize fights and learned bears and strong men and babies in bottles, pickled."

The last touch was right; Barbara squealed: "Oh, Michel, of course I'll come, are there any flying pigs?"

"Why naturally, of course there are," Michel lied.

"Thank you so much, when can we go?"

"Not to-morrow, I sit with the Pole at his cadé, but the next evening, if it suits you, would be splendid."

"Oh yes, come to dinner first and perhaps my aunt and uncle will join us."

Michel was charmed and determined to tell her he loved her on the flying pigs; she had called him Michel and thought of him in her bath. It was all too good to be true.

CHAPTER FIFTY-TWO

The Selbys thought of going first to the fair but decided to go off on a spree by themselves; middle-age was very dissipated in this family, and so was youth judging from tales of Virginia's daughters.

Before Barbara and Michel started off, Mrs. Selby for the sake of her own guilty conscience said a few words to the boy, thus: "Saint-Amant, I trust you as if you were my own son; don't let Barbara go up in the swings or fall into the water shoot, bring her home at twelve sharp, and don't for Heaven's sake let her win any rabbits and bring them here to live. Do you hear me, I speak seriously, you are an old man of twenty-eight and you must prevent her from being too fooh ish." Michel felt like hugging her, but refrained and said Barbara shouldn't go near any of the attractions. Mrs. Selby looked at him and added: "Now I didn't say that, only don't bring her home sea-sick or full of fizzy lemonade."

They started off in great spirits, Barbara sang "Old Black Joe" in the taxi and Michel whistled "Old Man River," making a perfectly beautiful harmony. It was indeed a heavenly scene when they arrived at the immense open square lined with double rows of glittering mirror-faced booths and merry-go-rounds. Barbara wanted to see the pickled babies at once but Michel, knowing there were none, said it was too soon after dinner. He bought Barbara a large gingerbread pig and the coster wrote her name on it, under her very eyes, in pink and white sugar. She liked this so much that she insisted on buying one for Michel, not so much from sentiment as to see the writing once more.

A raffle came next, you paid a franc and had the chance of winning an alarm clock. After trying forty times, they won it and went off triumphant, the clock ticking loudly under Barbara's arm. Then came a beautiful round of cows who pranced up and down to the tune of "Ramona." That was almost too much pleasure for Barbara, who sat between their gilt horns, while Michel rode on the velvet saddle; his hat flew off and into the very arms of a pickpocket, but this was a trifle not even to be noticed at the beginning of this evening of evenings.

Barbara was enchanted and in a melting mood; Michel, who was as wax in her hands, let her do every single thing that Mrs. Selby had forbidden, including two bottles of lemonade which came out of their eyes in bubbles, also their noses; it was so acid that their jaws ached, at least Barbara complained of sharp pains "where my ears begin" and Michel felt badly too out of sympathy. He looked wildly for the flying pigs and, would you believe it, found a merry-go-round with a circle of them, alternating with a garland of rabbits who ducked and bowed in happy unison. It was midnight and they were miles from home.

Barbara climbed on a pig, Michel on a rabbit, and off they went. He looked affectionately at Barbara and tried to say something, but shrill whistles from the pigs drowned his carefully prepared speeches. Meanwhile Barbara stuck on to her pig for ten turns and, I regret to relate, wore her other pig around her neck on a dirty string, all but the feet, which she had eaten. Finally, like Cinderella, she gave a shriek, looked at the alarm clock which she still hugged, and said: "Michel, it's half-past one, what will Auntie say?"

"She'll never let you go out with me again."

"Oh yes she will, I never enjoyed myself so much in my life."

Michel stopped a wandering taxi and they threw themselves into it, worn out with so many pleasures.

"Oh Michel," wailed Barbara suddenly, "the pickled children, we forgot about them."

"Never mind, we can see them another time, this fair goes to Neuilly next."

"Do you promise to take me again?"

"As much as you like," then plunging in quickly before he was too frightened, "Barbara, I must tell you something very grave."

Barbara stiffened.

"I want you to think it over in your bath to-morrow, I have loved you ever since I first saw you, you are the only," etc., etc.

Barbara said sleepily: "That's very nice of you, Michel, I must say I did not know it; are you sure, you know it may be only the pigs?"

"The pigs?"

"Well, I mean this lovely evening."

"How can you," etc., etc., etc. "I knew I loved you from the moment I saw you in your lovely blue dress, mixing juleps."

"It is a nice dress," said Barbara complacently, "now what are we going to do about it?"

"Can I ask your aunt for your hand?"

Barbara was surprised, but not too much so, as sleep was rapidly closing her eyes. "Wait a moment and I can perhaps tell you myself, let me think it over. No come to tea with me day after to-morrow."

Michel was dumbfounded with joy; after a strange and to him beautiful silence he was about to haggle with Barbara for an answer to-morrow morning, when he felt a soft weight on his shoulder. Barbara was fast asleep; he kissed the top of her hat and sat quite still, full of the hopes and fears of the all but affianced one. He helped her out at her door, walked up with her to the flat and breathed a few impassioned but whispered sentiments on her before he left. Then he drove home himself, too tired even for joy.

CHAPTER FIFTY-THREE

The next morning seemed very commonplace to Barbara after that glittering evening; she lay in bed until twelve, successfully fighting her aunt off until then. Mrs. Selby had appeared indignantly at ten o'clock, bearing a bottle of castor oil: "I see, Barbara Winship, that I can't trust you even to spend the evening with that sweet, gentle boy; it's a great worry for me to have a niece with no idea of the time. Would you rather have some castor oil now or calomel this evening?"

"Some calomel this evening," said the prospective fiancée, playing for time. She did not know what to do about Michel. She liked him a great deal but was not attracted to him as she would have been to someone more spirited, more disagreeable and less in love. She knew on the other hand that she would never meet anyone so nice again; even a foolish girl felt that instinctively about Michel. Greatly troubled, she resolved to consult Suzanne de la Huppe, who always gave good stout sensible advice. Michel telephoned at lunch time and his voice was a great point in his favor, also the flattering things he said.

After lunch, Barbara finished eating her gingerbread pig and walked it down by crossing a good bit of Paris before she reached the rue de Lille. Suzanne had just had a baby and reclined on a beautiful new sofa, part of her redecorated apartment in her father-in-law's house. She had left her parents' favorite epoch, the glorious eighteenth century, for modern furniture, but not wholly for her heart was two hundred years slow and she had a wholesome awe of her mother's taste. The La Huppes had noticed that all the beautiful ladies in Roger's circle had had a suite of rooms done over "to express their personality," so Suzanne, urged on by Roger, who wanted to show his friends "my wife's latest fancy," wrote to a decorator who understood the case at once, having helped on the "personalities" of a dozen worshippers of Louis XVI furniture.

In this case, Monsieur Lejar produced two beautiful rooms and one hideous one. Roger had several typical French characteristics, one of the nicest being not to spare expense if you want something really good. The bed-room already had fine old panelling in it painted gray; in for a penny, in for a pound, as Lejar remarked, as long as the walnut was tinted why not find a color that suited Madame de la Huppe's complexion? So the walls were painted shrimp pink, just the shade for blue-black hair and green eyes. Old La Huppe howled with anger over these image breaking ways, but, as he was as obsolete as a sedan chair or a bicycle, no one listened, although it was his house. The bed had no visible woodwork but lay in a curved niche of mirror engraved in patterns. The bed, armchairs and couch were made of thick, quilted and buttoned white taffeta; white rugs on the floor, a profusion of cut glass vases, some with lights inside, some with pink flowers, and that was all.

The sitting-room was painted or rather frescoed with scenes of Suzanne's life; one wall showed her buying lovely enormous bouquets of flowers, another a flat brilliant landscape with a boat, in which she would travel presently wafted on by fat bulging sails. Then Suzanne had her fortune told by a fat cupid, and on the fourth wall she chose clothes from a beautiful dressmaker, the dresses swirling madly around in various gay colors, but headless and legless; all most amusing. Low black wood bookcases, pale gray divans and arm chairs, big silver lamps, a profusion of glass trinkets and boxes made this room lovable and comfortable.

The third room was horrible, a small unofficial dressing-room, boudoir and hanging closet combined. The walls were ground glass, there were two iron chairs, cushionless and comfortless, two square glass tables, one cubist picture of an autopsy, and rows of cunningly contrived cupboards bound in aluminum. A gramophone seemed the only human touch to which the soul clung; one felt naked and cold in this barren chamber, and that at any moment a surgeon might have appeared from one of the cupboards, sharpening a couple of knives and grinning: "Next, please." Of course they do not behave like this in real life but they do in nightmares, and this room was one.

Suzanne lay on her shell-shaped couch the prey of an old lady in rusty black who made a hideous note in the pure light room, something like an oversized bluebottle. Hag-like, she was laughing at poor Suzanne's new suite, croaking: "*I* had a group of palms on a stand in the center of *my* drawing-room when I was a bride and a comfortable circular sofa below them; my bed was black peartree, a lovely wood, a good but not slavish copy of Louis XV. The mirrors back of your bed are indecent; my mirror was in my big wardrobe, only dressmakers use bits of looking glass in the wall." She finished up triumphantly: "And all the rooms were hung in deep red brocade, chaste, warm yet rich."

Suzanne was delighted to see Barbara, who said loudly in case the old lady should prove a little deaf: "These are the prettiest rooms in Paris, everybody thinks so and if I have an apartment of my own some day, I shall copy you, my dear." She bent over the baby who was sleeping in a little shell the replica of his mamma's couch, prodded him until he awoke howling and remarked: "Why, he matches the color of the walls exactly." In fact he was a lively pink, but young mothers don't see jokes. Suzanne had him removed by a terrifying English nurse, retorting that little Roger was becoming paler every day.

The old lady departed, still shaking with mirth, a most unbecoming proceeding, for it showed her single yellow fang, and the girls were left together.

"I must talk to you about something very important," began Barbara, drawing her chair up eagerly.

"I am so glad," answered Suzanne, "but you had better hurry before another old dodderer rambles in to make fun of my rooms; they make me feel wretched."

"Don't you worry, it's only malice, evil speaking, lying and slandering," from Barbara, who did not like old ladies very much. "Now listen to me, you who are as full of gossip as a concièrge. What do you know about Michel Saint-Amant?"

"Let me see, he writes for a paper, doesn't he? I know his mother, she is very youthful looking; that reminds me to put her on the party list."

"She has gone to Biarritz."

"Oh no, she is giving a charity bazaar in her beautiful house this week, she sent us a card, curse her; besides she would not dream of going away during the season."

"Well," said Barbara, a trifle perplexed, "what about her son?"

"I have only just met him, he is nice-looking but so quiet. Of course the family is excellent," in a very important voice, an unconscious imitation of Roger's, "and when his mother dies he will inherit her large fortune. Then she is very young still. Oh yes, and—you aren't in love with him, are you?"

"No, indeed."

"Well, before the baby was born, I looked so hideous that I used to make Roger take me out to dinner as a proof of true love, and twice we saw Saint-Amant with the most beautiful girl, but dressed, my dear, you would have died laughing ..."

"I'm sure I would," interrupted Barbara grimly.

"Dressed like a poster, all yellows and reds and you know this is a black and white season, so you can imagine that she looked like an exclamation mark; not a query, because it was easy to guess what she was. Roger says she would be a great courtesan if she could be less dashing, but there are so many real ladies to spoil the market for her. But in spite of his loud tastes in girls, Saint-Amant is very nice, everybody likes him."

"He asked me to marry him yesterday."

Suzanne looked a trifle concerned: "You should have told me that first; of course you must accept him. After all what does it signify? Anyone can go out to dine with a chorus girl."

"Anyone," agreed Barbara. "How do you like my new dress?"

"Lovely, is it true that sports clothes will no longer be worn after one P. M. sharp?"

"Quite true, why, Suzanne, let me tell you about the collection I saw …" so the conversation was neatly directed to other channels.

Barbara promised to come back two days later and went home pondering. Was Michel a deceiver? Why had he removed his mother from Paris to Biarritz and why did he dine out with beautiful girls when she at best was only pretty? She was annoyed, but more interested in Michel, since she perceived a worldly, perhaps baser side to his nature.

He telephoned again at dinner time and the Selbys had quite a lot to say about inconsiderate people who disturbed others at all of their meals.

CHAPTER FIFTY-FOUR

The next day, Barbara was still undecided, and as Michel's appearance on the scene became a question of hours, then minutes, she felt a sinking feeling in her stomach which she fancied was hunger.

Michel rang at a quarter to five, and entered the room eagerly with his hat and gloves on, surely a sign of great mental disturbance in such a polite young man. He beamed at Barbara in such a loving manner that it forced a smile to her lips.

"Barbara, I can't believe you are going to refuse me; why did you think it over? Anyone would refuse me on mature reflection."

"I must speak to you first."

"First?" very dolefully, for Barbara did not look very affectionate.

"Well, before we say anything definite."

A beam of hope came into Michel's eyes which he suppressed instantly: "You know, we have very little to talk over; my mother and your aunt do all the boring talking in case we ..."

"Michel, let me speak and don't interrupt me any more or I shan't be able to get it out. There is something that worries me, I am afraid that you are keeping things from me, little things of no importance but that might keep us apart."

"But Barbara, I have nothing to hide from you; you know very little about me, but there is nothing much to impart except that I adore you, in case I haven't told you before."

Barbara looked embarrassed and said feebly: "But are you sure you love me?"

Michel came and sat by her on Mrs. Selby's cherished sofa. "Would I want to marry you if I didn't? What possible reason could there be; don't be foolish, you dear little thing."

Barbara drew away her hand, a little ashamed of what she was about to say: "Then if there is nothing to hide, why do you persistently prevent your mother from meeting my aunt and why do you go out to dinner with beautiful girls? You must be interested in her and in that case why do you propose to an insignificant person like me?"

Michel drew a deep breath full of pent-up misery and finally answered: "Perhaps you won't understand about my mother, yet a sure proof of my love for you is discussing her with anyone in the world. I love her a great deal, but she loves me too much; remember she is a widow and all her interests apart from mundane matters are centered on me. I go to see her every day and she asks me questions about the most trifling matters; if I forget quite a small thing and she hears about it afterwards from an acquaintance she is heart-broken. Once I had a drink after the theater with Lemerre, you know, the friend who got me my present post. I omitted it in the synopsis of my day, she found it out and now worries about my becoming a drunkard or secret drinker of all sorts of horrid drugs. I am telling you all this because I prefer you to anything in the world and I don't want to lose you for the sake of a few silly questions. I was so much attracted to you on the day that Berry brought me to call that I wanted to see you again at once, and hit on the pictures as an excuse. I have never mentioned you to my mother since and had she known that I were in love with you, she would have insisted on knowing your aunt and asking a million questions about you all, which would have put you off forever. Remember also that in her generation, people were not nearly so simple about affairs of the heart as we are and no marriage was possible without numerous go-betweens enjoying themselves thoroughly. My mother has made me morbidly sensitive about questions. I cannot bear not having my word accepted as the truth without questions. I wonder if you follow me?"

"Yes, I think I do, but what about the beautiful girl?"

"The beautiful girl has been out to dinner with me twice, she is not interested in me and we will probably never meet again. I was forced to take her out. Please believe me, Barbara."

"I do believe you."

"Then you will marry me?" Michel and Barbara were overcome with shyness and looked at each other; his face was suffused with joy, like a nice-looking edition of the rising sun, and hers a little self-conscious. She smiled and slipped her hand through his arm: "Yes."

The sound of Mrs. Selby bustling about in the hall, cursing her maid, her husband and the world generally, brought them back to the avenue Henri-Martin.

"Not a word to my aunt," whispered Barbara.

Michel nodded, only too pleased to avoid another explanation for a few hours.

Virginia sailed in crossly: "How are you, Saint-Amant? I didn't know you were corning this afternoon" (she did because Barbara had told her). "Won't you have tea? How glum, you both look; in my day young ladies were taught to converse with callers. I have lost my passport, my bag with all the housekeeping money in it, the keys of the Andrésy house and my Spanish mantilla. I suppose you are going to sit there, both of you, and watch me break my heart over it all without even offering to help me."

They had jumped up long ago. Barbara, who was quite used to her aunt's losing all her belongings at least once a week, turned over a cushion and discovered the bag.

Virginia: "Well, trust you, Barbara, for finding the least important thing. What do I care for money? It's my mantilla that I mourn for, George brought it to me from Barcelona when we were engaged."

"Auntie," said Barbara casually, while Michel turned up all the cushions in the room wildly, "when you put your furs away in the camphor chest, did you look in the pockets?"

"Of course I did, what an idiotic question; I'll go see though, just to satisfy you, miss, that your aunt is not such a fool as you appear to think."

She flew out and Michel insisted on kissing Barbara. The latter seemed very pleased but said quickly: "I will tell you the rest later; remember, not a word yet. I must telephone about the passport and the keys, perhaps Uncle George has them."

She defeated Mr. Crosby successfully, for he never put anyone through to Mr. Selby if he could help it. "Hello, Barbara, what's that? Why, bless you, I always keep the keys right here, they weigh a ton. Your aunt's passport? Such a joke on her, just wait until I can waddle home. She need never say I'm absent-minded again. Yes, you love me? Why, of course you do, but this is so sudden; you didn't say you love me? Well, I'm getting deaf in addition to all the other attractions of age. Never mind, I'm bringing home two surprises for dinner. Tell your aunt the passport is one of them."

Mrs. Selby burst in again, this time quite mollified: "The mantilla was with the furs. I believe you and your uncle slipped it in to plague me." She turned to Michel with a radiant smile: "They play silly jokes on me, not funny ones either, just to make me feel old and stupid."

"Auntie, the keys are at the office and Uncle George has found your passport."

"I knew he had it, the old fool."

"May Michel stay to dinner, Uncle George is bringing home a surprise?"

"I know what that is, a heavy duck pie. That means a sleepless night for me," sighed the martyr, who adored duck pie herself. Then addressing Michel, who listened delightedly to all this: "You have no idea what I go through with that man; he tosses and turns, roars like a bull and frightens me to death, walks in his sleep, all because he will eat heavy dishes in summer; in the morning he wakes up fresh and gay while I recover the next day from a nervous headache. Yes, of course you must stay to dinner and please eat as much duck as you can and think of me."

They all laughed, particularly Virginia, whose sleepless nights were a highly colored exaggeration, as anyone could guess.

Just then Uncle George appeared, waving his pie, just as was expected. He greeted them all effusively and sat down with a wicked expression on his good-natured face; he drew out a large leather case, extracted a passport which he held out at arm's length reading: "Virginia Selby, born in 1879, nose blue, eyes straight, lips pale, complexion …"

Virginia snatched it away: "And why did you hide my passport in your office?"

"Hide your passport? Do you know who brought it to me this afternoon? Honestly, I was so pleased I gave the man twenty francs. A sallow youth from the Y. M. C. A. It was found in a parcel of books you sent them yesterday. Remember, you made poor Crosby send it off from the office, all tied up in knotted strings and old papers; the fellow was ashamed of that package and I don't blame him."

Everybody enjoyed this scene, including Michel, who liked his prospective family more and more. Mrs. Selby bridled, tightened her lips and said:

"Indeed I may have my faults but I am not a liar like some people and I bet you slipped my passport in among the books just as Barbara hid my mantilla."

Indignant denials and slight wrangling which lasted until dinner time. The duck pie was eaten unto the last crumb, largely partaken of by Michel, who so far did not understand the beauty of hominy and bacon.

After dinner the Selbys burst out laughing and fell into each other's arms, as they usually did after tiffs. George bent down under the sofa, drew out a backgammon board and challenged his wife to a rubber. She accepted rather distantly, whistled through her fist for luck and threw the dice: "Double six, I begin, don't even throw, George." She grew warmer in manner and cheerily addressed the young ones who stood behind her chair watching: "You see your poor uncle needs relaxing to-night, Barbara, I'm going to beat him blue; what are you children going to do? Not breathe down my back all evening I hope?"

"We thought we might walk down the avenue and back for exercise," said Barbara.

"All right, but no good appealing to your sense of time. Saint-Amant, march her right straight back by ten-thirty, please; otherwise this is the last time you go out together."

They assented and disappeared, Barbara merely needing a couple of beribboned lambs to look like a poster for spring.

George rattled the dice, coughed and said: "Barbara, of course, is your own niece and you know best, m'dear, but it seems to me she goes out a good deal alone with Saint-Amant, considering it's barely two months since they met."

"Oh, it's all right," said the usually circumspect Virginia; "I would trust him around the world; he's in love with her, which handicaps him a little, but I expect she'll end by marrying him."

"I wish she would, I'd be proud to have those articles in the family. Notice how devilish hard that fellow is on the Jews?"

"Yes, but that's not a popular subject with me. It's your turn, rattle and shoot."

"Really, sometimes I'm quite proud of my distinguished wife; to hear her takes me back to the dear old days in Denver City or any good honest repair for gamblers. Was your grandfather a forty-niner? I forget."

"My grandfather, George Selby, was the gentlest and best man in the world, he ..." She stopped and looked at her husband, "you're not getting a rise out of me this evening, it's all jealousy because I'm winning, anything to take my mind off the game."

CHAPTER FIFTY-FIVE

Meanwhile Barbara and Michel walked downstairs and sat on a bench under the trees; not a very distinguished place perhaps, but mighty convenient for a serious talk.

"I wanted so much to tell your uncle and aunt, Barbara," said Michel tenderly, "why can't I?"

"I want to get used to it all by ourselves first; it takes all the bloom off of news for everyone to know. Let's wait a little and tell them all at one fell swoop. I planned it all during dinner."

"So did I. Tell me your idea first; you have such lovely thoughts."

"Well, don't tease me, Michel, but I thought that we might be deliciously and secretly engaged until August or September, then announce all and be married in October." The truth was that Barbara wanted a big wedding and a lot of excitement.

Michel's face fell. "I thought of announcing it at once, to-morrow, June ioth, marrying quietly in August and we would have all the holidays for traveling." Michel wanted a quiet wedding, his gentle soul recoiling already at the thought of all his mother's guests.

Barbara suddenly thought of last year's little trip with Georges and her heart sickened. "Somehow I don't want to travel much in summer, not for our first journey together, the autumn is so much gayer somehow. Let me break it to my aunt when the spirit moves me, I am very intuitive, you know."

"Yes, I know, but tell me in time, my mother must know it at exactly the same minute."

They fell into the usual lovers' conversation that the very birds in the trees above them use for courtship, ending up thus: "And you shall do exactly as you like always."

"Even when I am old and ugly?"

"Of course, but you never will be."

Barbara returned at eleven-thirty; she found a card pinned on the front door reading:

> Mrs. George Oglethorpe Selby
> Thanking you for your punctual behavior,
> signed: the key under the mat.

CHAPTER FIFTY-SIX

The Polish gentleman's name was difficult to spell. He avoided it himself and preferred "Monsieur Stanilas" as an abbreviation. As is the custom of Poles, he drank a good deal but with great dignity; when much inebriated he begged the waiters to call him "Stani"; if they foolishly did so, he immediately knocked them down, paying for damages to their black alpaca jackets with great liberality.

There are three or four huge cafés on the boulevard Montparnasse that reign supreme; there artists, real and imitation, flock with their belongings. Monsieur Stanilas went to each of these cafés for a season in regular rotation, most afternoons and every evening. He wore a large fan-shaped beard, very white, to suit his seventy-five years; the rest of his features were hideous, particularly a tiny pair of hard, china-blue eyes. Being tall and massive, he was called a fine-looking man. He dressed neatly and well, although he insisted on donning a top hat, made of rough beaver, on all occasions. He had known everybody and still did, had ranged the world, knew Africa intimately and averred that never in his life had he viewed such a monstrous and entertaining spectacle as that of his three cafés. He explained all this to Michel, now his most favored audience:

"Great gentlemen like myself have always had a leaning for low life, so infinitely varied in its expressions. I assure you that even Port Said, which has a reputation, does not possess such an excellent collection of rag, tag and bobtail as this restaurant. And the passers-by, why, dear Saint-Amant, look at them; it's a kaleidoscope performance of the rogues' gallery."

"Oh come now, Monsieur Stanilas, you exaggerate."

"Well, of course, they may not actually be scoundrels, but they pine to appear so; look at that Negress with her wool dyed orange. And the man she is with, pray; his shoes laced up with string and an opera cape on his jockey shoulders. I beseech you to gaze on the old gentleman in a kilt, with plaid, sporran, cairngorm brooch and dirk, a complete disguise; he lives at Passy, is a virtuous French bourgeois, but loves this knavish atmosphere. What an opportunity for dear old-fashioned Freud! Why, all the world's inhibitions crowd here, perfectly happy, perfectly harmless, most of them crazy."

He turned and looked at the many sitting inside: "Some of the women are lovely, look at the group back of us." Michel turned, and to his horror recognized Mrs. Baxter. He bowed and saw with relief that she only favored him with a brief nod.

"Ah, you know one of them, I see."

Michel explained who Mrs. Baxter was.

"You see," triumphantly from the Pole, "you say she is perfectly respectable, yet outpaints and outdresses the most flamboyant light of love. Quite mad, like the rest of them; you must introduce me some evening, I wish to add her to my collection of freaks."

They rose and went to Monsieur Stanilas' dusky flat in a side street nearby, where after much searching among his papers he produced a letter from Gladstone on Home Rule, a rough draft of a treaty between Ireland and Germany penciled by an august hand, and a volume of Poe's Tales for Barbara. Michel had told him of his engagement under oath of secrecy. Monsieur Stanilas answered solemnly:

"My dear sir, I know the world, you will never be great, you are too delicate and too retiring, but perhaps you will be happy. Trust me as a friend, you do not know the lengths a Polish nobleman will go to prove it. In honor of your engagement, I will drink a bottle of old and tempered vodka with you, according to the custom of my family. Wait a bit."

Stanilas tore off his clothes, put on a brocade dressing gown, begged Michel as a favor to help him off with his boots. Michel, who was a milksop compared to this hardy son of kings, watched him open a quart bottle of vodka by neatly knocking off the neck against a marble-topped table.

"Now," said Stanilas gravely, "watch me. In my family good news is celebrated by the two friends drinking out of the same bottle, each one drinks as much as he can without drawing breath; you begin."

Michel gingerly took a sip out of the least dangerous corner of the neck and almost exploded; with tears in his eyes and a brave smile he handed the bottle back to the old man, who had thrown himself on his regal four-postered bed.

"Is that all? You will never be a great man. Look."

He tilted the bottle and in anguished silence Michel watched the liquid disappearing down his throat. When the flask was quite empty, Stanilas sat up, gave a warning cry, Michel ducked his head as the bottle whizzed through the window pane and crashed into the silent court. Stanilas cried, "Vrooska," probably meaning good luck; he shook hands ceremoniously with his guest, said it was the happiest evening of his life, calmly remarked: "I see the window has been opened by the bottle, let yourself out quietly, the concièrge hates noise, so do I. I will compose myself to slumber."

He did and was sleeping like a baby before Michel tiptoed and stumbled his way out.

CHAPTER FIFTY-SEVEN

The more she saw of Michel, the better Barbara liked being engaged to him. The Selbys breathed never a word and let him come as often as he liked, which was very frequently. Barbara, who was as intuitive as she had boasted, found out that there was far more to him than she had grasped at first. Ridiculously generous in thought and deed, most amiable and even-tempered, he had a strong will bordering on obstinacy. He responded to any sign of affection, told her his most secret thoughts unasked, and shut up like a clam before the most innocent question. She learned never to ask where a new tie came from, his face would cloud over and he would answer: "Oh, just from a shop near here, I don't remember where exactly," when she had only commented on it to please him. He found her perfectly angelic in every respect.

After a month of this delightful intercourse, with Michel to dinner on all the evenings when he did not consort with the Pole, the Selbys became very restive. The truth was that Barbara's presence at the August fashion openings was a great trial, for it meant that one of them had to remain in Paris with her for at least three weeks of that detestable month. They secretly hoped that Barbara and Michel would be engaged by then, she would throw up her job and everyone would be happy at Andrésy. Virginia was vexed with herself for having insisted on Barbara's sticking to her absurd work.

By the fifteenth of July the Selbys were beside themselves with impatience. They hated being parted even for a few days, and when feeling loving, lapsed into angry bickering. After an unusually lively dinner during which Virginia had accused George of a great-grandmother from Boston and he had retorted things about her Uncle Alfred, the most ominous silence reigned in the sitting-room.

George broke it by singing a song at least ten years behind the times:

"Life in Reno's simply great
Grant divorces while you wait,
I'm going out to Reno, I'm never coming back,
And if I do, I sure do hope the car runs off the track."

Virginia burst into tears and cried: "Barbara, your uncle's going to leave me; I don't deserve such hardships at my time of life."

George rose and played "Reno" on the piano with many flourishes.

Barbara suddenly felt intuitive, cleared her throat, clapped her hands and shouted: "One, two, three, the play's about to begin. I want to announce the engagement of Barbara Winship to Michel Saint-Amant."

The Selbys got up in a body, as it were. George danced the fandango; he called it that, anyway, it comported a number of twinkling steps and great snapping of fingers. Virginia fell upon her niece's neck and said solemnly: "My dear, you've helped to soothe a broken heart. I wish I could marry him myself; I would, too, if I were not old enough to be his mother and tied to a monster besides."

George beamed: "Virginia, I forgive you."

"Forgive me indeed, curse your impudence, you know very well she came from Boston."

"Virginia, the poor woman, rest her bones, has been dead a thousand years; forget about her. I have a scheme, I want to go and congratulate Saint-Amant this minute; if he isn't here," with an arch smile, "he must be with his second love, the Pole. Let's all go and be nice to him, I declare, I'm so happy."

"So am I," said Virginia, falling into his arms. They looked even more pleased than Barbara as they whirled round the room madly. Then George, who was in a songful mood, besought his wife to:

> "Put on your old gray bonnet,
> The one with the purple on it,"

and they went forth guided by Barbara, to whom Michel had explained exactly where he sat.

CHAPTER FIFTY-EIGHT

The taxi deposited them in front of the noisiest scene imaginable, dozens of little tables grouped on the broad sidewalk, and it seemed to Barbara that hundreds of eyes looked her over. No Michel to be seen. Mr. Selby secured a table and suggested that he and Barbara should glance inside, "because I know he's here somewhere." Mrs. Selby sat down and ordered something, her heart full of relief and expectancy.

The inside was noisier than the outside and very stuffy. At a very large table near an open window sat Michel, the picture of misery and the center of a rowdy group. On one side was the Pole, wearing his top-hat, as the corner might be draughty; on Michel's left sat Mrs. Baxter, in full fancy dress, her arm slipped through his, talking into his face with a languishing, familiar expression. Some Americans, male and female, filled the rest of the table in various attitudes of abandon. Barbara took the whole scene in with photographic swiftness. One always registers unpleasant things immediately and in the minutest detail. Michel saw her too and jumped up delighted as he always was to see her.

She turned away and would have walked out if her uncle had not seized her arm: "Hold on, manners first, there's Baxter, I must speak to him, never look as if you were running away and don't be too quick in your judgments, m'dear."

He ambled up to Baxter: "Hullo, my dear fellow, I haven't seen you in an age of peanuts." Baxter, who was Selby's age but always called him "sir" as to an old gentleman, shook hands cer-emoniously and introduced him to his wife. She nodded sweetly and swiftly, then with an eye on Barbara said:

"May I present my dear friend Monsieur Saint-Amant, the only person I love in France, except Mr. Baxter," she added, so coyly.

"We know him very well," answered George very affably. "Michel, we just popped in to say howdydo but we must be off again, my wife and the drinks are waiting for us outside."

Barbara noticed that her uncle had not introduced her to the terrible Baxters and continued smiling at Michel without a word. He whispered: "Darling, I can't leave these people now, let me telephone in the morning."

She said, "Of course," brightly, too brightly, and left without a glance at the party. She heard Mrs. Baxter ask as loudly as she could "Who is that washed-out, stuck-up hussy?" but she unfor-tunately did not hear Michel's reply: "The nicest and prettiest girl in Paris."

Virginia, not being blind, saw that something was wrong when they joined her and wisely refrained from speech. The Selbys finished their drinks in silence and a very gloomy trio drove home. Barbara's face from pale was red; red and hurt, so hurt that she knew she would cry if a word was uttered. She said good-night very quietly and crept to bed to enjoy a night of insomnia, similar to the ones of the Georges Lemoine epoch.

Mrs. Selby brought her breakfast in next morning at eight, made cheery small-talk to the miserable, silent object in the bed and said finally:

"Look here, my dear, your uncle told me what happened last night. You wouldn't let a vulgar, pushing woman destroy your happiness, would you? You know, nothing in the world is so deceptive as appearance."

"But, Auntie, if you can't count on appearances, what can you judge by?"

"Barbara, I believe everything, truth is far stranger than fiction; I am certain of one thing, that boy is devoted to you and to no one else."

"Auntie, this is not the first time. Michel does not seem able to explain things; appearances are always against him." She told her aunt about Georgette, his mother, his dread of questions, everything. She finished up with: "I may not be very experienced but I know that those are the things that count, if I can't be perfectly happy with Michel, I would rather be miserable without him. He is to telephone this morning; tell him I can't see him any more."

Mrs. Selby pondered some time and said gently: "Very well, my dear, you shall arrange your affairs to suit yourself, no one can ever settle them for you. You are very wise, now stay in bed a long time, it is my remedy for all ills." She stroked Barbara's curls. "Some day perhaps, this afternoon, maybe, I'll tell you of all the horrible doings that took place before I became engaged to George. You would be surprised." Barbara looked hopeful. "True love not only never runs smoothly, but means a lot of watching and forgiving. After lunch I am going to drive you out in the Bois and you shall have a surprise."

Barbara, like the rest of the family, adored surprises and felt vaguely interested.

CHAPTER FIFTY-NINE

Mrs. Selby had the only telephone moved into her room with its yards of cotton coil and waited. She chafed and gave many signs of impatience. Finally after three false alarms and conversations with her daughters which she made as brief as possible. Michel rang through: "Is that you, Barbara, I have been trying to get you for an hour."

"No, this is Barbara's aunt; I know," very sympathetically as to someone in deep mourning, "the line has been busy all the morning with stupid people."

"Good-morning, Mrs. Selby, may I speak to Barbara?"

"Well, she is still in bed. I am going to do something very extraordinary. I want you to come and talk to me."

"With pleasure."

"And I am going to be stranger still; will you meet me outside, on the avenue Henri-Martin? I hope you don't mind a rendezvous with an antiquated coquette?" She laughed gayly. "It will be our first meeting as aunt and nephew."

"Oh then …"

"Yes, Barbara told me, I am delighted. Can you be here in half an hour?"

"Certainly."

"Then you will know me by an ostrich plume in my hat and a bouquet of red roses in my left hand." She laughed again and hung up the receiver with a weighty sigh, thinking that no one ever understands the workings of the human heart, especially with a generation between.

She peeped into Barbara's room, the poor girl was fast asleep. "That's an hour or two gained over this vale of tears," thought Virginia, quite gloomy at the prospect of the day that lay before her.

CHAPTER SIXTY

It was one of the stifling days to which Paris occasionally treats itself. Not a breath of air stirred the dusty chestnut trees. A woman went by muttering to herself and presently a poor old tramp joined Mrs. Selby on the bench a few yards from her door. He removed a large board, announcing the finest kennels in Paris, from his aching shoulders. Mrs. Selby made room for him sympathetically, gave him five francs and told him in the most atrocious French that she wished she were dead, in a nice cool grave, or at Andrésy. He stared at first, but seeing she was a harmless, foreign lunatic answered that he preferred to live, that he would have lunch on the grass in the Bois at eleven and that she was a very nice lady and charitable to the poor; could he count on her if he ever got into trouble? Mrs. Selby said no, that she was merely passing through Paris, and spying Michel, jumped up and left him to meet her new relation.

"Oh, I was so worried last night," he burst out, unable to stop for more than a hand-shake.

"And well you might be," thought Virginia. She answered Michel: "We do not consider your engagement with Barbara at an end, but she does, alas! Now don't let us waste our time in pompous words or conventional talk. Just explain to me what your apparently strange behavior hides."

Michel looked staggered, then angry: "It is so difficult to explain extraneous factors."

"Of course you realize that I am not prompted by curiosity," resumed Virginia, a trifle tartly. "You love Barbara and she cares for you far more than she thinks; you will admit perhaps that if you were in her place, there might be things to misunderstand."

"I would easily admit it, only before we became engaged I impressed on Barbara how sensitive I am on the subject of being trusted; she said she understood."

"So she does, but with her mind only, not with her heart; she does not trust you thoroughly, because she has never been greatly loved before. Don't blame her for playing Doubting Thomas after the careless way she has been brought up. Faith is a gift that you give to others, not something they bestow on you. But enough of this elevating talk. Tell me the circumstances, if you can bring yourself to have confidence in your aunt-in-law."

Michel related at great length his hideous pact with Berry and very briefly his mother's character.

"Why on earth didn't you tell Barbara?"

Michel looked stupid and obstinate, which is the same thing. "Because I want her to believe me in spite of ridiculous incidents. I could easily explain everything but I won't; I have told her that I loved her better than …"

"Bibles," put in Virginia.

"Than Bibles," conceded Michel seriously, "and she must take it for granted; otherwise all my childhood, which could have been so happy, will pursue me again. I was wretched in spite of many pleasures and loving care, for my mother never believed me without a proof and doubts me even now; I am marrying Barbara to be happy."

"I hope, to make her happy too," from Virginia very dreamily.

"Naturally, and if we begin our life together like people in a wood, hiding behind trees and occasionally peeping out, we will be miserable."

"My poor Michel, you are as foolish as you are young. I see your meaning dimly but I feel that you are preparing a very dismal time for us all."

"Do you think it will be all right finally?" asked the big man pathetically tailing off into the small frightened boy.

"I will try to help you but, Michel," very persuasively, "won't you explain just this once and begin the doubting exercises in the fall only; it is so hot and we might be so happy at Andrésy."

"No, Aunt Virginia, I cannot, I am a coward and if I give in now, I will never have sufficient courage to take a stand later."

"Very well, but you are about to cause me great trouble and expense. I am going to leave you to your own devices and step in later like the Olympian goddess that I am. Only remember that if I were Barbara and twenty-two, I would feel as she does. You must work this out between you. This is our last meeting until things take a turn, mind you, I don't feel very optimistic."

She sighed and walked on a few steps. Then turning to her silent companion: "My husband and I are devoted to you, which is very nice of us considering you are making our niece wretched."

"But don't you think things will take a turn?"

"They always do, but never the way we expect; goodbye, dear Michel, this is my taxi I think." She jumped in, gave an address and said to herself: "I think that I have depressed him to the proper level, now for George."

CHAPTER SIXTY-ONE

George had an office "down town" in a quarter that was just beginning to be fashionable in the seventeenth century; he spent half of his waking life in a beautiful circle called the "Place des Victoires". A crescent of noble houses, as Mr. Pepys says, surrounded a prancing equestrian figure of Louis XIV, looking very proud of himself, his horse, his victories and his houses. He bore his hooky nose tilted in the air, not deigning to notice the signs and lettering that defaced his stately mansions.

Mrs. Selby went up a beautiful, low stone stair-case with wrought-iron bannisters; an 1880 hand had added a red velvet rail to the ironwork which ruined everything. She paused at the first landing, opened a small door concealed in the woodwork and let herself gently in. Observe, no bell and no brass plate for the King Cotton Company; George hated publicity, the concièrge could direct people to his office. The little door looked rather shabby and clandestine when the immense square ante-room with splendid panelling was revealed. Louis XIV would have been furious if he had seen what Mr. Selby had made of a fine lady's apartment. The usual varnished pinewood desks, chairs and tables, the typewriters and telephones looked their worst against a background of inlaid floors; finely modelled cupids and nymphs sprawled on the pale gray and gold walls in semi-relief. Photographs of the King Cotton works, from the plantations to the mills, maps of the underground, and dreadful, uninviting views of European cotton ports were stuck here and there in the flatter portions of the woodwork.

Boxes of linters and bales of cotton littered the sample room and the fragrance of dead and gone cigars made the place dismal. Virginia was met by Mr. Crosby, who tried as usual to prevent her seeing her husband, not from any reason but the desire to appear professional and businesslike. He disapproved of Mrs. Selby's incursions into his realm for he was king of the clerks and ruled them with a mental rod and bowstring. He incidentally bullied Mr. Selby as much as he dared, but Virginia he could do nothing with; she waved her hand at his approaching figure and darted into her husband's sanctum. George was reading some papers and jotting down figures on a pad. He was glad to see her and as she expressed it, "always delighted to fling down his tools." He greeted her as a long lost wife; although they had parted two hours since.

The office was as cool as the grave, yet very cosy with a Turkey-red carpet and slippery armchairs that exuded a faint delicious smell of old leather and George's eau-de-Cologne.

The pair had a long confidential talk with never a harsh word, barring the fact that George demurred about something and was called a mean, stingy, heartless old man for his pains. Then they went home together and cheered their unhappy niece as they could.

CHAPTER SIXTY-TWO

Virginia, in view of impending events, begged for a short nap after lunch. After which preparation for the fray, she took her pallid, washed-out niece for a drive in the country. There she unfolded a most stupendous tale regarding her amours with Uncle George. A very black picture in which domestic bliss was attained at the price of many scenes, disappointments, humiliating pardons and she wound up: "But you don't know how grand the reconciliation scene was! My dear, I wore a white muslin dress all starched and flounced with two petticoats; your uncle was sitting at a round table with his head buried in his hands, I could just see one mustache peeping through his fingers as I entered. I stood in the door and screamed loudly (for I wanted to test his love, having broken off our engagement that minute for the third time): 'George, George, help me, I am dying!' He leaped up looking frightened but pleased and thinking it over now, I imagine he did not entirely believe me; then he rushed to meet me and caught my swaying form in his arms. We were reconciled and married immediately before we could change our minds again." The last sentence was a case of absent-mindedness, not meant to be in the narrative at all as it gave a strange picture of the instability of true and requited affection.

Barbara was feebly interested and said: "Oh Auntie, don't talk to me about love affairs, I don't like them very much, I don't understand men very well and I am always getting my feelings hurt."

"You realize that you are too sensitive?" said her aunt eagerly.

"Not this time." Then after a long pause: "Tell me about the surprise."

"We are to fetch it this minute."

They drove for a little while among the strange jumble of town and country that makes up part of the Parisian suburbs. A beautiful old park was being cut up into small bits and tiny houses run up in great disorder, giving the appearance of turning their backs on everything in the landscape but the railroad track. This they all insisted on facing at some angle. Just off the road was a small old-fashioned white villa, with rows of lilac and laburnum bushes leading up to the green front door. The little garden was full of prim, neat flowers and Barbara wondered whom she was calling on.

An old gentleman with a benevolent face opened the front door; he was dressed in white, like a surgeon, and wore gold rimmed spectacles; he peered over them at Barbara, whose heart sank; she thought that her aunt had brought her to a home for disordered nerves, and here was the doctor. She had never forgotten her unexpected stay at Madame de Malassis' institution.

Aunt Virginia bowed: "Good-afternoon, I am Madame Selby, I telephoned after lunch, may we see Mademoiselle Mirza?"

"Certainly, Madame, come this way, I will send her to see you."

They walked into a cheerful little bower with fat armchairs ranged around the walls, a table with a large bowl of sugar in the center of the room and many photographs of smiling ladies and gentlemen each with an animal in their arms. All sorts of animals from snakes to bull dogs. By and by the door opened gently, Barbara expecting the dull Mademoiselle Mirza, did not look up until she heard the patter of tiny paws. A small white poodle was in the room; she ran up to Barbara immediately, shook the wooly curls out of her black eyes then inspected Mrs. Selby, chose Barbara for her own and jumped on to her lap. Miss Mirza wasted no time on preliminaries, but looked up once or twice before settling down as much as to say: "Barbara, see my beady black eyes, made up to match my white curls, the finest in France. That old gentleman has just bathed me in tar water. I wish he wouldn't, I smell so much nicer when I am cream."

The vet walked in very much pleased: "She is my most affectionate poodle, Madame, I picked her out when you said it was for a young lady; now she has many accomplishments, she knows how to count five pieces of SUGAR"; sugar pronounced very loudly and clearly. The dog jumped up, shook itself in an embarrassed manner, leaped on to the table and pawed five pieces of sugar into a heap; she looked expectantly at the vet, then at Barbara, hoping for the obvious reaction. It came. "Mademoiselle Mirza, you shall have the first prize for cleverness, your mistress will give you a small piece of SUGAR." Mirza and Barbara were delighted with each other as Mrs. Selby had hoped; the dog was squeezed until it squeaked in the car going home and the color of her new bow seriously discussed. Mrs. Selby suggested several shades but assured Barbara that crimson was the only possible color for Sundays.

CHAPTER SIXTY-THREE

L etter from Michel to Barbara received the next morning:

My darling Barbara, I shall always call you that, because you are.

I want to write you the nicest letter in the world, yet I feel that nothing looks quite right on paper. You will not see me and much as I grieve over it, I cannot beg you to do so.

There is nothing changed between us, nothing altered in our relations, you are the sweetest and prettiest creature to me, the instant choice of my heart and I cannot cease to consider you so because of a stupid incident, that has nothing to do with my love for you. I could write pages on the subject, not to convince you, but for the pleasure of telling you over and over again that I adore you.

If you do not trust me and choose instead to believe a trivial illusion, I must abide by your decision and wait until you can consider me what I am and always will be,

Your despairing but faithful

Michel.

Letter written the same day by Barbara to Michel.

My dear Michel:

It is difficult also for me to write letters, particularly in French; I know that I am not very clever and that is why I do not understand you. Or it may be that I do not grasp the French attitude in love affairs. As I do not, I feel most humiliated at your apparent deceptions and may I add, your indifference. You seem to me to consider only your point of view and not to bother at all about my feelings in the matter. Do you seriously believe that any girl could think herself engaged to a constant lover when she sees him sprawling in a horrid café with a woman, and such a woman!

I am sure that you will hate me from now on, but I would prefer you to do so than to think me a poor spirited creature that will swallow anything. I enjoyed every minute I spent with you from the minute we became engaged, but what you really want, and won't find in me, is a *fiancée* with second sight.

Barbara.

No more letters after this from either party.

CHAPTER SIXTY-FOUR

Michel the stubborn was wretched in the classical manner after having been the classical lover. So was Barbara. In a few more days the dreaded fashion openings with an exhaustive discussion of winter models would begin.

At the end of July, Barbara, Virginia and George were drinking coffee after lunch. George took a telegram out of his pocket, Virginia who was an artist in her way, asked Barbara for some more coffee to make things appear natural: "and two lumps of you know what, I dare not mention the article before one who shall be nameless." Mirza the unnamed looked up suspiciously from her footstool as she heard the faint rattle of sugar tongs and then went to sleep with one eye open in case anything should happen to her advantage.

Virginia read the cable with shrieks of surprise: "Why did you decide without consulting me? I thought you were only crossing in October."

"This will be a better time as Lovitt will be in New York and I won't have to trundle down to Charleston; I need only be a week in New York and the ocean trip will be a tonic, I'm really going for that. Meanwhile you can take your wicked old liver down to Vichy; you frame up some sort of an excuse not to go every year, this time you've got to."

"I believe I will go to Vichy, only what to do with Barbara?"

"Oh I'll be all right," said the hermit, "I want to be alone."

"I've had an idea," cried George, "Barbara shall not have the monopoly of thought in this mansion, she shall come with me, the ocean ozone will work marvels with her too."

"But, Uncle George, my openings?"

"Read the cable, daughter," (a very tender form of endearment from Uncle George, only used on rare occasions, he once called the station master at Andrésy, thus, when he recovered his long lost steamer trunk) "and see exactly what it says."

"Expect you New York end August, delighted, drinks are on you, Lovitt." Barbara read this and added dismally: "But you'll let me come back, Auntie, you aren't sending me home because I give you so much trouble?"

"Of course not, child, you don't give me nearly so much to worry about as my own girls, and you are not half as deceitful. When I think of the way Margaret used to lie to me! 'Where are you going, Margaret?'—'Just to a lecture, Mamma, and tea with old Madame Galignani.' I can hear her innocent voice now. And in her engagement book which she had left *open* on my desk were written the strange words: '3.30 studio P. 4.30 dance A.B. 6.15 tea with old Jew Simon.' You are a clear blue sky compared to those dreadful girls. George, do you remember the time we had when Evelyn ran away with the old waxed and dyed tenor Musini? I don't wish to put ideas into your head, Barbara, but she tried to commit suicide with a dental pain-killer when I discovered all and brought her home. No, you shall live with us as long as you like, I am getting quite attached to you. You too, George, aren't you?"

"Yes indeed, but I do love my own daughters, too," spake the loyal parent; "now Barbara, work like the devil at your articles, get all your clothes ready for a trip on a nice steady eight-day French liner, we leave in three weeks."

Barbara worked very hard, went to all the dressmakers including the ones that were beneath contempt and notice, a habit that does not grow upon the jaded fashion reporter, but then we are only young once. She wrote faithful reports home and prepared all the articles for September to be sent off weekly from Vichy by Aunt Virginia. The latter went off kicking and scuffling accompanied by Mirza and a large mutton bone to keep the young lady quiet in the train. There was nothing the matter with Mirza but she was fed on carrots at the hotel like all the rest of the liverish ones.

Barbara embarked on the "Jean-Bart," a steamer chosen by her uncle because the meals were long, elaborate, numerous, and delicious. Her passage was paid out of the party fund although she never knew it. Michel in the meantime, too weak to struggle, had been borne off by his mother to Evian where he gloomed all day and wrote letters all night, obligingly filling the wastepaper basket for the housemaid the next morning.

CHAPTER SIXTY-FIVE

arbara's log-book, discovered by the purser who pored over it for several journeys but could not make heads or tails of it; he had only lived seven years at Saint Louis, so had picked up very little of our barbarous tongue. It was just as well, as this document would have given him a strange idea of the quiet young lady who dined at his table. Here it is.

Second day out: Lay in bed a long time this morning and read Revelation. I feel very frightened, I must never be wicked any more. That is why I am writing all this. I heard two women at the Lafolie opening discussing all sorts of disgusting things. I listened to as much as I could, but I did not hear everything. They talked about strange cases. One lady who sat on a red hot stove because of the delightful sensation of getting up and no longer burning. They agreed that this was a case that was carried very far but the more learned one of the two had a good recipe for diverting your mind. She said: "All you have to do instead of leaving things concealed in your mind to worry you is to put them down on paper; as soon as they are expressed they stop bothering you." The second answered that this was an old plan, but not bad; she had a better one: if you are interested in someone, and that is always a sure source of worry, just sit down and write to them in a familiar manner as if you were talking to them and expected an answer. I shall try both these plans;

they spoke of something else too, which I did, but I will write about that later. This trip is going to be dull, I must have something important to say each day. I hope I will have enough evil thoughts to last the whole journey. I hope that I am not practising black magic. I asked Uncle George what it was exactly but he looked at me over his spectacles and said he really did not know what I was talking about, that there was no such thing.

I hope this cabin is not haunted; what with Revelation and that awful ghost story about the ship that was haunted by a wet sheet, I had the horrors last night and woke up screaming at four. I heard a swishing sound outside, just like the sheet walking but it was only the sailors swabbing down the deck. I am very unhappy, but in a numb way, not at all like last week; I hope that it keeps up; anyway there won't be anyone on this boat to fall in love with.

Third day out: Slept very well last night, in spite of Uncle George's intimacy with the purser. We have moved to his table and I wish Aunt Virginia could see what we devour. Uncle George says it is the sea air, but I don't think he ought to eat three quails in addition to the regular dinner. He says he has to as they were ordered as a compliment to us.

I am sitting in the reading room, there is a young man reading with his back to me, his ears are pointed like M. S. A's. I feel quite hot, supposing it were he? I know he would apologize and I would be so happy. I would drop into his arms just like in Aunt Virginia's reconciliation scene and the buyers that are returning to their small home towns, full of drinks and dresses would be very shocked; well they might be, it is not refined or genteel to behave thus. Uncle George would not mind, he is always natural, he is asleep by my side, pretending to read a cotton report.

The young man has just turned around; he has beady black eyes and a broken foot-ball nose. All this is not what I meant to write at all. "Just let yourself go" the woman said. I must write a love letter to M. I write splendid letters when I know that no one will ever see them.

Fourth day out: The people on this boat are awful, very ugly and so sociable! One woman says she is public-spirited, I remember there was one on the ship when I came to France. She wants us to be one big family, I want to be miserable all by myself. I feel very good to-day, perhaps I am getting rid of all my bad thoughts. To-morrow I will put down some more. The public-spirited one has extracted a cake of soap from me and my fountain pen for a lottery for the sailors orphans; then she made me buy ten tickets for same. Uncle George took fifty, he is much nicer than I am. I wish that woman would leave me alone she is called Mrs. Winterbottom and the name suits her to perfection. That's another evil thought I have extracted and put on paper.

Fifth day out: Wrote a lovely letter to M.; I almost kept it, it was so beautiful, I cried a little as I wrote it, but I burnt it finally hoping the magic will work.

I had such a disappointment at lunch; a wireless was brought to me, I hoped it was the answer at last. Instead a silly message from Berry; he is meeting us in New York. I don't want to see him, he is the cause of my knowing M. How does he know we are coming? Uncle George swears on his honor as a Georgian (why that's almost a joke) that he knows nothing about it. I have made friends with an old Austrian, who undresses for dinner, that is, he takes off his yellow boots and adds purple flannel slippers embroidered in cross-stitch to his green plus fours. He raises canaries and teaches them how to sing. I wish I could yodel like him and whistle through my fist. I walk around the deck with him in the evening, the other passengers cold shoulder him and think him common, so he is but in a far more kindly, amusing way than Mrs. Winterbottom. Why are vulgar people of your own race so much harder to bear than those of less familiar countries? Anyway, Herr Jagerschmidt says love affairs are very easy to arrange, provided they don't last too long. He is going to teach me the German waltz if they give a ball, we will be a very funny couple.

Sixth day out: How I hate the sea, I never look at it unless I can help it. To see the ship ploughing through that awful, swelling, blue water terrifies me. On gray days it looks solid like jelly and the thought of falling in and getting my hair, eyes, nose and mouth full of it makes me dizzy; I think of it and long to throw myself off the deck. A wave knocked me over when I was a little girl bathing. I opened my eyes and saw the green glassy water all around me like a wall, I shall never get over my horror.

Uncle George looks better and better, he is friends with all the passengers, I wish that I were less stand-offish and cold; he disappears into the Captain's cabin every day before lunch and comes out, so merry; then he also treats large parties at the bar. Cocktails give me a headache, so I sup pose all this criticism is jealousy. There is a conjurer on board, he has taught Uncle George some new tricks with which to frighten Aunt Virginia; she will never find her bag and keys anymore if he succeeds.

There is one thing that depresses me even more than the rest; supposing I should meet Georges Lemoine in New York. Face to face, for instance at the hotel. I should faint. He is horrible when I compare him to M. but he still has a fascination for me, I know I shall see him. Writing those letters to M.

may be a good thing, yet I notice that I think of him far more than usual and he is becoming in my memory like my love letters, not like himself. How I wish I knew why he deceived me with such horribly dressed women, I mind that more than anything else. Suzanne says that those are the women men prefer at heart. Then why do they also make love to the drab ones like myself?

Seventh day out: Well, two days before we sailed, I went to see the woman who goes into trances and sees your future. I must write it all down carefully because I still dream of her at night with her eyes rolled up and her vacant face. She lives way off at Montmartre in a dreadful street full of squalid children and blind alleys. There was no concièrge but the sign on the door said "Star hotel, lodgings for the night, furnished rooms to let." I hesitated a long time but those buyers at Lafolie's said she was so marvellous and told them dates, lucky days, etc., that I summoned up courage and knocked at a door on the first floor. Two little children opened and said that their mother was out and that they had never heard of Madame Mazella. On the second floor a card read: "Jim O'Connor, boxer and Miss Florence King, manicure." I hurried by; on the next landing a door flew open as I paused for breath and a woman with red hair leered at me and asked me to come in and rest for a bit as the stairs were steep. This sounded fishy to me so I said, "No thank you" and just then a man in his shirt sleeves lounged out and looked at me hard. I asked them if they knew Mrs. Mazella, they answered "No," roughly and banged the door. Then I decided to try just one floor more; there was no door on the fourth landing, just a looped up curtain of many colors, the entrance of a coal black room with a shaded lamp burning in the middle; a Negress came out and without wasting any time on questions told me

Madame Mazella would see me in a few minutes. I sat down in this black cavern with my heart beating wildly. By and by a very commonplace clean little Frenchwoman bustled in and beckoned to me.

I mentally said goodbye to Uncle G. and Aunt V. and followed her into a very bright, cheerful kitchen. We sat on straw chairs facing each other, she looked at me very sharply and said: "I always tell my new clients two things; first that I charge a hundred francs, secondly when I am in a trance, I describe everything I see, pleasant or not; does that suit you?" I agreed, she put her foot close to mine, took my hand in hers and after a series of shudders and grimaces her face changed into a sort of pallid mask, her eyes rolled up until the whites alone showed and she said in a colorless far-away voice:

"*Voilà*, give me a letter or glove belonging to the person you wish to know about." I gave her that last horrid letter from Michel. She pondered over it for a while then said: "This man is unhappy and stubborn, he loves you far more than you love him; never ask him for explanations, he will not give them. You will go across the water before you see him. A man older than yourself and a woman will arrange all for you and if you take my advice you will avoid wearing green. Ask me just one question now, please."—"Will I marry the person I am thinking of?"—"Naturally but you will end by loving him too much; if you are jealous, you had better not marry him." She shuddered again and came to, filling me with misgivings, the worst being the hour, for it was half past seven. I tore home and found Aunt Virginia pacing up and down the avenue and Uncle George hanging out of the dining-room window.

That beastly woman's prophecy torments me, that's why I put off confessing my visit to her until the last day on board; even if I marry him she says that I will be wretched; she also mentioned "I would begin with twins"; not a very alluring prospect. This is the end of my diary, because we land tomorrow; the buyers are very noisy, smashing up the bar and singing patriotic songs. What man and above all what woman are to arrange my future?

CHAPTER SIXTY-SIX

They landed on a day that broke all previous records for heat. Lovitt and Berry bore them off and they drove through the sordid streets that surround the docks in a state of collapse. Berry looked well and tanned; he said that the expression "as brown as a berry" had been widely used in his village that summer.

All four had rooms at a nice quiet hotel much patronized by Southerners and after a few comforts had been pressed upon the travelers they felt better and more able to cope with Berry, whose constant jocularity was a little irritating to the weary.

"How long will you be in New York?" asked Berry and Lovitt simultaneously.

"An easy week," answered George, fanning himself with a palmetto leaf brought by Lovitt who knew his requirements. "Then we take sail on the 'Surcouf', the 'Jean-Bart's' sister ship where I hope to find exactly the same purser, same food, same stewards. The captain too has a twin I hope, he was a remarkably well-informed fellow, specially well up on statistics, why, he tells me Lovitt. …"

They fell into a conversation of passionate interests, punctuated by "you don't mean to say so," "really you surprise me," "I had no idea that Asia produced such quantities of—"

"Listen to them," said Berry to Barbara, "and some folks say that business is not interesting. Do you know of anything but statistics and bales of cotton that can produce that rapt expression on two faces for hours?"

"Well I suppose so," very absently.

"Now hear me, Barbara, before you can ask me to take you to Grant's Tomb or Coney Island, which I refuse beforehand, I want to know if you will stay a few days at Springfield with us? I wish your uncle would come too. What's this dull town to me, Robin is not here," he carolled. "By the way Robin is here; I mean your old friend Georges. He is engaged to Betty van Camp the bankeress and believe me, I feel sorry for him. She collared him when he landed, so to speak; he put up a brave fight but collapsed almost at once in those golden hands. I've lunched with them once or twice and it would make a cat laugh, much less you, to see them together. She says 'I' when she means Georges, but he is such an ambitious cuss that he swallows it all with the rest of his business training. He hopes for a revenge when they get married, but even then Betty will wear the trousers of that concern. I haven't done a thing to help him because I love you true," finished off Berry expecting a volley of thanks from Barbara.

She looked rather pleased, but still felt a little prick in her heart when she heard her first love's name mentioned. She was not sentimental but she had a splendid memory.

They all four had dinner on the roof and pretended that occasional hot gusts from the asphalt below were ocean breezes. Messrs. Selby and Lovitt enjoyed themselves immensely. They did not feel the heat much and besides there was much to relate, all the cotton and rice failures, the bank and real estate booms and collapses of the coast. This was solemn gossip, cheered with a list of the dead. Uncle George called the roll for Savannah and Charleston, beginning with old ladies and gentlemen who had criticized him from their piazzas when he was a small boy playing in the square. He enjoyed going back forty-five years and hearing: "dead" from Lovitt to every question. It was a great satisfaction until he reached his own generation which was still fairly healthy, but then as Lovitt remarked rather apologetically: "we don't have yellow fever any more."

Barbara and Berry melted away with heat and boredom. Barbara begged her uncle to go to Springfield with her. He refused even the week-end as he wanted to finish his business and go home.

"But Uncle George, you were confided to me by Aunt Virginia, you can't spend all your evenings alone, I won't go away and leave you."

"Don't you worry about me, I am going to spend my evenings with Lovitt." The latter nodded solemnly and murmured something about a great privilege. "We are writing a book about the war."

"Of course you must have had a great many interesting experiences at the Neuilly ambulance," said the gross and wicked Berry.

"You know very well what I mean, Berry Johnson; when I say the war, I mean the war, not that last European tussle. Anyway my book will be called 'The Recollections of a Reconstruction Baby,' because that is what I am."

Berry wanted to laugh immoderately, but hedged in as he was by three fierce fire-eaters he muttered instead: "Yes, sir. But let Barbara come. In fact I told my family we were all arriving to-morrow morning. I only wish you could come too," the last remark including Lovitt whom he found confoundedly slow and dull.

The declining ones thanked him profusely and mentally blessed him for taking Barbara off their hands; she was to be returned to Mrs. Cataway's hotel a week from that day to the minute.

CHAPTER SIXTY-SEVEN

Berry, like many other Americans, prided himself on his snappy efficiency. As you may have noticed, he invariably thought of the most complicated short cuts such as a Latin mind would scorn; his mother had left little trace of her influence except when it came to understanding the French which he did thoroughly and loved accordingly; he prided himself on his behavior during banking hours when he added horn spectacles to his cheerful face and a very solemn manner. He said that what he really needed was a mask as among the people who came to consult him, doubtless taken in by his severe looks were innumerable old ladies. The idea of anyone old and doddering worrying about surplus income was to him unspeakably grotesque, and their appearance when they waddled in from remote districts threw him into internal convulsions which were very bad for him. He sometimes looked so ill that ladies would press lozenges and tablets into his hand for immediate relief, which of course had the opposite effect and give him hysterics.

It was just as well that he had private means and that Mr. Baxter did not hear his advice to bewildered old crones who wished to invest their money. Here is a sample of his counsels to the more hopeless cases: "Madam, the best investment in the world is gold; keep your money like the forty-niner in your belt or your cholera band. A banker is like a doctor, excuse my blunt terms. If you do not wear one, a big leather purse worn under your petticoat in the middle of the front is what I advise my clients to invest in. No, they don't show at all unless you are very rich, then they do bulge a bit. But if you are rich everything about you is admirable so why should you care? You would like to consult Mr. Baxter about the purse? Mrs. Springlove, he cannot see you at present he is negotiating a loan with sh ... I must not even tell my best customers."

So when Berry found that Mr. Selby could not come, instead of taking the train to Providence and changing for Springfield, he decided to take the willing Barbara in the train to Yonkers, borrow a car from a friend there and drive from there to Springfield. When they got into the car and felt cooler. Berry's conversation became most fantastic:

"I want you to have some picturesque side-lights on your native land, you ridiculous foreigner, returning to this lovely country for a week. Which would you prefer, the miser's house at Plumdale or the lost village not far from Yonkers?"

"Both of course."

"That's my brave girl; well I can't stop to find the village but I will tell you about it. Figure to yourself as Michel says, how is Michel, do you see anything of him in Paris?"

"Never lay eyes on him."

"Liar," shrieked Berry, "no, I don't mean you, Barbara, bless you, I wouldn't dream of such a thing, I was talking to the throttle. Well to return to my village, at the time of good king Washington, it was in a very fertile spot, but cut off from the main road by a belt of pines and sandy soil. The villagers did not care much, they did not use the road much themselves and had few visitors. They raised sheep, ate the meat, made clothes out of the wool and lived like hundreds of other loyal subjects to the King in the backwoods. Well, pinch me if I get too poetical, but by and by, the main road was discarded and a big thoroughfare, far better, broader and more practical was built nearer the coast. The villagers saw that their road was out of repair and the parson who rode up once a month complained of it a little but they simply couldn't be bothered. Besides they heard there was a war on and they were too proud to fight. When the parson died he was not replaced because the village had been forgotten. They were by nature a stupid, timid folk and they never ventured far from home; they went on wearing their woolly clothes, raising a little corn and eating mutton. Barbara," covering his face with one hand and driving carelessly with the other, "it grieves me unspeakably to tell you that they weren't even married and began courting their own grandmothers. Now you know the Prayer Book particularly forbids you to marry your grandmother?"

"I didn't know anyone ever wanted to."

"Well, they did, the result being that when I discovered them, in company with other savants in 1925, they were hopeless idiots, too stupid to realize they had been republicans for a hundred and fifty years. They were garbed in full peasant's dress, lads and lasses of 1775 and—"

"How did you find them?"

"Because we lost our way, found traces of the disused road, stumbled through the pine waste and came on this broken-down hamlet."

"Did they talk through their noses?"

"Yes, indeed, they did not use modern slang, to be sure, but were difficult to understand. The American government was not very pleased with my find. First, because it is untidy to discover an eighteenth century village in the suburbs of New York; next, they were expensive idiots with no property, to be cared for until they popped off, and thirdly, they had not paid their taxes for a century and a half."

"Berry, how can I believe you?"

"Well, if you don't, I won't show you the house that was found full of dead misers."

"Please tell me about it now, what a lovely drive this is."

"Isn't it, and aren't I a perfect host? The miser tale carries a great lesson with it: keep up with the times. Imagine a big square timber house in the fashionable part of Plumdale, about 1800. A whole family of rich people live in it, proud and taciturn. The father dies, the two sons die, one daughter marries and has three children who never leave the house. The rents of many other houses are brought to them every quarter, in gold by a bank clerk (Berry's favorite mania). The town changes and moves west, the house is now in the slums but the misers don't know it, they live on barrels of unappetizing stores from a grocer who finds a pencilled order pinned to the back door. They still take the air in their back yard, in the clothes they find in the house, and very funny their neighbors found them.

"The children grow up and only go out to bury the old misers; they continue adding gold to their hoard; finally one quarter day the bank clerk brings the money in a very pretty bag done up in gold and green ribbons and. ..."

"Now Berry, how do you know that?" said Barbara rudely interrupting this entrancing tale. "I was so interested and then you go and spoil it all by ridiculous details."

Berry stopped the car at a drug-store, very indignantly: "Look here, have I slaved all my life in a bank or not? I suppose I ought to know the color of the ribbons on the miser's money bags. Come in and have a sundae or some plain ice-cream. I never eat anything else on my travels, so we won't have any meals to-day, just stop now and then for an iced drink. Don't you think so, it is so much more pleasant not to be a slave to time or the stomach; I suppose you prefer roast pork and plum pudding?"

Barbara was delighted with the idea of living on ices and hurried into the store; she had two sodas and the morbid Berry bought her a cigar to smoke on the way. She knew nothing of the country, but he did, and thought that by driving hard all day they might reach Springfield in the evening at about eleven. He telephoned and informed his family of a change of plans and to do them justice, they were neither surprised nor ruffled.

When they clambered into the car, each with an icy brick in their boiling stomachs, Barbara begged very meekly to hear the end of the miser story.

"Aha, Miss, you want to know in spite of suspecting the veracity of my narrative; well you are my guest, rude as you are. The clerk knocked at the door, rat-tat-tat. Silence. He put an eye to the key-hole. Nothing. An ear. Nothing. Then his nose. A faint but dreadful odor caused him to take off his nose and put it in his pocket. I suppose even you, poor gull, won't believe that. Well he merely turned his nose away, very disgusted and informed the Society of Hygiene."

"What is that?"

"Why the police, don't they keep us clean, mentally and physically? They opened the house and thought it smelt strangely too. Now in spite of your yearning glances, I am not going to describe the state of the misers' house. Suffice for me to say it was dirty and untidy, without even a flower to make it homelike. In the kitchen sat the last miser, shivering and hungry. On two chairs were two long rolls, rugs or matting you suppose? Quite right, but inside each carpet a dead and gone miser. The remaining one had forgotten what we do with the dead but as he was neat in his habits, had made a parcel of his brother and sister. Off to the hinatic asylum he trundled but the State was pleased this time because it found an immense treasure and made the house into a museum."

"New England is not at all the way I imagined," said Barbara reflectively.

"That's your Southern pride; you think in your stuck-up way that you have the monopoly of romance in America. Now we are not only poetical but crazy, as you see. Of course everybody would not tell you these details but true they are. Before we get to Springfield I will tell you plenty more folk-lore. Just you wait. Let me know when it is time for another sundae or will you light your cigar?"

"I think I'll wait until I get to Springfield."

Berry tore the cigar out of her hand: "Just what you can't do. You don't suppose I want my family to meet a cheroot-smoking Parisian. I bought it merely to break the journey."

Barbara answered nothing to that. After a pause: "Berry, what is your family like?"

"Wait and see; I have purposely said nothing of them for they are terrible, icy, purse-proud, go to church twice on Sunday, which is to-morrow, and have breakfast after prayers lasting twenty minutes. Did I tell you that breakfast was at six-thirty sharp?"

"Impossible, I don't believe a word of it, or anything else you say, Berry."

Berry took out of his pocket a post-card representing a fierce, forbidding man in uniform; his face looked vaguely familiar to Barbara who turned the card over curiously. "Give me back my card, its unladylike to read other people's mail". He tried to snatch it away, but too late because Barbara had seen the name, Hindenburg. "All right, don't believe me, wait and see, wait and see." He made the last words into a very sad song punctuated with sobs. Barbara became quite mournful for night was drawing in and they had struck the road along the coast.

"Pity you can't see this road, Barbara," said Berry presently, "we are driving through a swamp; this is where King Philip lived, the nicest of Indians. On either side of us are rhododendron bushes, simply growing in the mud; one slip and in we sink until the mire fills our lungs." Barbara gave a shriek. "Then the local gentry comes along in rubber top boots and pulls us out for a quarter apiece."

After a while they left the swamp and came to a bleak barren stretch, the sea on one side, bleak rolling hills on the other; neat old villages were passed, here and there a big lonely house and grounds silvered over by the powerful moonlight.

"Did you know," said Berry presently, imitating Lovitt's ponderous voice "that Rhode Island is the most densely populated State in the Union?"

"It doesn't look like it by moonlight, particularly this part. I feel as if the Indians might come for us at any moment."

"Well, they won't, here we are." Berry opened the gate by pulling a rope and they drove up to a pretty white wood house, with 1797 inscribed over the fanlight door. In the big comfortable hall, a boy was reading, lying on his stomach; two good-looking, tall women came forward to meet the travelers.

"This is my fiancée, Barbara Winship, the toast of twenty clubs," turning to Barbara who looked furious, "Barbara, this is Aunt Penelope and this is Aunt Phoebe, both virtuous ladies, so be careful in your conversation, that negligible boy is my brother Penn." The aunts greeted Barbara cordially and said in a breath: "I hope you know our nephew well enough not to be surprised at his astonishing behavior; he is too awful, the country air agrees with him and he is worse every day and more of a liar."

"So I am, but so gay! I hope you have not prepared supper for this unworthy person, she's been eating all day."

The family looked puzzled then indignant as Barbara explained the day and her bill of fare.

"Please don't tell your uncle about this lunatic, Miss Winship," said Aunt Penelope, "come and have supper; then you shall go straight to bed and your breakfast will be brought up to you to-morrow at ten. I hate to think what horrid lies he has told you about us all. No, don't tell us now, I want to sleep to-night without wringing his neck first."

CHAPTER SIXTY-EIGHT

Barbara, next day, saw that the grounds were lovely and the garden around the house full of flowers. As she walked with Aunt Phoebe, she discovered that Berry's father had been dead for years, that breakfast was at nine and that his family was easygoing and agreeable. His stories about the village and the misers were more or less true. Berry had gone to church. After the usual Sunday dinner, he said he would meditate for an hour in his room but wished to take Barbara for a walk at five. "Important matters to talk over," he added waving a much creased cable.

The truth was that Berry did not know what to do; he had received a mangled telegram from Mrs. Selby reading thus:

> Murder wil out arrange bro kenengagement Michelbar bara make Barbara apologize arriving New York Jean-Bart thirty firstloves Elby.

He had spoken to Barbara several times about Michel without getting even as much as a civil answer and now he must beard the lioness in her den and extract the truth from her. Who had broken the engagement and why? He received a letter from Michel about a fortnight after he landed, cursing him for Mrs. Baxter and Georgette but as usual he had not answered, so knew nothing from that quarter. He was in a quandary and floundered about on his bed with a lurking suspicion at the back of his brain that his girls might have something to do with all this. He planned a conversation with Barbara carefully with a choice of suitable opening sentences such as:

"Would you rather have a boy or a girl, I think girl babies are just too cunning."

"My poor child, the cable is from the *concièrge*, your aunt passed away in her sleep." No, no, that wouldn't do, too brutal.

"Michel has been run over, fatally I think." No, too sudden.

He decided on the following manly effort. "Barbara, your aunt has suddenly become a gentlewoman in reduced circumstances, she wants to get rid of you." Very much satisfied with this, he fell asleep and awoke at six: "Damn it, that girl does nothing but vex me!" quoth he, struggling into fresh clothes. By the time he was ready it was seven o'clock and off they went to a picnic on the beach with a great many other revellers.

Barbara enjoyed the barbecue, as she savagely called it, and was only too delighted to put off her heart to heart talk with Berry. They were always unpleasant for one of the party at least and she determined to avoid it as long as possible. She made up her mind that he was not going to talk about Michel, as he had only alluded to him in veiled terms as a lady-killer.

Berry made another appointment with her for the next morning at ten. He came down in time for the rendezvous but long after the others had breakfasted. He found Barbara in earnest conference with his aunts; she liked them and under oath of secrecy had imparted as much about her love affair as she knew. Berry bowed low all around and bellowed in the direction of the pantry that he only wanted coffee, he had no time for more.

"Please don't hurry for me," said Barbara, "because I am going to play golf with the Mac Donalds. Can we talk this afternoon? It seems to me that we said so much driving down from Yonkers."

"There is much more to impart; who told you to drive my car down to the club anyway?"

"Your aunts said I might."

"Oh, in that case it is less impertinent. Aunts, I give you fair warning, that if I don't have an interview with Barbara this afternoon at four there will be trouble, wigs on the green, blood on the moon perhaps."

"Not this afternoon, Berry," said Aunt Penelope, "I am giving a bridge party, make it to-morrow morning."

"To-morrow morning at nine sharp then."

"Yes, unless I go to Harvard with your aunt Phoebe, let's make it day after to-morrow, Wednesday, fifth of September."

"All right, let me look the car over before you go, fancy playing golf in this weather. You must have some crime to forget or fresh wickedness to perpetrate."

CHAPTER SIXTY-NINE

On Wednesday morning, the book cases were found in great disorder; Berry had arisen early, determined this time not to allow Barbara to give him the slip. He was most affable at breakfast and suddenly produced a small volume bound in watered green silk:

"Let me read you some gems of American thought. This book is a brilliant collection of maxims, anno 1895, reserved for private circulation; what a pity when I see on the first page the following powerful verse:

> 'When this you see,
> Remember me.' "

His aunts rose with great agility and sought to rescue their book: "Berry, is nothing sacred for you, even our schoolgirl follies? Give back that book at once or you will be sorry, remember you aren't the only facetious member of this family."

Berry galloped around the room reading: "Here is a very sacred bit 'Never forget the fourth of March 1896,' in fact that's almost improper in its mystery; but here is a jewel of the first water:

> 'You ask me to write in your album
> But I hardly know how to begin,
> For there's nothing original in me,
> Excepting original sin.'

"Berry, do you know who wrote that? One of our dearest friends, Mary Steinway, and do you know where she is now?"

"Dead, at any rate I hope, but here's another one:

> 'The hours I spent with thee, I never can forget,
> Would that I lived with thee, or we had never met!' "

Berry gave a groan; "That last sentiment was lovely, speaking of which, step this way to the garden, Maud." He took Barbara by the arm firmly and off they went.

The aunts looked at each other and said: "I think he deserves a lesson and with the help of that poor girl he is now pestering to death, I bet we can arrange something to our mutual advantage."

CHAPTER SEVENTY

Berry put his banking spectacles on the tip of his nose and addressed Barbara. "Barbara, were you ever married before?"

"No, why these idiotic remarks?"

"Because I am leading up to my subject artfully, ever been engaged? I don't count Georges?"

"I don't wish to answer your impertinent questions."

"Ever been engaged to Saint-Amant, for instance?"

"Berry, just what do you know?"

"Everything except the reason that made him break it off."

"He didn't break it off."

"Oh, then you did; come now, be reasonable, if it wasn't he it must have been you. Now, Barbara, he is my dearest friend although I bait and annoy him. As I can't run you through the body with my rapier, you owe me an explanation."

"Unfortunately, I haven't an explanation on me."

"Oh, come now, yes you have. You must have hurt his feelings; you don't know how sensitive he is. You ought to be ashamed, fancy that sweet creature wasting his affections on you. Why he is not only the nicest man in France but the most loving and the most constant."

"I agree about the loving; so much so that it prevented the constant."

"Now what on earth do you mean, you silly girl?"

"Simply that I am not going to live with a Don Juan."

Berry looked genuinely alarmed: "Don Juan? Michel? Why, when I knew him, he was reserved and far too delicate minded to deceive anyone."

"Well he deceived me," bursting into tears, "and Berry, if you could have seen my rivals, it is rage that is making me cry over them."

"Rivals? Do you mean to say there were several?"

"I know of two at least, both beautiful and dressed like sin, no worse than that, like pedlars' vans."

"But did he flaunt these scarlet women openly?"

"Yes, and he won't give any explanation, except that they have nothing to do with him."

Light dawned on Berry. He looked for four-leaved clovers in the grass with absorbing interest. "Were they really terrible, tough-looking females?"

"Well, the one I saw was and Suzanne's description of the other was just as bad."

"Then Barbara, they are mine, not Michel's."

"Yours?"

"Yes, the only kind I really like; my chosen ones must look like cart horses at a fair."

He explained the legacy of the flat and its codicils; Barbara's heart grew lighter, although she kept a severe and gloomy face, repeating, now and then: "You don't expect me to believe you, do you?" Berry finally said:

"If I show you a begging letter from Georgette Leblond and a list of errands from Mrs. Baxter will you be persuaded?"

"Mrs. Baxter, that's the one I saw," cried Barbara, "yes, I believe you without the letters."

"Now," said Berry, relaxing and lighting a cigarette, "you must apologize."

"That's my business," spoke Barbara firmly, "if ever a mischievous ass needed a lesson, it's you."

"Never mind about me, but don't give Michel a lesson because I play practical jokes."

"Don't you worry about Michel; only I'm not going to have any interference from you. To think of the weeks of misery I have been through!" Berry looked abashed. "In fact I don't know if I am ever going to speak to you again." Berry held out a paw which Barbara ignored and she rushed into the house.

Berry for once felt that he had gone too far, and further had not arranged matters for his belovèd Mrs. Selby. He wandered about quite sadly, while the female inmates of the house were busily sending a cable to France. Aunt Penelope insisted on telephoning the message under cover of her pillow, as she always did when Berry was prowling about.

When he came in finally, prepared to apologize to the whole world, he was told that Barbara had gone to bed with a headache. Aunt Penelope said she was quite worried, that Barbara had rushed in crying that she wished she were dead. Aunt Phoebe kept up the conversation by adding that she was delighted to leave this gloomy hotbed of lies and mischief-making the next day. She was to visit a friend in the Adirondacks, although this was news to Berry.

"You used to be so fond of me, Aunts," said Berry in the whining voice of a beggar, "now you don't love me anymore. Have I done anything to offend?"

"No, dear," they answered in a chorus, "but we wish you wouldn't bring the love-lorn to visit us, just as we are getting to the comfortable time of existence when all is pleasure and no deceptive amours can prevent us from enjoying life."

"Why, I thought you liked Barbara," he exclaimed much mystified.

"So we do, but somehow she's so tragic to-night, we can't help thinking that something awful might happen at any moment."

"Nonsense, you worry about nothing; I have arranged things beautifully for that ungrateful hussy; mark my words she'll be as merry as a grig to-morrow morning."

They shook their heads sorrowfully.

CHAPTER SEVENTY-ONE

Next morning, Berry sat eating a huge breakfast with Penn and Aunt Penelope. "Everything I love for breakfast," said he, "nice scrambled eggs, do you think I would pop off if I had a little more ham? A day that begins like this is a perfect day, where's Barbara?"

Aunt Penelope said she was a little late, she supposed. A quarter of an hour passed. No Barbara.

"Why don't you run up and knock at her door, Penn?"

He did, loudly, but came down saying no one answered. Aunt Penelope arose and flew up the stairs. Berry went on eating and when possible, singing merrily.

His aunt came back very slowly with her napkin pressed to her face: "Berry, Barbara is not in her room, the bed has not been slept in!"

He still looked unconcerned: "She's gone out for an early walk and made her bed up first, she's such a tidy creature."

"Very likely," agreed his aunt, "she'll turn up presently; meanwhile if you have quite finished, will you drive me over to York? I want to buy some candles at 'Ye antick dove and distaffe shoppe'; I hate to patronize a place with such a ridiculous name, but I particularly want candles with gold flecks in them."

Berry wiped his mouth, sighed and strode off to the garage; he ran back to the house as fast as his breakfast would allow:

"The blue Chrysler I borrowed from Joyce at Yonkers has gone."

"Never mind," said Aunt Penelope "my runabout is there, isn't it? I daresay Barbara borrowed the car for a drive."

Berry was becoming a little thoughtful, but his aunt seemed most lively and talked in high spirits on the way to and from York. Lunch came, no Barbara.

"Do you think we could telephone to a few people and find out if she's been anywhere near them?"

"But aunt," objected Berry, "she has only known you for four days, she would not go off without telling you, she isn't a very familiar or unconventional girl."

Tea-time came, an English habit indispensable to Johnsonian life, dinner time, and no sign of the girl. Aunt Penelope declared solemnly:

"I am now quite alarmed, Berry, I suppose you warned her of the swamps?"

"Well, yes, that is, no. But I tried to frighten her with them as we drove here."

"Perhaps you had better give a glance in that direction after dinner," very glumly.

Berry looked horrified: "But Aunt, what do you mean, you must be joking, besides she is an excellent driver."

"You must admit that her staying out all day is very strange; as you remarked, she does not know us very well."

Berry stuffed a sandwich into his pocket and patrolled the swamps, lakes and all. The moon was full and they had never looked more sinister, the water glistening like silver and the dismal undergrowth a mass of wicked black shadows. When he returned, his aunt said wearily:

"Well, I can see from your face that you have not found her. How long does it take for a car to sink into the swamp?"

"About two hours, oh Aunt, how gloomy you are!"

"This is Thursday night and the poor girl was to sail Saturday at noon. If we hear nothing by to-morrow morning we must inform the police. How I wish that Phoebe were here, she has such a level head."

Berry spent an all but sleepless night; the graphic way his aunt had described Barbara's face after her interview with him in the garden, made him tremble. "And to think of the cable I sent Michel," he groaned. It was indeed frightful; he had wired: "Postpone our wedding until November, I want dear Berry to attend, Barbara." The next morning he patrolled the roads and hills, as pallid as he could be under many coatings of tan; he refused to inform "those silly cops." He was rapidly losing all self-control and suddenly burst out.

"Have you thought of Mr. Selby, he sails to-morrow, you know?"

"I have thought of nothing else all day, Berry, you will have to ring him up to-night."

Berry almost cried: "Aunt, I can't, you will have to, I never felt so badly in my life. I'm afraid something dreadful has happened after all and I was fond of that girl at bottom."

"Don't say 'was' as if she were dead, it's too sad."

"Aunt, give me until to-morrow morning before we telephone to Mr. Selby." Berry was quite humble and a changed man from his cocky, gay self. "I still have this afternoon and evening to find her."

He returned too exhausted to eat at ten o'clock: "I found this tag in the rocks by the sea at Westover," he said drearily.

His aunt saw the name "Barbara Winship, 29 Avenue Henri-Martin, Paris," and buried her face in a cushion on the sofa.

Berry slept splendidly, too worn out even for worry; just after dawn he tiptoed down in his pajamas, called New York, the Cataway Hotel and finally Mr. Selby.

"Who's that? Oh, is that you, Berry, calling me at this unearthly hour? Why don't you know it's been as hot as Tophet all night and I am getting my first snooze?"

"Well, Mr. Selby, you must excuse me but I am in such a state …"

"Why call me when you go on jamborees?" Mr. Selby was plainly annoyed.

"Mr. Selby, it's about Barbara; she isn't with you by any chance, is she?"

"Look here, Berry, I tell you solemnly, you're tight, don't you realize it's half-past five in the late night or early morning, whichever you choose to call it, and I'm lying in bed? Of course Barbara is not with me."

"Well, sir, I might as well tell you the whole truth, I've lost her."

"Lost my niece, what the dickens do you mean?"

"Yes, she disappeared on Wednesday and I have been looking for her ever since; I am desperate with worry."

A long pause, then over the wire Mr. Selby pronounced: "Now Berry, I confided my niece to you for a few days, if you've lost her, you've got to find her. Only I give you fair warning that if she isn't here by noon, I sail without her. You will have to return her when you find her at your own expense. You can't borrow my niece and not return her, it's grotesque, goodbye." He rang off.

Berry, stunned by Mr. Selby's heartless acceptance of the news, went back to bed. He slept again and woke up rather ashamed at his being able to do so. He was awakened by the voices of his aunts, talking and laughing together without a thought for the tragedy that hung over his head like a heavy pall. "I am the only person in America that has the least feeling for that poor girl, and even I fell asleep." He gulped and went down just as he was, much touzled and dishevelled:

"Hello, Aunt Phoebe, when did you get back?"

"A few minutes ago by the twelve o'clock train," answered that lady tranquilly.

He caught sight of a pink felt hat on a table and pointed to it silently.

"Why, what's the matter with you, Berry, can't you speak? It's only Barbara's hat."

"*Only* Barbara's hat," he repeated dully.

"Yes, she lent it to me for the train, mine was unbearably tight, although it wasn't very suitable for a lady of my years."

"I feel I shall go off my chump," said Berry elegantly, "if you don't explain yourself; don't you know Barbara's probably dead?"

"Well, she wasn't last night," cried Aunt Phoebe cheerily, "she decided Wednesday night late to drive me over to the Anderson's camp; she said the Chrysler was the only car she knew how to handle. Then we got on so well on the way we thought we would go straight to New York as the camp proved a bit far for two lone females to attempt. We arrived at Mrs. Cataway's entrancing hotel late on Thursday evening. Then I had a delightful day Friday, shopping for Mrs. Selby and making Uncle George's acquaintance. I came away early this morning as I couldn't bear to see them off."

"I see," said Berry slowly. He looked at them a long time. "You've made a haggard old man of me, because I read your album."

"No, no, Berry, but in memory of Barbara, Michel and all the alarms and skirmishes you have enjoyed since you came home."

He rose stiffly. "Well, I can kill Penn, at any rate. He scattered the tags and pieces of stuff among the rocks and swamps, I suppose?"

"Answer correct, only he has departed for the day."

"Bed is the best place for me," declared Berry. "You have won the first game, but the worst is yet to come." He departed looking quite crushed.

His aunts tittered. Penelope: "Well, that was rather a cruel joke, but it was worth it, don't you think?"

Phoebe: "Do I think so? I'm worn out but I feel even with him for once. When I remember the valentine he sent Mrs. Slingsby from me, and in May too, it makes my blood boil!"

CHAPTER SEVENTY-TWO

The first idea for a novel must have been taken from real life, because even now occasionally strange situations present themselves as they do in fiction. The poetical mind that decreed that life was like a piece of knitting, unravelled by means of a single conducting yarn, was quite right but it should have added another simile: existence viewed as a piece of mosaic, all the little odds and ends fitted together to form a pattern. The cement that seals the pattern down, morsel by morsel, is called coincidence. The sad part is that you can only see the completed design when life is over, and very funny it must look, inspected from the other side.

All this rambling talk is to impart that Michel Saint-Amant was sitting with his mother at Evian, on a terrace overlooking the too perfect lake. He was explaining to this lady for the twentieth time why he did not like mountains. She, who never listened to anything much, suddenly said:

"Michel, are you going to marry the girl I mentioned at lunch? I only touched on the matter because the dining-room is so noisy, I am going to change my table. I don't like our waiter, I am sure he drinks the wine, the bottle is almost always empty in the evening and you scarcely touch it. What was I saying?"

"We were talking about mountains, I think."

"About mountains, no we weren't, I remember now. I have had answers from several old friends about Mademoiselle de la Paume-Rimbaud and her references are excellent."

"You sound as if you were engaging a housemaid, not a daughter-in-law."

"Don't interrupt me. Marie writes that she is an orphan, very pretty, no inherited diseases, a million and a half dowry, two estates in the country later and very few relations. ..."

"I don't think I ought to deprive some other young pretender of this marvel. No, Mother, I do not want to marry anyone. As to this girl, how can you expect me, retiring as I am, to wish to spend my life with her? By the way, what are the drawbacks? You know that in your favorite game, marriages of convenience, you begin just as in other bargains with a list of advantages, cunningly concealing the defects until the prospective buyer is properly seduced."

"Really, Michel, you talk in a very trivial way, you must have consorted with a great many journalists lately."

"Is she a hunchback?" asked Michel pitilessly.

"Of course not, there are no faults except perhaps a trifling impediment in her speech."

"Do you mean that she stammers? That would make me very nervous."

"Just a little, a great many people find it most attractive."

"What else?"

"Augustine also writes me that there is nothing unpleasant to say about her whatsoever. You know that I am very broadminded. She is a devout Catholic, her mother was a Jewess, but that side of her family does not show at all and the Paume-Rimbauds are above suspicion."

"I am sure they are, and if I wanted to marry anyone in the world I would certainly choose a stuttering Jewess, but unfortunately I am a confirmed bachelor."

Madame Saint-Amant looked a little disappointed but promised herself she would arrange a "chance meeting" and for the time leave things as they were. The *concièrge* came towards them bearing a pile of mail. All the letters but one were for Madame Saint-Amant, she being a violent correspondent, the books and papers and one enormous grimy envelope for Michel, the last addressed in a sprawling, illiterate hand. As he opened it, his mother looked up and gave a little cry:

"Why, Michel, what a collection of telegrams!" She picked up the envelope, "I hope they are not urgent, that fool of a *concièrge* sent them on as letters."

Michel tore open four cables, trying to shelter them from his mother's ardent gaze and at the same time not to show too much surprise, a difficult and unsuccessful achievement.

The first was Berry's facetious message.

The second was from Barbara and read: "Believe you forever and ever forget foolish letter love Barbara."

The third said: "Arriving Paris September fifteenth with Barbara Uncle George."

And the fourth: "Cancel first cable writing forgive jocular Berry."

Michel's brain revolved madly; although all this news was strangely mixed and he was surprised to learn Barbara was in America, he ended by taking in the gist of it. Berry had explained matters to Barbara, she had resumed their engagement and was coming back. It was a great relief but not perfect happiness because after all Barbara only believed him now she knew the truth. Nevertheless he had been too unhappy without her to bargain with fate and gave himself up to joy. Just then his mother said: "Another letter from Marie, she writes that Mademoiselle de la Paume-Rimbaud's uncle is dying and she will inherit his historical château at once. Doesn't that tempt you, Michel?"

"No, even that does not change my decision, at least as far as your Jewess is concerned."

He picked up his cables and walked into the hotel in as unconcerned a fashion as he could. He put in a call for Paris, hoping to reach the Selbys before they left for Andrésy; this was the afternoon of the sixteenth, he was a day late, owing to the stupidity of the janitor. In a frenzy of impatience he packed a bag, love and excitement giving him the courage to leave his mother at a minute's notice with a very meager, vague, unsatisfactory explanation. She gathered as they parted that he was going to Paris to see a strange American called Selby on business.

It was Mrs. Selby who answered the telephone, she sounded a long way off, at the bottom of a well. All he could make her understand was that he would be at her house the next morning at nine.

CHAPTER SEVENTY-THREE

When Michel arrived he found the Selby family waiting for him in force. Mrs. Selby in a very elegant dressing-gown of mauve satin embroidered in white birds, although she secretly preferred a nondescript red flannel garment. The mauve creation was reserved for unexpected events such as fires, communist revolutions, burglars and various excitements. This was her first and excellent opportunity of wearing this wrap and made her feel very important. Barbara, bronzed and attired in a fashion plate costume of blue tweed called "on the links" looked charming, Mr. Selby was arrayed for business in iron gray cheviot. He was pining to get down to his office and hear the news, though this impatience seems incomprehensible, as Mr. Crosby took a very gloomy view of cotton and painted matters in the blackest colors.

George thought it right and proper to greet his new nephew with the slight tinge of solemnity due to a great occasion. He had warned Virginia not to be too merry and she had retorted sharply to leave her alone, she knew Latins better than he did, that she and Michel got on splendidly together, and that if she had been engaged to him there would never have been any trouble. All of which was perfectly true.

The interview passed off very well; after due congratulations and official confirmation of the engagement, the affianced ones were left to themselves and the Selbys departed to their various occupations.

Like happy countries, Barbara and Michel had little to relate, only too glad not to talk of unpleasant past events.

"Now we can get married at once."

"Certainly," said Barbara thinking the wedding would be in October as she had planned. "Have you told your mother?"

"Not yet, I took a train as soon as I telephoned your aunt, not stopping for explanations. We must call her up at once and ask her to return to Paris. She hates leaving Paris anyway, so any excuse will satisfy her."

"Do you think she will like me? Have there ever been any Americans in your family?"

"No foreigners of any sort," answered Michel, rising to telephone, "you can't imagine how French we are. Anyway, Mamma thought you were charming as Berry's fiancée, so think how pleased she will be to have you as a daughter-in-law." He was not as convinced as he sounded, but he hoped so.

Barbara pursued the topic: "Please tell me how French you are."

"Well", after a long pause, "I don't like American food very much; I prefer my meat served separately with vegetables, one at a time, after; I don't like sitting in a draught. I hate strong drinks that make me say foolish things and I love disgusting jokes as long as they aren't cruel."

"I am very disappointed," said Barbara, "I expected much worse, you don't sound unlike a human being."

"Thank you very much, oh here is Mamma at last."

Mamma sounded curious and mystified. Michel, knowing they would be cut off in a moment, burnt his boats and said with the calmness of one facing inevitable death: "Maman, please come up to Paris by the first train. No, nothing dreadful but something most important, has happened. I am engaged to Barbara Winship, a very nice American girl," he tore the receiver out of Barbara's hand, she very naturally wishing to hear her future mother-in-law's reactions. Michel continued: "and you must come up and see her uncle and aunt at once. I will meet all the trains from Evian until you come, so hurry, Maman." He then artfully pretended to have been cut off and replaced the receiver hurriedly. Michel was so relieved:

"Now we have nothing to worry us, you don't mind waiting for Berry do you, Barbara darling. He arrives early in November."

"No, especially as he must have worried dreadfully over my disappearance." Michel looked blank and then enjoyed the joke as only the oppressed could; then flaring up with independence declared: "I am not going to put off my wedding to suit Berry Johnson, he can come over a little earlier."

Barbara and Michel flew about like butterflies, leaving all the hard work to their relatives. They told a great many people of their engagement and bought the most extraordinary presents for their loved ones. Michel purchased an uneatable woolly pineapple and a dozen pomegranates for the Selbys, as connoisseurs of exotic fruit; a new harness and bow for Mirza, Longfellow's poems for Aunt Virginia, who detested them, an expensive English Tantalus for Uncle George who lost the key promptly and could not use the bottles. They showered fantastic gifts everywhere. Barbara, who ought to have known better, was worse, if possible, and knitted a shawl for her mother-in-law; this smart and nimble lady gave it to the *concièrge*, who loved it: a long fringed square of purple and black zigzags. As Aunt Virginia ungratefully remarked: "Never mind, we will all be even with them when the wedding presents pour in."

Barbara bestowed her articles on Mr. Crosby. Whether he wrote the fashions for Canada from that time forth, or farmed the position with someone else, I cannot tell you, as even the Selbys never discovered. Virginia would have given her eye teeth to know, and invented conversations with Crosby the fashion expert which were the source of hysterics for her family circle.

Michel, not to be outdone in folly, asked Monsieur Stanilas to take charge of his articles until Christmas. The Pole was delighted to do something for Michel and said he would make them sensational, original and inspiring; this sounded frightful to his young friend but he did not care very much as the wedding was fixed for October the twenty-third. Berry had graciously consented to appear as best man and announced his arrival early in October, he even offered them his flat. The offer was rejected contemptuously by Barbara who wished to be at least as grandiose as her friend Suzanne; fate favored her as you will see.

CHAPTER SEVENTY-FOUR

The Selbys loved excitement but were getting a little too much of it. Next to excitement they enjoyed grumbling and they did a great deal of that.

Very early in October, after a glance into the next room where Michel and Barbara were addressing invitations and laughing at their presents, Virginia squirmed in her large square armchair and appealed to George who reclined on his sofa, a curly black leather affair that combined sunken springs with great comfort:

"George, do you think we will live to see Barbara married?"

"I hope so but all these ceremonies, arrangements and family parties are killing me. You are lucky to have had a cure at Vichy."

"Vichy!" snorted Virginia, "that's one of the reasons I am so low in my mind. I ought to be resting after my cure. Instead of which my liver is all stirred up and working harder than it has for years, and think of the excitement ahead of us; three dinner parties for forty people this week."

"Oh, Virginia, did you say three?"

"Yes, my dear; we are the bride's family. First a dinner for the engagement, then a dinner to the family-in-law, next a third dinner and party for the signing of the marriage contract." A groan from the sofa. She went on revelling in the horror of the next three weeks: "It's too frightful; next thing to look forward to: Michel's mother will return the compliment with a banquet at least and each of the fifteen couples we are inviting here will ask us to a dinner or party. Then comes the wedding. I give Barbara a strong tonic night and morning but I doubt if we old ones pull through. Southerners are so delicate."

"I suppose so," said George, in a depressed voice, "it seems to me we didn't have such a tussle when our girls were married."

"No, because one married an Englishman in England and the other, the only Frenchman living who could persuade his family to a quiet wedding. Even then we did a good deal of heavy-as-lead entertaining. I exonerate Michel, it's his mother. I have never met anyone widi so many relatives or such a thirst for solemnities."

"Now, Virginia, brace up and tell me how your first interview with Madame Saint-Amant went off. We never have a minute these days to exchange views or have a good laugh."

"Well George, if you hadn't meanly gone off to a committee meeting you could have helped. As usual, poor frail me was left to bear the burden and heat of the day."

George composed himself to an hour of sheer delight: "This is as good as a play. Don't you leave out a single detail. I want to know how she rang the doorbell and entered the sitting-room."

"Let me see, George. She was beautifully dressed in black trimmed with ermine, a mild but ceremonious form of half-mourning suitable for great events, and she arrived at three, precisely the calling hour. I wore my new gray georgette dress and thought I looked very nice until I saw Madame Saint-Amant. To begin with, she might be my daughter, she is so fresh and youthful, but you know that. You are also aware of how ridiculous my French is. It was never so shocking as when I answered her perfect, polished sentences, rounded periods and neatly turned phrases."

"Couldn't you repeat some of it in French, just a sample?" begged George anxiously.

"No, you would enjoy it too much; but when we had finished complimenting each other on the happy circumstances about to unite our two families, Madame Saint-Amant (or Madeleine as I must call her from now on) said that she would speak frankly as one woman to another. I knew that something horrible was coming and held my breath. Of course, she went on, she knew nothing of Americans although she respected them as a nation of self-made emigrants and admired them for their money-grubbing propensities ..."

"Oh come, Virginia, she didn't say that!"

"Well, not exactly that but she insinuated it so strongly that there was no room for doubts; not a single insulting remark, mind you. Then she gracefully told me that much as she would have preferred her only son to marry one of her own race, she was prepared to capitulate before my charming niece who was the great exception in every way to the average American girl."

"The chairman demands the answer; go to it, Virginia," cried George, sitting up on his rosewood sofa.

"Oh, I didn't say much," answered the modest Virginia. "I merely remarked that I too would have liked my niece to marry an American but that I had not been consulted. That I considered Michel a perfection but that Barbara, although my belovèd niece, could not be described as anything extraordinary, just a mediocre American with all the faults of her race, flighty, generous, extravagant.

"Madame Saint-Amant seized this opportunity gracefully and said that Michel, thank goodness, was well provided for and would later on inherit his father's fortune. 'As late as possible,' says I bowing gracefully. 'Thank you, Madame,' says she with an affable smile. But what about dear Barbara? What could the young couple count on from her side? I looked very innocent and answered, nothing at all. Nothing? Madame Saint-Amant laughed like a chime of bells and said that she realized how wealthy Americans were, but what we considered trifles were important sums in francs. 'Madeleine, when I say nothing, I mean nothing; I mean that Barbara is penniless'."

"Excitement is killing me," cried George, "how did she react?"

"Madeleine continued unruffled that she understood the American idea was to marry without a dowry; but her future inheritances? I pretended to be rather embarrassed. Alas, no legacies in the future, all her uncles and aunts had large families of heirs, direct ones too. I was surprised that Michel had not mentioned it.

"That was a staggerer, but to do her justice she rallied gallantly: 'Michel is very vague and never discusses money, but certainly, as it is a love match, it does not matter at all.' I chipped in then to say that Barbara wrote extraordinary articles of real literary value (may Heaven forgive me) and could perfectly well continue to wield the pen if there was any financial shortage; also that the young couple could be our guests perpetually.

"Then she became really charming; Michel would never consent to his wife touching a pen for anything but pleasure. She herself was very rich and could do anything for them in reason. She gave me a few figures that startled me. Why do we always consider foreigners impecunious? She said, and I believed her, that this embarrassing conversation was only a formality which she would gladly have spared both of us, but that it was always better to begin things on a monetary basis, never to be mentioned again. All this couched in lovely language. Then Barbara was called in, she embraced her affectionately and pressed a large box into her ready hand: 'Just a little souvenir for my daughter.' I had a moment of panic, I was so afraid that Barbara would throw herself on the present like a savage and disgrace me. She was very tactful, however, laid the parcel on the table and responded very prettily to her mother-in-law's advances."

"Cut out the sentiment, what was in the box?" from greedy George.

"Why, George, you know, the most magnificent diamonds, set to perfection, and such quantities of them."

"Do you mean to say those stones are real? I hope you mentioned Barbara's mother's pearls and her island."

"Speak of that marsh full of ducks on the coast of Georgia? Why, a tidal wave might destroy it any day, I should think not. The pearls will come as a surprise, also those chests full of Winship silver, I have written to the bank for them. Barbara has also received a small fortune in checks but she and Michel are so silly, they have probably spent them already."

"Very likely, m'dear, do you blame them, it's such fun to waste money that drops from Heaven, so to speak. Madeleine sounds quite nice. She probably only wanted Barbara to have money for the sake of her friends. I must admit, it is aggravating to have one's son choose the poorest American in Paris for his bride. To a French mind a poor American is an anomaly difficult to grasp. To-morrow we must discuss the menu of our first dinner, I don't feel strong enough to-night."

CHAPTER SEVENTY-FIVE

Barbara, too, began to feel the weight of grandeur and thought that a quiet wedding would have been less tiring. But, like her mother-in-law, she had a taste for pomp and parties, so the three weeks that elapsed for the publishing of the banns were not such a nightmare for her as for the Selbys.

For the first dinner in honor of the engagement, the poor wretches found themselves presiding at a table for forty. The Selby contingent was eight, with their daughters and the fiances, the remaining thirty-two composed the most valid part of Michel's family; it came forward as one man, from Paris and remote provinces alike, all spurred on by the vivifying impulse of family ties and intense curiosity over the American bride. Naturally marrying a foreigner was no longer an unheard of occurrence, and since the war the golden, western world had ceased to surprise.

Taken as a whole the relations were kind, polite and very gay, excepting a few old people who hobbled in to criticize with much gnashing of false teeth and blowing of ear trumpets. Madame Saint-Amant received the clan privately, told them as much as she knew of the Selbys and Winships and besought them on no account to talk about the war debts and loans. They all promised except one old senator who said his manners were formed and he needed no lessons.

What cut the Selbys to the heart was the enormous expense. Do not judge them too harshly. Remember that all these dreadful parties were to be paid for out of the party fund and that diamond ring had only provided one private orgy, the rest swallowed up in quite unnecessary and tiresome ceremonies, including Barbara's ocean passages, the latter incurred so that Berry could explain.

The pearls, a complete set of necklaces, ear-rings, brooches and bracelets, were magnificent, and excited great admiration, Barbara going up in value every minute, except in Michel's eyes for she was perfect already. Uncle George pondered daily over his wedding present. He addressed Barbara: "You don't care what we give you, but I must impress that old dame in the jet bonnet. What would be the most enormous and effective present?" Barbara consulted Michel. The old lady being his grandmother, he said promptly, a car, for though she was immensely wealthy, she could never bring herself to the expense of a chauffeur. "All you have to do is to send us the photograph of a motor," Michel added laughing. "A very good idea, my boy, I shall buy you the real thing at once." On the installment plan, he thought to himself, but he kept the parenthesis a secret, for this very American mode of living is one that shocks French people vastly; used as they are to buying only what they can afford, they do not hand out all their money every month for luxuries as any sensible Anglo-Saxon does as a matter of course.

The dreaded engagement dinner took place in a private room at a good hotel. The hour was fixed at half-past eight but as early as seven-thirty the older members of the party arrived, giving themselves up to pleasure. As they lived all over France and seldom traveled, the more candid would have admitted, if asked, that family events were their one chance of enjoyment; whether christenings, weddings, confirmations or law suits, it mattered not. In fact a good large funeral was about as much fun as anything else, and once the corpse had been decently disposed of, great cordiality, even a little genteel mirth reigned among the mourners, pleased to meet their old friends and so delighted to be alive.

Anyway, Mr. and Mrs. Selby received the thirty-two in a pompous boudoir adjoining the feast, with carefully prepared sentences, which they both meant to use again and again until the wedding was over. Then the younger, smarter members of the family drifted in, enlivening the jet and black atmosphere of the great-aunts and grandmothers. All the old gentlemen wore decorations and orders; all the old ladies, dirty old-fashioned jewellery of immense value. Barbara, dressed in white tulle, did her best to act the part of the perfect betrothed maiden; Michel looked as if he had been drowned, so far away and absent did he appear from the congratulative platitudes that were showered on them both.

The doors of the dining-room were flung open by the most respectable looking butler with mutton chop whiskers, and in they trooped. The questions of age, precedence and rank had been beautifully settled by Virginia. As always, the unimportant members of the party, such as Mrs. Selby's daughters and Michel's gay young cousins, had a very good time, clustered like flowers at an undertaker's. The fiancés were flanked by the oldest and deafest.

Mrs. Selby surveyed the long table decorated with oval pieces of mirror, clusters of wax candles (considered a great extravagance by the retrograde) and garlands of white roses. It looked lovely. She sighed and turned her attention to a general on her left, smiling at him most coquettishly. Although he did not understand her opening remark very well, he responded with great gallantry. After he became accustomed to her French, he found her a witty and original neighbor and the American nation went up a great deal in his estimation, especially as Virginia at an appropriate moment mentioned Lafayette with tears of gratitude in her eyes. On her right she fared worse. There sat a senator, a conservative of the deepest dye who addressed his usual dinner party remarks to her at stated intervals, principally at a change of courses, when he had nothing to gobble and could spare the time. His conversation being a series of proverbs, which he considered a safe opinion ever, Virginia kindly interpreted a few English sayings culled from the wisdom of nations for his benefit. They stuck firmly over "Penny wise and pound foolish." Impossible to make the senator comprehend this deep remark; besides it sounded perilously like the exchange. The Chinese version supplied by the coarse Virginia, pleased him better: "Go to bed to save candles and have twins." He guffawed long and loud with an alarmingly red face, trimmed with swelling blue veins on the brow. Virginia's end of the table was rapidly becoming brilliant. She was winning the conversation prize in spite of French as a heavy handicap.

George beamed at her and succeeded in interesting the women on either side of him in a long and complicated narrative, diluted with numerous considerations and details. It was all about a journey to Turkey in which he had been the prisoner of a distinguished brigand. George hoped with luck to spin it out until the cheese and then, if hard pressed, to give a faithful rendering of a bull fight. All went very well, a few romantic remarks about Andalusia and old Madrid found their mark also; George was safe until the coffee.

Barbara and Michel, each in their own way, behaved disgracefully. Barbara ate enormously, drank of all the wines—five were served—and did not pay the least attention to her neighbors, both distinguished men, beyond an occasional smile. As the dinner proceeded, the wines gave her moral poise and great impertinence; she openly defied her aunt's furious glances and signs.

Michel, who sat by an ear-trumpet, had started out bravely with a remark on the weather: "Louder, please, that's not the right tone of voice," shrieked she. He tried again, with no success, and, as he found that he was becoming the cynosure of all eyes, as they say in old-fashioned novels, he had a fit of humility and handed back the trumpet. On his other side sat the fast lady of the family, who considered him a milksop, and gazed ardently at him through a *face à main* whenever he addressed her. In great mental agony he ate and drank nothing, and furtively consulted his new wrist watch, a present from Barbara. Still two hours before midnight.

Mrs. Selby thought that a little music after the coffee would finish the evening without too much effort. The programme was appalling, but short, and arranged to suit the worst bores, as the young ones giggled in the corners anyway, delighted to be together. After copious liqueurs which fixed the high red blush of dinner in every cheek, the concert began with some comic songs contributed by a well-known artist from Montmartre. Everybody liked this much better than talking, and they all knew the songs, which was also a comfort.

Then a tall stout matron with slick black hair parted in the middle thundered out a poem by Victor Hugo about some drowned fishermen. This struck the right note of pathos, indispensable to the digestion of a huge dinner. As the Yorkshire farmer remarked in his simple, hearty manner every evening: "I've had a good dinner, I don't care who hasn't."

Just as everyone wiped away a furtive tear, the prima donna of the evening flew in with a bunch of imitation violets in one hand and a roll of music in the other. She had a rollicking, girlish manner as she bowed to the audience which turned to grim attention as the first cords on the piano were struck. In a menacing manner she bellowed "Pagliacci." Heavily encored, she grew worse—no, no, she grew sadder. The supersensitive diners were treated to the intimate details of "Louise," the grand scene of the love affair, in which she explains matters in no uncertain way; they liked it very much.

Libations of an innocent sort were served to comfort them and to crown the evening. They were followed by a general stampede of the guests. As soon as one decided to leave, the others fought for the pleasure of shaking hands with the Selbys, and then for their wraps.

Virginia pretended to faint when they had all departed and Michel asked Barbara quite seriously if they could not elope, in the face of many other rejoicings. "Oh children, how I wish you could," sighed their immoral aunt. "But you can't in France. Three weeks' residence in the same parish and a civil wedding at the Town Hall. By the way, Michel, have you arranged about getting a dispensation for marrying Protestant Barbara in a Catholic church?"

"Yes, I have, and the wedding will be the worst of all, when I think of those rows of gilt and velvet armchairs all waiting in the choir to be filled by the family!"

"Oh, it won't be so bad, I'm looking forward to Berry, he is such a ray of sunshine in spite of his wickedness; and Michel, if you don't cheer up about your wedding, I'll insist on your being married in the Episcopal church too. That will be three ceremonies instead of two."

CHAPTER SEVENTY-SIX

The other parties were much the same as the first one. Barbara forbade her own friends to give any for her, and began worrying about a roof to live under when she returned to Paris after her honeymoon.

This is where Madame Saint-Amant stepped in. She recognized a pliable, sweet-tempered nature in Barbara and resolved, as she liked her, to make the most of it in order to retain her grasp on her son. As her daughter-in-law's worldly tastes were somewhat like hers, the ground was prepared for mutual good feeling, strengthened by gifts, attentions and kind words to which Barbara responded as the heliotrope turns to the sun. Most students of nature overlook the fact that this flower also drinks a lot of water; in this metaphor, the water was Michel. He also influenced Barbara greatly, in quite another direction, that of polite, smiling obstinacy, and a determination not to be wheedled and coaxed into too great an intimacy with anyone but Uncle George and Aunt Virginia. The Selbys were a proud, independent race, familiar with no one, not even themselves or their families.

The result was that when Madeleine Saint-Amant, in view of the dearth of apartments and the repulsion they had experienced for the closet-like flats they visited daily, offered them a whole floor in her big house, they accepted with alacrity. Like beggars they appeared most ungrateful asking for a private entrance, a lift to the second floor which was theirs and several bathrooms. Madame Saint-Amant agreed to everything except a private gymnasium, as her old house would not stand the strain. She did not care, for in this way she would see her son every day, and know exactly how the couple lived. It may as well be said that that part of her scheme miscarried, for though Michel and Barbara were properly dutiful and affectionate to her, she saw no more of them than they wished. It became a game on their part to envelop themselves in a cloud of mystery as far as their parent was concerned. She became accustomed to it and enjoyed their daily visit very much.

What time they could snatch from introductions and blessings, they spent in devising a home to be quite unlike anything they had ever had before. No more museum furniture for Michel, gorgeous chests of drawers, severely inspected each day for a guilty nick or scratch; no more armchairs that had belonged to Madame de Pompadour and therefore could have no springs or cushions on the seats because these comforts did not belong to the period. Barbara yearned for rooms like Suzanne de la Huppe's and between them they furnished their immense suite of rooms in the most fantastic manner, yet the general effect pleasing: light, warm colors, fine rugs, pretty lights. Certainly they made a few mistakes but not irreparable ones. Barbara had all the doors leading from one room to another removed and replaced by brocaded curtains. When the floors creaked in the old house at night and the furniture snapped and cracked two rooms off, they were frightened to death; they contracted colds and stiff necks from draughts impossible to avoid in huge rooms that were difficult to heat, in any case, and very chilly without the doors. Instead of curtains, the window panes were engraved in imitations of billowing ruffles, which is lovely in a friend's house but too fancy to amuse long in one's own home. They bought too many etchings, which they discovered later to be a life-less form of decoration. But these were trifles and they became even happier than they had imagined, which is saying a great deal.

Some of their wedding presents they could use but most of them were placed in a small dark room christened the chamber of horrors; they pasted the name of the donor under each gift, to avoid regrettable mistakes, and sent them on to their acquaintances as they mated.

Berry had arrived and insisted on their begging his pardon before he bestowed his blessing on them. They gave in for the sake of peace and he presented them with a costly traveling bag, with tortoiseshell and crystal fittings as a joint present for them both, "so they could fight forever after" as he kindly remarked. There is nothing more irritating than sharing toilet necessities, even with a loved one, and he knew it.

Another present from Berry which Barbara appreciated far more than Michel was a mystery room which he fitted up in their flat at his own expense, as he constantly reminded them. He found a small disused cabinet, a sort of trunk room at the end of a passage; here Berry revealed himself as a master. The horror of this room was unsurpassed, but could only be shown once to each visitor as no one but a lunatic would have been induced to return after one performance.

You went in with either Barbara or Berry, never Michel; he had been so frightened that he warned his friends, which only increased their desire to go. When you opened the door all sorts of things happened in this black chamber; if you turned the door handle slowly you were sprayed with icy water, not enough to ruin your clothes, but a sufficient amount to make you furious. If on the other hand you entered boldly, music rent your ears, factory whistles blew, cuckoos called, "unpleasing to the married ear" as Berry pointed out, owls hooted and a puppy howled. A little upset, you walked in: quite a nice, primly furnished little room. You walked over to examine the curious ornaments on the mantelpiece, the floor in front of it caved in, engulfing you to the knees. If, obstinately, you smiled and picked up one of the china dogs, it stuck out an enormous tongue and hit you in the face. That was usually enough, but bold spirits have been known to sit on an innocent chair which straightway screamed like a mandrake and crumpled up, depositing them on the floor. This chair was made of rubber, and was invented by Berry. As the months went by fresh "attractions" were added but always in very bad taste, most people considered.

CHAPTER SEVENTY-SEVEN

The great day approached; after having seemed a long way off, it was swiftly there. The day before, Barbara, Michel and the other thirty-eight had gone informally to the town hall for the civil wedding without which the French government would have considered them concubines, paramours and other horrid things; much as the religious French despise this legal ceremony, they are not properly married without it. They all sat down in a large bare room decorated with palm trees and a white plaster bust of the Republic. Michel, Barbara and their witnesses (Monsieur Stanilas and Berry) signed a paper declaring their marriage. The mayor, a tricolored sash tied around his fat waist, congratulated them in a short halting speech which touched on a multitude of subjects, all uninteresting. After this, the last dinner took place. The Selbys went home to toss and rave with fatigue, Barbara took a sleeping draught which took effect the next afternoon only, but why discourse on these too familiar events of civilized life?

The next day was fine, mild and clear, the anniversary of Uncle George's pneumonia. As Barbara drove to the church in a handsome carriage decorated with white flowers, she scarcely realized it was her wedding. Again she had the feeling that all these festivities and horrors could not possibly be for an insignificant mortal like herself.

The outside of the familiar, shabby yet pleasing church of Saint-Honoré-d'Eylau was gaily decorated with a red and white striped cotton canopy over the door. As she, on Uncle George's arm, walked over the red carpet stretched over the sidewalk, the doors of the church were flung open, a magnificent red and gold beadle in a cocked hat and padded white cotton calves met and preceded them up the aisle striking the ground solemnly with a gold topped cane. The organ crashed and pealed something ugly chosen by the organist, and Barbara and Michel found themselves kneeling in front of red velvet armchairs, just as they had expected.

Back of them walked the bridesmaids and groomsmen, then came all the family, two by two, carefully paired off according to the etiquette of family ties and importance. The church was full. Much singing spun out the ceremony interminably, for this was an important wedding with a great many flowers and candles. The family clustered around on red velvet chairs of honor in the choir and the guests composed themselves to slumber when the kindly fat priest began his homily. He touched lightly on Barbara's family of heretics and foreigners but lingered interminably over Michel's, raking up all his ancestors, remote and near, extolling their virtues and commending Michel and Barbara to resemble them all, a difficult feat, and if he had known all the truth about them, not a very good idea.

Fully married at last, they walked into the vestry, with the family always, and stood there an hour. The male guests with their top hats on sticks, the female ones pushing and fighting, joined them, to congratulate them for the fiftieth time and shake hands with all they knew. As the wedding took place at twelve and it was then two o'clock, a reception was held at a hall conveniently near by, made for the purpose, where an elaborate and delicious lunch had been provided by the now much impoverished Selbys.

This was Barbara's last public appearance for several weeks; she sat in a corner, as a bride should, her immense white satin dress billowy around her; Michel stood by her, smiling and relieved to think he was about to resume a fairly safe and agreeable existence. He thought a great deal about Barbara and glanced fondly at her nodding head. She was overpowered by fatigue and veronal and could only smile wanly at the guests. Not that they expected or wanted more from her; it was their party and they had assembled to fight at the buffet, and talk about each other. Berry and Aunt Virginia managed to smuggle her away, Michel glad to tear off his dress suit, promptly followed, and no one missed them except Monsieur Stanilas who brought them champagne (which they poured onto some convenient plants) every time he had some, about every ten minutes.

When Michel and Barbara were ready to leave, the bride opened the door of a bedroom where she had changed her dress and called Berry who was hovering about, waiting for her: "I want to say goodbye, dear Berry, and thank you again for the mystery room and …"

"But, my good girl, don't thank me, besides I am going to see you off."

"No, you aren't," said Michel, suddenly springing from behind the door which Barbara locked while her husband knocked Berry down. Then she returned to see them struggling on the floor, slipped Berry's legs through a thick rubber ring not painful but very tight. The rest was easy. They wound a sheet around his indignant form and tied it securely with pillow cases. The pillow itself was placed under his head and tied over the face, leaving a tiny hole for breathing in the middle, the feathers deadening any calls for help. This satisfactorily arranged, they laid him on the bed, tied down with the remaining sheet, kissed the pillow over his face goodbye and locked the door.

So they departed, to begin a new life, happy to be together and delighted to frustrate Berry, whose overcoat pockets still bulged with detestable inventions such as sticky paper confetti and garlands of celluloid flowers which exploded under foot.

CHAPTER SEVENTY-EIGHT

Letter from Berry written six weeks after:

Darling Aunts:

A merry Christmas to you both, although you don't de« serve one and won't get it without me anyway. A great many things have happened. First of all, Mr. Baxter and I have agreed to disagree and so we part; he will be sorry some day he has let the only ray of sunshine in the dour Vendôme Trust leave him. He is a slow old poke and never did understand modern banking. Business is now conducted as an agreeable pastime, not a stern duty. The fellow has no poetry in him and perhaps not even a soul on him. I told him so but only after I had resigned; then he said mean things about your Berry. So now I am a broker and sell the most beautiful stocks and bonds, all warranted to wear well and bring in profits of a handsome sort. Let me choose you some with pretty names, Anaconda, Rio Tinto or Malopolska? My first client was sweet, intelligent, considerate Mr. George Selby, magnate.

That reminds me, I can see you even as I write, looking your worst, eyes popping out, tongues lolling with excitement. I have forgotten to describe Barbara's wedding to you. No, I didn't forget, I did it on purpose to punish you for your behavior, not only now but always, ever since I was a small orphan, defenceless in your vindictive Yankee hands.

Well, the marriage was only the culminating point in a series of rejoicings that would put your humble junketing to shame. For three weeks we never sat down to dinner less numerous than forty or forty-one, for I was included in each feast. I behaved very well always and the Selbys now allow me to call them uncle and aunt. They worked hard for the glory of the Star Spangled Banner and managed to give quite a natural air to the most ghastly family reunions. Aunt Virginia knows just what to say and she imparts it in atrocious French, but so graphic. Of course the enemy tribe (for the Montague and Capulet atmosphere is always the proper one for a marriage) were too polite to smile.

I gave your wedding presents to Aunt Virginia instead of Barbara, I thought that she deserved them most. So she gets the herb pillow against insomnia and the night gown sachet with which to impress Uncle George; don't thank me, it was no trouble at all and even if it had been, I would not have hesitated to do the right thing.

Barbara did not deserve anything, she just smiled and smiled, leaving her relations to do all the hard work. Yes, they had a villainous looking detective to look after the presents; some were beautiful, others could best be described as striking, I liked mine best.

Barbara was married severely and tightly, first by a Mayor, a wholesale butcher in private life, then by a Catholic priest. Do you hear me, at a Catholic church, and she promised that all her children would be papists. I looked very nice in my tail coat and top hat and escorted a beautiful bridesmaid in pink rustling stuff, I may marry her myself some day and then I can have a Catholic wedding too. Barbara wore a white stuff dress, I don't know what the material was, nothing very warm, as I noticed she looked cold and hungry. She had on besides, a long train, a mosquito net over her face trimmed with lace.

Then we had a grand party at which I was most conspicuous; I brought refreshments to the halt and the blind, conversed with the deaf and dumb and gave all concerned the impression that a kind American gentleman is really a noble work.

After a while the bridal couple and I indulged in a few harmless pranks all in very good taste and so we parted. I think I wrote the same sentence about Mr. Baxter, but you can't repeat a novel term too often, besides I invented the phrase, short, terse yet full of feeling. I was sorry to see them go, yet glad in a sense; believe me if you can, I didn't say a word when they kissed me goodbye, I was so moved. They will return in a few days and something tells me it will be their turn to be speechless with emotion.

Please send my Christmas presents in time, so I won't feel too lonely without you. Even the Selbys cannot replace you, bad and hard as you are. And both of you knit me some more socks, my customers like them and I think are impressed, particularly by the green heather mixture.

Your loving orphan nephew,

Berry.

CHAPTER SEVENTY-NINE

t was eight o'clock when the Selbys, alone, surveyed the ruins of the reception rooms. Virginia dropped into an armchair. The guests had departed, leaving great havoc and disorder behind them. The air was heavy and lifeless with cigarette smoke and scent, the banks of flowers looked wilted and crushed as if heavy weights had been thrown against them. Under each chair were glasses and plates. In the adjoining room the scene was somewhat worse; where a long table had looked so hospitable a few hours ago, with piles of sandwiches and cakes, ices and big ornaments of spun sugar, inviting pitchers of soft drinks and many heady beverages, a loathsome spectacle reigned instead.

Virginia closed her eyes: "George, do I look like a broken lily?"

"Yes, m'dear, you do; and do I look like a tramp? I feel like one."

"No, you seem very presentable still; how I wish the angels would call me!"

"Oh come now, Virginia, things aren't as bad as that, are they? You'll be first-rate to-morrow morning."

He roamed about nervously, peering into corners and bending down now and then.

"George, do come here and rest for a moment. What are you doing, you make me feel so nervous."

"Just fishing around and collecting trifles that people have forgotten. I once read a very interesting article about what passengers leave in trains, but this party beats all records; look at this first haul. Some of the things I don't even recognize."

Virginia feebly opened her weary eyelids.

"Here are two kinds of spectacles, a pince-nez; here is a silver thimble, a rubber overshoe. God bless my soul, what's this?" He held out something black.

"An ear-trumpet," answered Virginia wearily, "there were several about; the one that looks like a telephone belongs to the general's wife and the pale green Venetian glass one was Mrs. Crashaw's. No, I don't recognize this one, it must belong to one of the waiters."

George went on: "Then comes a Prayer book, English, and a scurrilous book, American; here's something very touching, an Anglo-French conversation book and Monsieur Stanilas' top hat. How it found a resting place behind a group of palms I can't imagine."

"Go on fishing, George, until you find me a box of cough lozenges, I am hoarse with so much cordiality."

"Will this do? A box of malted milk tablets?"

Virginia took two and handed the box to George who helped himself. After a long silence, she sighed, stretched and said she felt better.

"George, I expect it is about time."

George consulted his huge old-fashioned gold watch. It was his favorite treasure, all his children had cut their teeth on it and here it was, as good as new, with a few little dents on the smooth surface, all that was left of long nights spent walking obnoxious babies, tiresome but adored, to sleep. George had been a tender parent and heard many a wail unheeded by weary nurses and Virginia.

"It is exactly twenty-six minutes past eight. Would you like to change your dress here?"

"Oh no, I couldn't, George, I haven't the strength."

"But, Virginia, think of what is ahead of us."

"I know, but I think a little dinner, just you and I, by our-selves would revive me. We must begin all over again, just the way it was before Barbara came."

"Darling, I think the *Brasserie du Coq* will be the very place; at last we can eat beefsteak and fried potatoes in peace and maybe a glass of beer. I hope we aren't going to miss that girl too much."

"I hope not, I want you to love me so much that there won't be room for anyone else, even for nieces."

"There never was, in one compartment of my heart, the big-gest and warmest. That has always belonged to you, ever since the first time I met you at Tybee."

Virginia looked very pleased. "Well, same here, George, the feeling is reciprocated. What worries me is that we may die some day."

"I expect we will. I expect before that happens I had better call for the bill, don't you?"

He did; the manager appeared, handed him a slip of paper, murmuring at the same time: "I can't understand what took place; your party has been the only one this week, sir. Would you like to see for yourself?"

George read the bill in silence, too surprised to speak; he pushed his spectacles back and handed the paper to his wife. Virginia read it over and over, the picture of amazement. What puzzled them was the following item:

"For wrecking and destroying contents of room number ten: 2000 Frcs."

"I can't make heads or tails of this," she said finally. "That was the room I engaged for Barbara so that she could change her dress and escape without notice. Michel had another room, natu-rally. Is there anything the matter with room number twelve?"

"Oh no, Madame, the room is in perfect order. Monsieur and Madame Saint-Amant left a letter for you."

"Well, I'm glad they only decided to annihilate number ten." Virginia tore open the envelope, hoping to get some light on the strange proceedings of such a quiet pair. It was just a little note from Barbara, very loving and tender, thanking them both for their affection in a way which showed unexpected depth of feeling. But not a word about the room, merely a postscript about Mirza, who had been sadly neglected at the last.

George said, much perplexed, that they would like to see the room.

The manager, still most apologetic, led the way to a really extraordinary scene of disorder. To begin with, the room was full of feathers blown out of the pillow by Berry in his efforts to breathe. Torn remnants of the sheets and pillow cases, cut by Monsieur Stanilas' knife, strewed the floor. The ornaments and clock on the mantelpiece, although marble, lay broken on the hearth and added to an atmosphere of crime, while a smashed chair and twisted light table gave the finishing touches. Berry's struggles must have been awful.

When Virginia could speak she whispered: "The damage is cheap at two thousand francs. Let's pay, George, and say no more about it. Perhaps some day, one of our guests will enlighten us. I know that Barbara had nothing to do with this."

George turned to the man and said something ambiguous about practical jokes. The manager pocketed his check much relieved and asked if they wished for a taxi, adding: "Your bags are quite safe, Sir, I had them put in my office."

The Selbys sank into their taxi and drove off.

Virginia put her head down on her husband's shoulder: "Never mind about the expense. This shoulder is the only place where I feel really at peace. Have we ever been to Venice before?"

"Not that I know of, m'dear."

"I think we deserve a second honeymoon, don't you? I am so glad we gave the Henri-Martin flat to Barbara and Michel. It is hard on the newly wed to travel after this terrible engagement. They can start off on their journey next week."

"In our lovely new car," said George proudly, holding his wife's hand. "I know we are going to enjoy ourselves on this trip. Even more than our first spree together, it was worth all this trouble to realize it."

"I want to kiss you before we get to the *Brasserie*," murmured Virginia, skittishly, "I feel like a bride myself."

THE END